ANCIENT VENGEANCE

ANCIENTS RISING SERIES

BOOK SIX

KATIE REUS

Cover Art by Sweet 'N Spicy Designs

Editor: Kelli Collins

Author Website: https://katiereus.com

Ancient Vengeance/Katie Reus.—1st ed.

ISBN: 9781635562699

For all the readers who look up and wish to see dragons.

PRAISE FOR THE NOVELS OF
KATIE REUS

"...a wild hot ride for readers. The story grabs you and doesn't let go."
—*New York Times* bestselling author, Cynthia Eden

"Has all the right ingredients: a hot couple, evil villains, and a killer action-filled plot. . . . [The] Moon Shifter series is what I call Grade-A entertainment!" —Joyfully Reviewed

"I could not put this book down. . . . Let me be clear that I am not saying that this was a good book *for* a paranormal genre; it was an excellent romance read, *period.*" —All About Romance

"Reus strikes just the right balance of steamy sexual tension and nail-biting action....This romantic thriller reliably hits every note that fans of the genre will expect." —*Publishers Weekly*

"Prepare yourself for the start of a great new series! . . . I'm excited about reading more about this great group of characters."
—Fresh Fiction

"Wow! This powerful, passionate hero sizzles with sheer deliciousness. I loved every sexy twist of this fun & exhilarating tale. Katie Reus delivers!" —Carolyn Crane, RITA award winning author

"A sexy, well-crafted paranormal romance that succeeds with smart characters and creative world building."—Kirkus Reviews

"You'll fall in love with Katie's heroes."
—*New York Times* bestselling author, Kaylea Cross

"Both romantic and suspenseful, a fast-paced sexy book full of high stakes action." —Heroes and Heartbreakers

"Katie Reus pulls the reader into a story line of second chances, betrayal, and the truth about forgotten lives and hidden pasts."
—The Reading Café

"Nonstop action, a solid plot, good pacing, and riveting suspense."
—RT Book Reviews

"Exciting in more ways than one, well-paced and smoothly written, I'd recommend *A Covert Affair* to any romantic suspense reader."
—Harlequin Junkie

"Sexy military romantic suspense." —USA Today

"Enough sexual tension to set the pages on fire."
—*New York Times* bestselling author, Alexandra Ivy

"*Avenger's Heat* hits the ground running...This is a story of strength, of partnership and healing, and it does it brilliantly."
—Vampire Book Club

"*Mating Instinct* was a great read with complex characters, serious political issues and a world I am looking forward to coming back to."
—All Things Urban Fantasy

CHAPTER ONE

R hodes urged his horse to go faster as he galloped down the cobblestone lane. The princess had left the castle and he'd been waylaid by a handful of street vendors who'd unintentionally blocked his path. Considering she had guards with her, he wouldn't be kidnapping her today, but he liked to keep her in sight.

As often as possible.

He shouldn't be in the Nova realm, definitely shouldn't be near their castle. But very recently the royal family had celebrated the marriage of their long-lost daughter and her return—and they'd opened up the realm to outsiders. Ares had even woken from his hibernation to see his daughter married. And it didn't seem as if he would be going back to sleep anytime soon.

Now that the oldest daughter was married, that left the youngest daughter, the petite Stella with bicolored eyes and an astonishingly small build for a dragon. He had overheard some females make a derisive remark about her size, but…there was no denying how attractive she was.

Or how kind.

Nothing at all like he'd expected—been led to believe when he'd been contracted by the fae king of the Domincary realm.

He slowed his horse as he reached the small town's edge, then tossed the reins back onto the saddle and patted the horse on its flank. It immediately headed back down the cobblestone pathway toward the castle—where he'd 'borrowed' it from.

Pausing by a bridge that would lead into the town, he eyed the long row of quaint houses on either side of the road, looking for any threats.

Even with the foot of snow covering all the front yards, candles and magical lights lit most of the windows. Sunset was perhaps half an hour away and everything had a soft feel to it. Though there were signs of people—footprints along the road, smoke from most of the chimneys— he didn't actually see anyone through the windows.

In the human realm, it was currently spring, but here it was still ice cold. Which was good for him as he had on a hooded coat that helped him to blend with the population. Not that he'd received any odd looks since arriving in the Nova realm a week ago. He'd been sleeping in the nearby woods in his dragon form, using his natural camouflage to stay hidden from the sentries around the castle and throughout the realm itself.

He was an assassin for a reason—he was naturally good at getting into places unseen.

Only months ago this place had been almost completely cut off from the rest of civilization but ever since the new mating and return of the older princess, they had opened up their realm and created an alliance with the territory of a human place called New Orleans. The castle's security was still tight, however.

But it wasn't good enough to keep him out.

He waved casually to a big male riding a horse through town and the male waved back. As he made his way down the street farther into the town, he inhaled deeply, easily able to follow her scent. She wasn't far now. Though she wasn't alone. He scented many, many others nearby.

Frowning, he picked up his pace.

Stella shouldn't have left the castle this late. Though her clan was a matriarchal line, with fierce female dragons running the realm, they kept her sheltered. Protected.

Rightly so. He wasn't sure why she'd come to this nearby town, why she was out near dark. He didn't like it.

Luckily he was a born tracker, was easily following her wild, sweet scent that reminded him of strawberries. He could practically taste her on the air—had fantasized about tasting her from the moment he'd seen her. Scented her.

It didn't matter that he'd been ordered to kidnap her, to bring her back by any means necessary. He wanted her with a desperation that defied logic.

He locked down that thought as he reached the top of another bridge. And that was when he saw her in a gazebo, talking to a handful of large dragon males. His dragon snarled, not liking that at all. Music played from somewhere, lifting on the wind, and the rest of the townspeople were laughing, drinking, having a large party.

The townspeople who lived outside the bailey walls, no doubt. The farmers and others who provided various necessities for the realm.

As he strode closer, the music grew louder, people laughing and singing and—a man stumbled before he clapped Rhodes on the shoulder.

Rhodes tensed, almost going into fight mode until the slightly smaller male shoved a tankard into his hand. "Praise be to the goddess and hope we see an end to this winter soon!"

"Praise be to the goddess," he murmured, taking the drink, the scent actually quite pleasing.

Which made sense. This was a realm known for their finery. Everyone here had an education, a roof over their head and was given the chance to figure out what type of job they preferred. They would not be drinking some of the swill he'd had the misfortune to taste in other realms.

Taking a sip, he neared the edge of the gazebo and turned from Stella and the two males as he leaned against the outside railing, watching the revelry. But he remained close enough to hear her, scent her.

"I promise that we're looking into what happened." Stella's lilting voice was soft, lyrical as she spoke. So very soothing. Her silvery hair hung down her back in a thick, intricate woven braid and she wore a simple navy tunic over loose navy pants, as was the style of the realm. It was clear her clothing was quality, however, given the elaborate silver stitching along the neck and hemlines. Her breasts were full, given her petite size, and they strained prettily against the fabric, making him wonder...all sorts of things. Like how soft her skin would feel if he were to caress her bare breasts.

No. He shut down that thought, forced himself to focus, to scan for her security—who was nowhere to be seen.

"Aye, we know that you are. And we appreciate you coming here in person to speak with us."

"Of course. I wouldn't miss the festival anyway," she said on a laugh. "You've outdone yourselves this year."

"We really have. So when will we be hearing an announcement about your engagement? Now that your sister is happily mated—"

Rhodes inwardly cursed as the ale sloshed over his fingers when he crushed the metal tankard in his hand. Luckily no one was paying him any attention.

Children—in dragonling form—were sliding over a frozen pond while their parents looked on. In the distance he could see slightly older children sledding down a huge hill and there was an ale tasting going on. Which made sense considering this little township provided the ale to the rest of the realm.

He funneled all of that out as he strained to hear Stella's response. An engagement? He'd heard nothing whispered about her getting mated. Not even a hint. And he hadn't seen her with a male, not romantically anyway.

She laughed, the musical sound a balm to his ears. "No engagement for me. I'm far too busy to even think about looking for a mate."

One of the males laughed. "Well, we were just curious. The wedding celebration was..."

Rhodes tuned out the rest of the inane conversation when he realized she wasn't engaged. Wasn't looking for a mate.

He shouldn't care, not considering he'd been hired to kidnap her and deliver her to the fae.

Not that it mattered what his contract said. Because he wouldn't be kidnapping her. His dragon had decided to keep her instead.

CHAPTER TWO

S tella waited in the shadows of the castle's hallway until the door to her sister's room opened and the big dragon male who was Juniper's mate stepped out. As soon as Zephyr was out of sight down the long stone hallway, she briefly knocked on the heavy door. "Juniper?"

"Come in," her sister called out even as she shoved the door open. Whew, her sister was fully dressed.

Juniper was newly mated and just back from her honeymoon, so Stella had been hesitant to bother her tonight. "You have a few minutes?" Juniper had told her that she was always welcome in her chambers.

But for over a hundred years everyone had thought Juniper was dead —Stella had thought she'd lost her big sister, the one who'd let her sneak into her room at night when she didn't want to be alone. Which had been often. Now she was back and mated to a wonderful dragon. And Stella was thinking of leaving for a while.

"Of course. You just missed Zephyr."

"Ah, I know," she said, laughing lightly as she shut the door behind her. "I thought you guys might be busy so I was waiting to see if he left."

Juniper snorted and pulled her into a tight hug. "You are such a wonderful weirdo. I've told you to please knock on our door any time. Ever."

She hugged her sister back, trying not to smell her too hard like a... well, complete and utter weirdo. But it was hard not to. She'd missed her so much. Which was why leaving for a little bit felt even harder. "I wanted to ask you something," she said as she stepped back, took in how neat and orderly their room was. She blinked. "Your clothes..."

"Are hanging up in our closet." Juniper's voice was dry. "Zephyr was going a little crazy with my mess, I think. I came back earlier this evening and everything looked magazine worthy."

It took Stella a moment to remember what 'magazine' was. They didn't have things like that here in the Nova realm, though she was learning a lot about the human realm simply from conversations with her sister. Of course, the human realm had recently undergone a massive change—thanks to a bunch of stupid, selfish dragons who'd thought to take over the world and had instead killed over half of it. The Fall, they called it. "Thank the goddess," she murmured. "It was making me itchy yesterday."

Juniper blinked, then let out a bark of laughter. "I didn't realize you were a neatnik."

"I don't know what that means. But I can guess. And yes, things have a home and belong in their home—not strewn all over the floor and bed and chaise with complete abandon." She mock shuddered.

Still chuckling, Juniper motioned for her to sit on the chaise by the stained-glass window. "So what brings you here so late?"

"I need sisterly advice. For a couple things." One of them was quite embarrassing so she was going to save that for last. "I've...never seen our parents so happy as they've been the last couple months. To have you back is everything." Their father had come out of Hibernation for his daughter's return and Stella was so happy to have him back as well. She'd had her mother and grandmother and many members of her clan, but she'd missed her father.

Juniper's expression was soft as she sat next to her. "It feels like you're stalling. I know our parents are happy."

"Gah, okay, I *am* stalling." She took a fortifying breath. "I wish to see more of the human realm. Any realm if I'm being honest, but the human one is fascinating and you have so many friends there. There's been talk of sending someone to New Orleans and—"

"And you wish to go?"

"Yes."

"And you're worried that it will bother me after being gone so long to have you leave?"

"Yes."

Juniper's smile remained soft, serene. Of anyone, she understood Stella the most. "I think it's a great idea for you to spread your wings. I've seen much of the world. Enough for multiple lifetimes. You deserve the same, to be less sheltered."

Tears immediately sprang to her eyes. She had been sheltered. Stiflingly so. Before it had been fine, or fine enough, but now she wanted to see everything. "You won't hate me if I leave?" she whispered. "It won't be for long," she tacked on.

She just had this burning need to leave, to discover, to do something *more* than what she did here. After a lifetime of being cooped up here, and of putting up with it because of the events that had led to it, the attack of so many... She needed to explore and see what she was made of. Because she was made of more than most people seemed to assume. She was small for a dragon and because of that, people viewed her differently. Even if it was subconscious, it still stung.

"I think you should go as long as you want and I could never, ever hate you."

Stella hadn't realized how much she'd needed to hear her sister's words until that moment. She hadn't been worried about her parents' reaction—they weren't going to like her leaving no matter what. The only person's opinion she'd cared about was Juniper's. More tears spilled over as she threw her arms around her sister and hugged her tight.

At that moment the door flew open so she drew back, wiping at her cheeks.

Her brother-in-law Zephyr frowned as he looked at the two of them.

8

"Who do we need to kill for making your sister cry?" he growled as he stalked forward, his expression murderous.

"These are happy tears," Stella blurted, even as Juniper started to laugh.

"You will be killing no one," Juniper added. "At least not tonight."

The tension in his shoulders eased immediately. "Ah...should I come back?"

Stella started to rise, to just leave without asking about the other thing she needed advice on, but Juniper nodded.

"Give us a few minutes? Maybe get me some of that chocolate cake from the kitchens? If there's any left," she added.

"The chef saved some for you," Stella said even as Zephyr nodded. Their chef loved having Juniper back as well—everyone in the castle did.

Once they were alone again, she absently smoothed over the embroidery along the hem of her tunic. It was time to ask about the other thing. "So...how did you know you were ready for sex the first time?"

Juniper's expression froze, her bicolored eyes going wide. "Wait..." She cleared her throat. "I mean..." Cleared it again. "Have you never, ah..."

"No, I've never had sex." Stella felt her cheeks heat but ignored it. "We have grown up very differently. There's never been anyone I could just freely sleep with. My every move has been monitored. As a princess of the Nova realm—"

"I'm not judging! I was just surprised, that's all. You're gorgeous and sweet and...anyway, yes, that makes sense. I guess I never thought about the rules and other stuff that would come from living in this castle."

Stella nodded, some of her tension easing away.

"So... Is there someone in particular? A male? Or female who—"

"There's no one! I do prefer males, however. But... I was hoping that if in the human realm the opportunity presented itself, I'd have a better understanding of... I don't know." She covered her face with both hands. "This is so embarrassing."

Juniper gently clasped her wrists, pulled them down to stop her from hiding. "No, it's not. Please don't be embarrassed." Then her sister shoved out a breath. "Look, there's no wrong or right answer for your first time. But I think it should be with someone that you have strong feelings for and someone who has strong feelings for you. He should respect you, treasure you—treat you like a queen," she growled.

Which just made Stella giggle. "You sound a lot like Mother."

"You spoke to Soleil about this?" Juniper looked a little shocked. It seemed it was still difficult for her to call their parents Mom and Dad since she had been gone for so long—hadn't remembered them when her memories had been messed with. Juniper had been raised by kind wolf shifters who she called Mom and Dad. And Stella adored her other parents as well.

"Uh, no. But many, many, many years ago, she told me that when I found my mate, he would treat me like a queen or be locked in a dungeon for all eternity." And Soleil, her mother, had meant every word.

"That sounds about right." Juniper nodded once, clearly agreeing. "You're a smart dragon. Trust your instinct where sex is concerned. And since you're asking for advice, I'm going to give you just a little more. When you talk to Ares and Soleil about leaving for New Orleans, don't ask. Tell them what you're doing. And don't back down. The way you handle this will set the tone for their reaction. And it'll set the tone for the new boundaries I know you're trying to set with them. So be matter of fact, tell them you're going and then do it. If you want your independence, you're going to have to take it."

"That is easier said than done."

"True. But you're ready for this. Even if they're not."

Stella nodded slowly, digesting her sister's words. Because she was right. Their kingdom had been invaded over a century ago, so many of them killed, and ever since then she'd been taught to fight, to kill with accuracy, but she'd also been incredibly sheltered to the point she'd never been very far from the castle grounds. Only allowed to travel to nearby towns and always with guards—who were never stealthy about following her. After Juniper had been thought killed, she'd been next in line to rule. Now Stella was back to being the second born, thankfully. She never wanted to be queen, she wanted to make her own rules.

If she stayed here, she knew deep down it would kill the flame burning inside her. That she would become a muted version of who she could truly be. Stella wasn't sure how she knew that, but deep in her bones, she knew it was time to find herself. So she hugged Juniper once again. "I'll be leaving tomorrow then." Saying the words aloud made it feel more real.

As if she was really going to have her first adventure—and she was going to prove to herself and to her mother and grandmother that she was as capable and independent as them.

CHAPTER THREE

Stella felt freer than she ever had in her life as she coasted through the skies of her realm in dragon form. She loved her clan, her people, but...she was on her way to somewhere new and wild.

By herself.

Her family hadn't sent a guard with her for this trip—they were trusting her to go to New Orleans and hunt down a thief from their realm.

All. By. Herself.

It wasn't a dangerous job, but still. This was her first official assignment alone and she was going to take every advantage of the freedom. She loved her family with a fierceness, but they could be smothering.

She dipped low, her dragon feeding off all her positive energy. She did a barrel roll in the sky, the blanket of stars above her a glittering audience as she dove and dipped, enjoying the wind rolling over her scales and wings.

Until pain ripped through her right flank, over and over—something had struck her.

Her vision blurred, flames erupting from her throat as agony speared through her in wave after wave of raw, fracturing pain.

She somehow forced herself to stop breathing fire, to continue flying, but it was as if tiny shards of glass were embedded under her scales, digging, digging, deeper. Slicing away at her insides until they'd started to boil.

Oh goddess, she was barely holding onto her dragon form. The sudden realization that she'd been poisoned slammed into her. And it was causing her to shift to human. She just had to hold on a little longer...

Fighting through the pain, she angled downward, the edges of her vision black as she struggled to maintain a hold of her beast. If she fell from a great height, she'd survive but likely break every bone in her body. She'd be weak, unprotected.

Fear punched through her at the thought.

The forest stretched out before her, thick, dark clusters of trees. No homes, thankfully. She was so close to the first portal she needed to take to get to the human realm.

There would be help there—healers. Or her clanmates guarding the portal door—they could help. She simply had to make it.

As she skimmed the tops of the trees, she let out a roar as her dragon almost slipped away from her. Whatever poison was eating away at her was brutal agony.

Hold on, hold on, hold on, she chanted even as she scanned the ground for a threat. *Someone* had shot her. They would have been on the ground, would be close by. Unless it had been a dragon from the sky...

She tried to slow herself, her wings flapping frantically as the ground greeted her with a startling quickness.

Unable to hold on anymore, her dragon form fell away, her human side taking over as she slammed into a thicket of bushes.

She cried out as brambles scraped over her arms and body, bit it off immediately.

There was a threat out there. She had to hide, to be silent, because she was in no shape to fight.

And she was also naked. Completely vulnerable. The females of her line had the ability to clothe themselves after a shift, but she couldn't even call on that small magic. This was so very bad.

Ice slicked down her spine as she rolled out of the bushes onto all fours, scratched and bleeding, waves of pain slicing under her skin. She tried to call on her dragon out of instinct, failed.

She shoved up, took a step forward. Then another. But with each step, it was like the glass embedded deeper into her skin.

There was nothing actually there, of course. But she felt the pain coursing through her veins all the same.

Blinking fast, trying to fight through the poison, she looked around at the forest, saw only shadows.

Fear like she'd never known punched through her, but she refused to lay down and die. She had to be...a mile from the portal. She would make it if she had to crawl the whole way.

There was no other choice. So she staggered forward, each step an effort.

A glowing light emerged from her right, a little blue orb floating through the thick trees.

Hide.

All her instincts screamed at her. She stumbled back toward a large tree that would have been called a redwood in the human realm. Clutching onto the thick bark, she hoisted herself up, started to climb.

"Don't bother, little princess," an eerie voice whispered, seemingly from all directions.

"You're ours now," another disembodied voice followed.

Ours? Oh goddess.

She couldn't even lift herself off the ground, couldn't climb. Her body weak, she fell back to the snow-covered earth with a thump.

A swishing sound sliced through the air and she waited for the blow, for the sword or blade to stab through her.

It never came.

Turning, she backed up against the tree and—stared.

A huge shadow moved so fast she could barely track it, battling with two tall, elegant-looking... Wait. The poison must be affecting her neurological function.

Two glowing beings who looked like fae warriors had swords out, were slicing at...air.

One let out a scream of rage, swiveled as they tried to fend off the liquid shadow.

She tried to keep her eyes open as blackness crept in.

But as she let it take over, the agony inside her subsided, beckoning her to slumber. She couldn't close her eyes though. Had to stay upright and alert.

A scream rent the air, then another.

Then silence.

She couldn't see anything now, could barely feel anything.

"You're safe, princess," a growly male voice rumbled by her ear as she went completely weightless.

She inhaled deeply, dragged in the dark, sensual scent, let it invade her lungs. Her dragon tried to reach for it, but just as quickly, blackness took her completely.

STELLA OPENED HER EYES INTO…DARKNESS. No, not total darkness. There was a crackling sound nearby. What was… A fire. Blinking, she tried to figure out where she was but could just make out a fuzzy pillow under her head.

Someone was nearby. She could hear them moving around.

A dull ache pounded through her body, but nothing like the pain from before when she'd been flying. When that male, the *unknown* male, had shown up. She hadn't seen him, but she'd scented him, could scent faint traces of him on her now.

She pushed up, the fluffy blanket that had been wrapped around her pooling in her lap. At least she wasn't naked any longer.

Immediately she spotted the large male crouched next to the fire in…wherever they were. A small room of sorts.

He moved lightning fast in the way of supernaturals—not that she'd doubted he was like her. Given his size, he had to be a dragon. Or maybe a bear. His hair was dark, cut close to his head, severely so. The way warriors often kept their hair. It certainly showed off stunning cheekbones—and a wicked scar across his cheek. He was so close to her and that scent—like rich, dark chocolate, wrapped around her.

"Princess," he murmured, his voice a low rumble that sent an odd sensation spiraling through her. He laid the back of his hand against her forehead, concern in his green-gold eyes. She'd never seen anything like his eyes and they seemed to glow, the fire making them even brighter. "You are still too cold."

He was…right, she realized. "I am cold." Her voice was raspy from disuse, but she continued. "Where are we? And who sent you?" She knew it had to have been one of her family members. She'd thought they'd finally given her freedom but it turned out they'd sent a guard with her after all. She couldn't actually be angry, however, when the male had saved her life. "Was it my mother?"

He frowned, eyed her in a clinical fashion. Oh yeah, he was a body-guard. All about duty and honor.

She sighed. "Or my grandmother? They said they wouldn't send a bodyguard for this trip," she murmured. "But I can't very well be angry that they did."

"How are you feeling?" he rumbled, that frown firmly in place as he watched her, worried she might break.

Which was sort of annoying. She might be smaller than the average dragon. Like, way smaller. But she was still a dragon. And she could fight like a demon when she wasn't, you know, *poisoned.* "You're just going to ignore my questions?"

He paused, looked into her eyes, and considering he was crouched right in front of her—and smelled like absolute heaven—she got the full impact of his green-gold gaze. A scar bisected his right cheek, telling her the original wound must have been deep since she was assuming he was a dragon.

"My name is Rhodes," he finally said. "And it's my duty to keep you safe."

Duty? Oooh, her grandmother must have sent him, she realized. Goddess, he was striking. She couldn't believe she'd never seen him around the castle, but she knew that her grandmother had a small, elite guard of assassins who lived in the shadows. And while she wasn't known to gamble, Stella would bet that was exactly what this male was.

"Your duty?" she murmured, reaching out and tracing her finger over his scar, up and down—he went very, *very* still, his eyes flashing to dragon. His beast stared out at her—intensely curious.

Oh sweet goddess, what was wrong with her. Blinking, she dropped her hand, beyond embarrassed that she'd just touched him without permission. "Apologies." Clearing her throat, she shoved up, needing to move, to put distance between her and this male who was making her feel off balance.

He didn't back up at all, gave her no space as she tried to stand. Instead, he set his hands on her hips as she found her feet, swayed. His big fingers slid higher, held onto her waist in a very possessive way, and at that moment she was aware of two things: (a) she didn't have any pants on, just a huge tunic that smelled like him, and (b) he was watching her with more than curiosity now.

Heat arced between them, a strange buzzing energy wrapping around her, through her. She swallowed hard, but didn't break his gaze. She wasn't sure what was happening.

She shifted slightly, taking a step closer to him, and the tunic slipped, falling off her shoulder, exposing her skin.

His gaze tracked the movement, and his eyes went full dragon, practically glowing. He looked away almost immediately, as if embarrassed, but he didn't let go of her hips as he...lifted her up.

She yelped. "What are you doing?"

He scooped her up, then gently set her in front of the blazing fire. "You will sit here and get warm. You are far too cold and I don't like it. I'm going to make you something to eat."

"But—"

"No. It is my job to keep you safe, to protect you, to feed you. Do not move, princess." He grabbed a blanket from a basket set back from the fireplace and wrapped it around her shoulders.

"Rhodes—" She stopped as he crouched in front of her, his gaze unreadable. "What?" she whispered.

"I like hearing you say my name." Then he stood and just...left.

What the holy hell had just happened? Was he...interested in her? He was a bodyguard, very likely worked for her grandmother. Maybe her mother. Which would actually be worse. He couldn't...want her. Well, maybe he *could*.

And why was she worried about that? She needed answers!

She let the blanket fall, then stood, almost fell as a dull ache rolled through her, made her bones feel tired. It was such a strange sensation. She didn't feel sick or in pain, but she felt so very weird. Something was wrong. Missing.

She took a few tentative steps, realized she could walk okay. As she followed after him, she also realized they were in a little house. A human one, likely abandoned given the layers of dust on everything. She'd been so close to the portal when she'd been shot out of the sky. And none of this looked like it belonged in the Nova realm. Nope, there was a television gathering dust on the wall as well. That was a human contraption.

Damn it, she needed to ask him so many things.

She stepped into a dark hallway, frowned at how very dim it was. Why couldn't she see well? "Rhodes?" She could hear the fear in her voice, hated it. But panic gripped her chest tight.

Then he was there, but instead of hovering, he'd crouched again so that he was closer to her eye level. "Why are you not by the fire?" His eyes were glowing, lighting up the darkened hallway.

"Something is wrong with me," she whispered.

"I know. You've been poisoned by fae."

She gasped. "In our realm?" She hadn't misremembered those fae, the glowing blue orb, her fall from the sky. Oh no. No, no, no.

"They are dead. I made sure of it." His dragon looked back at her now, the switch from human eyes to dragon instantaneous. The green-gold was even brighter. "I sent their heads to your family."

She swallowed hard. "They shouldn't have been able to get into our realm."

"I know." His expression was dark, his jaw set tight. "They will never harm you or anyone again."

"Do you know...what kind of poison?"

18

He paused. "Not for certain, but I can guess."

"Am I going to..." She didn't want to say the word.

"No," he snarled. "I've already given you a small injection that should combat the full effects until I get you to a healer. It is the only reason I didn't take you back to the Nova realm immediately. As soon as you've eaten...I will return you to the Nova realm and you will see a healer." Too many emotions crossed his face as he spoke and she couldn't grasp on to any one of them.

She shook her head. "No way. We crossed the portal obviously. Right?"

He nodded.

"We continue to New Orleans then. There's an ancient healer there, she'll heal me. And we're at the halfway point anyway so it's no farther to go there."

"You don't wish to return home?"

"I was sent on a mission and I'm not stopping until it's complete. You can come with me or not, but I'm not returning home." In reality, he could probably force her.

"I will go where you go, do whatever you command."

Oh. *Ohhhh*, she liked the way he said that way too much. He must have been ordered to listen to her, which made sense. Even so, the way he said the words sent a frisson of heat spiraling through her. She had so much more to ask him, however. "Do the guards at the portal know of the fae in the realm?"

He paused, then nodded.

She wasn't sure what to make of the pause. "What?"

"I punched one of them when they would not listen to me. But when I tossed the head of one of the fae in front of them, they stopped acting like assholes. They raced back to the castle with the heads and bodies so your family knows about the breach."

"What did they say about...me?" She was surprised they'd let him pass through the portal with her unconscious.

"I did not tell them about you," he said matter-of-factly as he suddenly scooped her up in his arms again.

She wanted to be annoyed, but she really, really liked the feel of him holding her so close. He had on a tunic, similar to the one he'd given her, but she could feel how built he was, the raw power of him. And her legs were weak anyway. "You lied to them?"

"No. I simply did not tell them about you. When they went to deliver the bodies and news, I left with you. I don't answer to them." His voice was a low, deadly growl as he sat her in front of the fire again.

"Who do you answer to?" She was hoping he'd finally tell her who had ordered him to escort her.

"You."

CHAPTER FOUR

R hodes watched the princess—Stella—closely. Curiously. She had surprised him in more ways than one.

He'd been fascinated from the moment he'd started watching her.

But when she'd touched his face earlier, he hadn't known what to do. So he'd remained still, hoping she would continue to stroke his skin.

Now she was staring at him with wide bicolored eyes—one a bluish green that reminded him of the Mediterranean and the other a silvery gray. As she watched him, it was difficult to read her. The fire created shadows across her face, her emotions flickering too quickly across her expression, too many for him to discern. Her silvery hair was in disarray, falling over her shoulders in loose waves. The silver was a familial trait the royal family shared. That and other magical powers.

Unfortunately her magic would be muted now because of the poison.

He wished he could kill those fae bastards again. Then again, for daring to hurt her.

"Me?" she whispered, hesitation in her voice.

"You're a princess." His princess. "Of course I answer to you." His dragon wanted nothing more than to make her happy. To an extent that it confused him.

Her cheeks flushed a delicate shade of pink and the scent that rolled off her—he wasn't sure what it was, how to read it. But he liked it, sweet and sensual, like strawberries.

"I would like to go outside then." Her voice was quiet, almost subdued.

And he wanted to argue that she stay right where she was by the fire. He didn't like how icy her skin felt. It wasn't that cold outside at least, not like in the Nova realm, where it seemed to be frigid all the time.

Growling under his breath, he scooped her up again, ignored her little yelp of surprise.

"I can walk."

"You have been poisoned." She would not be doing anything until she got to a healer. He wasn't certain why she wanted to go outside but there was no one near this little farmhouse he'd found. It had been abandoned long ago and other than the animals in a nearby forest, there were no humans he could scent or hear.

She laid her head against his shoulder as he strode out the front door and onto a large porch covered in pollen and dust. He tried not to focus on the way she'd curled up against him so naturally. He knew he shouldn't get used to this, shouldn't enjoy it at all. Not when she'd been injured. It was the only reason she was leaning on him.

A half-moon hung in the sky and a blanket of stars lit up everything around them for miles.

"Put me down," she murmured, wiggling in his arms.

He shoved down a groan. He didn't want to let her go and had to lock down the direction his thoughts were headed. Gently he eased her down, liking the way his tunic looked on her even if it was too big. He knew she must have brought a bag with her, but he hadn't been able to find it in the forest and there hadn't been time to extensively search for it. He'd wanted to get her to safety in case there had been more fae lurking.

She pushed the tunic up on her shoulder, but it fell down again. "Can you turn around please?"

He frowned down at her as she nervously twisted her thick hair around her hand, just watching him with that inscrutable expression.

Did she...realize he hadn't been sent by her family? That he wasn't really a bodyguard? Her assumption had been fortuitous, but maybe he had betrayed himself somehow. He hadn't been raised in the castle, hadn't been raised by dragons, so perhaps he'd done something small and she'd picked up on it. "No."

She blinked at him, her mouth falling open slightly. Her bottom lip was lush and he had the urge to lean down and bite it. "What? Why not?"

"It will be pointless for you to attack me. You are too weak right now."

She blinked again, her head tilting to the side ever so slightly. "Attack you?"

"I will guard you, keep you safe. It would be foolish for you to venture out on your own."

Groaning, she scrubbed her hands over her face. "You were definitely sent by my grandmother," she muttered. When she looked back up at him, her jaw was set. "I would like you to turn around because I'm going to get naked, not because I'm trying to escape or whatever nonsense you've cooked up. I can't feel my dragon right now and I'm close to freaking the fuck out." Her voice rose with each word, the sharp scent coming off her scraping against his senses in large swipes. "And I know most dragons don't care about nudity but I feel weird being naked in front of you!"

Oh. Now he was the one to blink. Wordlessly, he gave her his back, even though he'd already seen her naked—he'd had to dress her. But it seemed wise to not mention that, even as he remembered exactly how strong and curvy she'd been. He'd tried to avoid looking at her, but he was only a dragon. Annoyed with his lack of control, he shifted on his feet as he heard a soft rustle behind him.

Then a gasp. Then...

He swiveled to find her silently crying, tears tracking down her cheeks, her expression haunted as she clutched the tunic against her chest. "I really can't call on my dragon," she whispered. "I thought it was weird that I couldn't see well in the house before but... I don't have any of my dragon senses. She's buried deep and I can't shift." Fear bled into her gaze as she stared up at him, horror in her eyes.

And he felt like the biggest monster in the world. He'd been hired to kidnap this bright shining star and though he hadn't, could never have, he still should have known the fae would send someone else. Should have realized and done something to intervene before the attack.

Should have protected her better. He was...useless.

He crossed the few feet between them, pulled her into his arms and was surprised when she buried her face against his chest.

The strangest sensation rumbled through him as he rubbed his hand down her bare back in a steady rhythm. He'd never comforted anyone before. "We will leave now," he found himself saying. "I will fly us to the next portal and you will see the healer soon." They could be in New Orleans soon, though nothing could be fast enough. "Unless you wish for me to cook something?" That was what he'd been planning to do. She needed food now, to keep her strength up. The injection he'd given her would only mask the effects.

A healer needed to extract the poison. Luckily they had time—one of the reasons he hadn't flown her back to the castle in her realm. He'd also been worried there might be more fae lying in wait. But the truth was, he knew if he'd taken her back, he'd likely never see her again.

He could not allow that.

"I would like to leave now," she murmured against his tunic before she lifted her face to look at him, wetness covering her cheeks.

He didn't care what kind of protocol he should be pretending to keep, he couldn't have stopped himself from touching her if he'd wanted to. And he didn't want to stop. Gently, he swiped his thumbs over her cheeks, marveled at how soft they were.

Her eyes widened slightly as she watched him and that strawberries scent was back, twining around him, filling the air.

He resisted the urge to pull her back into his arms. Instead, he took the tunic from her hands and looked to the side as he held it up. "You need to dress now."

She slipped into his clothing and though he could see flashes of skin out of the corner of his eye, he waited until she was fully clothed.

He was not a good male, but he would never take what wasn't offered freely. Wouldn't look at her naked until he'd been given permission. But if she ever gave him permission...

"Will you sit by the fire while I pack up?" he asked as he lifted her in his arms once again. She fit perfectly and he couldn't stop his fascination with holding her so close. It was as if she had been created just for him.

Which was foolish nonsense.

"Yes. Thank you, by the way...for what you did." Her voice was soft, thready.

He just grunted a response, hurrying inside to grab his small pack. Then he scooped up a couple blankets before heading back outside with her.

"You know how to..." She blinked rapidly as if trying to keep her eyes open. "Ah...get to the other portal I take it?" She weaved once on her feet as he set her down and his dragon roared inside.

The injection should have staved off the effects for much longer. "I do. I'm going to shift, then pick you up in my claws and carry you that way." Because he didn't think she could stay on his back in her weakened state. Holding her would mean her ride was bumpier but he'd be as careful as possible.

Nodding, she wrapped one of the blankets around herself as he shifted to his dragon. His magic, dark and wild, swirled around him, his shift seamless. He didn't wait a moment longer than necessary before he eased her into his claws and took to the skies.

First step, get to the portal, get her to New Orleans—and then to the healers. Then he would keep her safe while he figured out a way to kill those who wanted her for their own.

CHAPTER FIVE

"Mother," Juniper said, instead of saying Soleil, her mom's first name.

That got the queen's attention since it was the first time she'd used it.

Soleil blinked, pausing from staring down one of the guards who'd just delivered two dead fae. "What?"

Juniper looked at the guard, a male named Marcus who was young and looked slightly terrified by Soleil, though he was doing a good job of hiding it. But her mother kept staring the guards down and she wanted to make certain they understood the entire situation.

"So, let's recap everything. A dragon delivered the heads and bodies of these two fae, correct?" Juniper asked, keeping her voice soothing.

He looked relieved to be talking to her. "Yes, my lady."

Ugh. Juniper wasn't sure she'd ever get used to that title. "What else did he say? Specifically? And did you see Stella in the forest?" Because they hadn't mentioned her sister and that bothered Juniper.

The male blinked. "Princess Stella? No, of course not."

"You didn't see her cross the portal?"

"No, but..." He cleared his throat, glanced at the queen, then at the other guard he'd arrived with who was standing next to him—Rye.

"We left the portal to bring back the bodies," the other one said. "And we searched aerially, looking for other fae in case they were staging an attack of sorts. We didn't see or sense anyone else in the forest."

"Why did you leave the portal unattended?" Soleil snapped.

"That male was there, he ordered us to take these back and said... Oh, he didn't actually say he'd watch the portal. I guess it was just assumed."

"So now you take orders from random dragons?" The queen's voice dripped with ice.

Juniper took a steadying breath. "What did this male look like?" They needed to focus on more important things.

"Large, like...well, your mate. He was a dragon. Dark hair, it was short and... I don't actually remember. He had on dark clothes, a tunic in the same style as us," Marcus said, motioning to himself and his compatriot. "I assumed he worked for Starlena, if I'm being blunt."

"Ah." Soleil nodded once. Then she said, "Return to your quarters now. I will deal with your breach of protocol later."

As the males hurried out of the large stone room, Juniper called out, not bothering to wait for her mother to do so. "Zephyr!" she called out to her mate—who'd opted to hang back when the two guards had come in because of some kind of protocol. But she knew he was in the next room, a similar one to this—all stone with huge tapestries hung up on the walls and a large fireplace to keep the room warm.

He strode through the stone entryway looking like the warrior he was. "My love?"

"Talk to Virgo, please order him to gather up a small search party. We need to search the forest for signs of more fae and figure out how they got into our realm. I'm assuming it wasn't through the portal, but that is a possibility." Especially since the two guards had already proven they didn't follow protocol. One of them should have stayed behind. "Also, we need to do a search for Stella. I'm sure she simply crossed over while those two left their guard station but..." She looked at Soleil, who was completely unreadable. "What?"

"I would like you and Zephyr to go to New Orleans after we do a search, just...check on Stella. I know she is capable and I know I

27

promised not to send a guard, but you're not a guard. You're her sister, so I'm not breaking a promise."

"Of course. But I want to be part of the search of the forest. Just to make sure they didn't miss anything. If I know Stella...she might have seen what happened and then snuck out of the realm because she was worried you'd make her stay after a fae breach."

Soleil's mouth pulled into a hard line. "I had thought of that as well."

Well that's what happened when you smothered your child. Juniper kept the thought to herself, however.

"I'll gather Virgo and some others and we'll meet you in the bailey." Zephyr moved ghost quiet out of the room.

"You really were born for this," Soleil murmured as she pulled on a cord near the fireplace.

"For what? Giving orders?"

Soleil simply lifted a shoulder. "To lead."

Juniper nodded, not sure what to say. She had led her own small black ops team for decades before discovering her birthright.

"I like that you called me Mother," Soleil said into the quiet, taking Juniper off guard.

Oh. Juniper wasn't sure how she felt about it. She cleared her throat and was saved from saying anything more when one of the staff hurried in—Valentina, her mother's right-hand woman.

"How may I help?" Valentina was a badass warrior who kept things running efficiently at the castle, Juniper had learned since moving here.

"Please alert Ares that I need him—we'll be out searching the forest for hours. So I want to make sure there's enough food ready for everyone when they return. I'm not certain how fae made it into our realm, but we need to make sure there aren't more and to assess the entire situation in general. Make sure the castle and surrounding areas are on high alert—and I need someone to send a message to my parents about what's happened."

Valentina simply nodded and strode out of the room.

"How long a flight will it be to get to them?" Juniper asked. Meaning, her grandparents. She was still getting used to the fact that she had them, had a clan and family. Though she'd always had family, even if they weren't blood.

"A few days at least, but if I don't send for them, my mother will not be happy."

"Why did Marcus assume the male who killed the fae was sent by Starlena?" Juniper's grandmother and Soleil's mother.

"Because she oversees an elite group of warriors and if the male dragon gave orders, he might have assumed it came from one of her people—otherwise he would have recognized someone from the regular patrolling guards... It was stupid of Marcus and Rye to assume but they're young, still learning."

"So you won't be too hard on them?"

Soleil's expression was like granite. "I didn't say that." Then she cleared her throat. "Are you ready? Do you need to get anything?"

"I'm good to go." She'd be shifting to her dragon form, didn't need anything else for a search. She wanted to get to the bottom of this, and she could admit she wanted to rush out to New Orleans, to chase after Stella.

But she also didn't want to be another family member who tried to smother Stella by being overprotective. The last thing she wanted to do was break the trust she had with her sister.

CHAPTER SIX

"You can stop pacing." Stella sat in a comfortable chair by the window in the bedroom she and Rhodes had been led to.

The healer's place in New Orleans was buzzing with activity and while she was exhausted, it was nothing like before, when they'd left that little home hours ago. The chill hadn't abated, however, and she hated how cold she was.

"Someone should be in here." Rhodes was a caged predator as he stalked back and forth near the door, his jaw a tight, hard line. He really was a stunning male and in the brighter light of the bedroom she could drink in every inch of him.

His tunic fit him much more snugly than the one she had on, his pecs and biceps clearly outlined, molding to his body. He was taller than she'd originally thought, perhaps even taller than her mother and father —and they were huge dragons.

"They've taken my blood to be analyzed," she murmured, not that she thought he'd forgotten. He was just *very* impatient.

He grunted in response, but at least he'd stopped pacing. Instead, he leaned against a delicate-looking piece of pale gray furniture, some sort of dresser, and glared at the door, as if willing it to open.

They'd arrived maybe fifteen minutes ago and the healer, Greer, was efficient and kind. Stella had no doubt she and the others working with her were doing everything they could to see to all their patients.

"Rhodes?"

He turned to look at her and she got the full focus of those green-gold eyes, felt pinned in place for a moment. She didn't know him, not really, didn't even know what clan he came from. He was clearly from her realm, but there were different, smaller clans that made up the entirety of the realm.

When he'd shifted to his dragon form, he'd been so dark it had been difficult to make out his form fully. And she found that she very much wanted to know everything about him. "Will you talk to me?" she continued.

Nodding, he moved away from the dresser and came to sit across from her in one of the other cushy chairs.

The room was large, as were the chairs, but he seemed to dwarf his. "What do you wish to talk about?"

"You. Tell me about you." She was far too curious about the male.

He blinked once, confusion flickering in those gorgeous eyes. "What about me?"

She wrapped the blanket tighter around her body, fighting off a shiver of cold. She knew it wasn't that chilly in here, but she had to push down her fear that the poison was doing irreparable harm to her body. "I don't know, tell me about your clan, ah, any siblings?"

His eyes shuttered then and he looked away. "I have no family."

Oooh. There was such a wealth of...not sadness really, but his tone was so bleak it sliced right through her. She swallowed hard, feeling like the biggest kind of monster for taking it for granted that he'd have a clan. Most dragons did and... Oh, if he worked for her grandmother in her elite guard then it made sense if he was a loner.

Going with her instinct—and not caring about stupid princess protocol at this point, especially if she actually was dying—she let her blanket drop and stood.

He stiffened in his chair, looking ready to jump up and help her, but he stilled as she dragged her chair closer to him, until the chairs were touching.

31

He frowned slightly, but settled back down.

"I'm sorry if I asked a painful question," she said, watching him closely.

"It's fine. It is not painful." His stiffly spoken words said otherwise.

She nodded, though it was clear he was lying or just in denial. "Okay."

He cleared his throat, then said, "What else would you like to know?"

All the things. Was he...single? He had to be. She hadn't scented anyone on him. But that might mean nothing because her senses were muted now. She frowned slightly as another shiver rolled through her.

He suddenly stood, his dragon flaring to life in his eyes. "I will get the healer."

"No. I'm just cold. It would help if you held me." A partial truth. He looked a bit lost, as if he needed something to do. And she liked the thought of his arms around her again.

He moved swiftly, shifting her to his lap in moments.

Screw princess protocol. She laid her head on his shoulder, a sigh escaping. She knew she should feel weird about this, but she didn't at all. She felt as if she was exactly where she needed to be. Even if she was behaving nothing like the way she'd been raised. "Can I ask you something else?" Hopefully less painful.

"You may ask me anything." The deep rumble of his voice was an aphrodisiac itself. Along with the heat of him, wrapping around her in tune with his dark, sensual scent.

"Earlier, why did you think I would attack you?"

He shrugged against her. "People normally do."

Well that was depressing. She hated that he must work for her grandmother, though she had no doubt he was good at what he did. She lifted her head, then patted his forearm gently. She started to respond when the door opened and Greer, the elegant healer with copper-colored hair, strode in.

She dressed the way many humans did, in jeans and a flowy shirt the same color as her green eyes. Her expression wasn't grim, exactly, but it was sober.

"Will I get my dragon back?" Stella asked before she could stop herself. She hated that the words came out unsteady, but she was terrified to lose that intrinsic part of herself. And if she wasn't going to, she wanted to know now.

Greer's eyes went soft. "Yes. But it will take some time. As you said, it is definitely poison in your blood. A nasty concoction, a mix I've never seen before. But, I can take it out and destroy it. All your magic will eventually return but it will take a bit of time for you to heal once the poison is gone."

"Then do it." Rhodes' voice was whiplash sharp. "That's why we're here."

Stella gently nudged him, but kept her focus on Greer as she murmured, "Hush."

Greer simply ignored him and focused on her. "Since you're my patient, I need to know if you want him in here while I go over your options."

He shifted underneath her and Stella could feel his anxiety even without looking at him. If her parents had been here, they'd have been shocked by her behavior right now. She was sitting curled up in the lap of her bodyguard like a wild dragon. And she didn't care.

She liked this male with a fierceness that defied logic. "He can stay."

Rhodes settled under her so she turned to him, found his face inches from hers. "Only if you stay quiet and don't snap at the very nice healer," she whispered.

Jaw still tight, he nodded, his eyes glowing.

Stella turned back to Greer, who nodded. "Okay then. You have a few options. One, I can remove the poison with my healing magic. It will be the quickest way, but it will also be the most painful. This poison...it's dark. There's no other way to describe it. I used some of my magic on your blood sample and was able to get rid of it, but it wants to fight back. It's why I took longer than expected. I needed to make sure I could truly destroy it."

"How quick?"

"Roughly two hours. I could sedate you, but I don't like the idea of giving you too much—"

"No sedation."

Greer nodded again. "Okay. Other options. I could also break up the sessions into shorter time frames if the pain is too much. My only fear is that if I do that, it'll spread back faster, and grow stronger."

"So this is more than a poison?"

"It's like a poison-virus. Partially made, partially naturally occurring. We could also try blood transfusions with healthy supernatural blood. I have a small supply of—"

"No." Stella shook her head quickly. "I don't want that." It scared her to think of other blood inside her, even though she knew it was ridiculous. "I can deal with the pain. Can you remove the poison now?"

"Yes. And we can do it in here where you're comfortable," she said as she tapped on a cell phone.

Stella knew what they were, but did not have one. Her sister had told her someone from King's pack would provide her with one to communicate once she arrived. But…she didn't care one way or another.

Before Stella could respond, Reaper, a large male, stepped inside, moved up next to Greer in a way that made it clear they were mated. He gently gripped the healer's hip as Greer said, "Rhodes, my mate Reaper is going to take you downstairs for a bit of tea. Stella will be fine with me." She spoke extra gently, as if expecting an argument.

"I'm fine where I am." Rhodes' grip around her waist tightened. He'd wrapped his big arm completely around her, was basically anchoring her to him.

"That's my mate's way of politely kicking you out." Reaper stepped forward, his dragon in his gaze. Waves of power rolled off him, the level similar to that of her parents. He was definitely a warrior dragon.

Stella turned to look at Rhodes, was surprised to see his dragon in his gaze. Oooh, he was definitely going to fight this. "It's fine. More than fine. It'll be easier for me if you're downstairs. I don't want…" She didn't want him to see her at her weakest. The dragon in her simply couldn't allow that. She was too vulnerable. "I would prefer to do this with just the healer."

He paused for longer than she expected, then finally nodded, his green-gold eyes back, the dragon faded away. "I won't be far." He looked as if he wanted to say more, but finally stood and gently set her back down before leaving.

As soon as the males were gone, Stella felt the loss of his presence immediately.

Which just felt...a little crazy. "We really can do everything here?" she asked, standing at the side of the large bed. Soft bedding in pinks and grays covered it.

"Yes. It'll just be you and me. I won't actually touch you, but my magic will. It will invade your system and pull the poison out, destroying it on its way out. If you need to make noise, to scream, you can. And if you need to stop, tell me."

"I won't disturb the other patients?"

"I work with a couple local witches. They've created a sort of ward around each room that mutes noises. It's gone a long way in helping with privacy, especially given supernatural hearing."

Stella shoved out a breath of relief that no one would be able to hear her in pain. Her weakness. She knew she shouldn't care, but she'd grown up in the palace. She'd always had to be strong, tough, to never let anyone see her as weak. That was what it meant to be part of the Nova clan, to be royalty. She was strong or she was nothing.

"Let's do this," she said as she stretched out on the bed, bracing for the pain. The sooner they got this over with, the sooner she'd have her dragon back.

CHAPTER SEVEN

"I do not care for tea." Rhodes kept his tone as civil as possible as he strode downstairs with the dragon named Reaper. Though the male was much older than Rhodes, he had heard of him, knew of his exploits—and was surprised such a lethal warrior was mated to a healer.

"Good because we're not drinking it. Come on." He kept going, striding past a couple smaller supernaturals, male and female, in a long hallway that eventually deposited into a large kitchen.

And Reaper kept going to a back door.

"I will not be far from my…charge," Rhodes said. He'd been about to say 'my female' but she was not his. Even if he wanted her with all of his being in a way he'd never wanted anything. She'd changed everything.

"We're only going back here." The big male motioned toward a smaller structure in the backyard.

It had no windows and looked sturdy. "I will not be easy to kill if that is your plan."

Reaper let out a snort of laughter. "Fucking dragons. We really are all obnoxious," he muttered as he opened a large door into what turned out to be a gym of sorts.

"What is this place?"

"My mate uses it for physical therapy with humans and shifters. But it is not in use and you need to stay distracted." He tugged off his shirt as he strode to a wall, picked up a long, blunt sparring stick.

Ah. Rhodes tugged his tunic off, folded it neatly and left it at the edge of the mat along with his shoes. "What are the sparring rules?" Or he assumed that was what Reaper wanted.

"We stay in human form. Obviously. No breathing fire. No claws. No killing or maiming. Just practicing."

"What is the point system? The goal?" He'd sparred in the past, many years ago, and understood how some warriors in clans practiced and kept their skills sharp. But he'd never belonged to a clan, did not fully understand all dragon clan rules.

"The goal is to keep your mind off your female. And the point system..." Reaper turned to face him, a grin spreading across his face. "Won't matter because I'm going to wipe the mat with you."

It registered that Reaper had called Stella his—and Rhodes was not going to correct him. He caught the long pipe that Reaper tossed him, felt its weight. Heavy, made for supernaturals.

This was a good distraction.

He squared off with the male and they began circling each other slowly, sizing each other up. Though Rhodes had no doubt the other male had sized him up from the moment he'd stepped into that room with Stella.

Where she was right now... Fuck. He couldn't think of her in pain. He wanted to be there, to be holding her and comforting her. To simply take away her pain.

"Stop thinking!" Reaper attacked, coming in low with his weapon.

Rhodes reacted swiftly, diving over him, going into a roll. Decades ago he'd learned various martial arts with humans in a small village, high up in the mountains of a place that was no longer inhabited by humans or supernaturals. The humans hadn't been as physically strong as him, but they'd taught him so much.

Reaper turned, struck out, missed him by a hairsbreadth.

Rhodes struck out as well, was blocked by Reaper, the clang of the pipes ringing out.

And it was on.

~

"Here." Reaper handed Rhodes a metal cup, nodded at the big water jug. "Where'd you learn to fight like that?" he asked as Rhodes filled up his cup with water.

"Here and there."

Reaper let out a laugh behind him, filled up his own cup and said, "Well, it's impressive. If you ever want to move territories, I have a feeling there's a place for you here. Or I know a clan up in Montana who'd appreciate your skills."

Rhodes couldn't tell if the other male was mocking him so he simply grunted, drank his water.

"What clan are you from anyway?"

He shrugged. "Don't have one."

"Ah." Then Reaper nodded. "I get it." He took a sip of his water, then eyed him carefully. "You're really not going to tell me where you learned to fight? I'm ancient and I've never seen some of those moves."

Perhaps he had been serious and not mocking after all. Rhodes did not interact with other dragons, or really anyone, enough to understand all social cues. He'd lived with humans long ago but after... *After*, he'd kept to himself for the most part. "From humans."

Reaper blinked, then shook his head. "Fine, don't tell me."

"I am being serious. From humans."

"Huh." He took another drink, still watched him with the eyes of a predator. "How old are you?"

Rhodes raised an eyebrow.

"Apologies. We don't know much about the dragons from the Nova realm and I was simply curious. You have a youthful scent but you fight like a savage from my time."

He cleared his throat, decided that telling the truth wouldn't hurt him. "About a hundred and fifty."

"Damn. You are young."

"How did you end up mated to a healer?" he asked, figuring that it was a fair question since the male had been asking him personal things.

"I try not to ask that question because I know I don't deserve her."

38

Huh. Rhodes was silent, continued drinking his water. He would never admit it, but Reaper had tired him out with the sparring. The clock on the wall told him that only an hour had passed, though it felt like much longer. His muscles were tired in a way that didn't often happen.

"Would it be possible to get some things for Stella?" he finally said. "So when your mate is done, she will have some ah, creature comforts?" She had nothing of her own and he hated that, even if he did like her wearing his tunic. But it would make her feel safer, more secure to have her own things.

"Of course. We have plenty stocked up for everyone who comes through here. First, you need a shower because I guarantee we both stink. So shower, then you can look through our pantry with all the basics."

He fell in step with Reaper as they headed out of the training and physical therapy area. "Thank you."

"Of course." Reaper showed him to a small bathroom downstairs and gave him everything he'd need. Though Rhodes had his own clothing, it was nice to have new soap. "If I owe you—"

Reaper simply snorted, and clapped him once on the shoulder. "You owe us nothing. And I'm going to offer you some free advice... If she doesn't scare you a little, she's not the right one for you."

Rhodes shut the door after him, contemplating the male's words even as he hurried to shower. Stella terrified him on many levels, so perhaps that was good.

~

"SHE WILL LIKELY SLEEP FOR A WHILE." Greer's voice was low, melodic as she spoke to Rhodes in the hallway.

He held onto the small bag of things he'd collected for Stella, anxious and needing to see her himself. "But she is okay? She will be able to shift soon?"

"Soon is relative, but yes, all the poison is out of her system. She needs rest right now more than anything for her body to mend. I'll have some food sent up for you soon and then again when she awakens. She'll be hungry when she wakes." The tall healer's cheeks looked more defined than the last time he'd seen her. She was paler. Drawn.

"I am not hungry. Go take care of yourself, please." It was clear that she needed rest. "And thank you for all you've done. I didn't mean to snap at you earlier."

She gave him a soft pat on his upper arm, a ghost of a smile on her lips. "You were worried, so I understand. And I will get food soon, but if you're going to be watching after her, you'll need to eat too. So eat what I send up." Her words were a gentle order.

He nodded before hurrying into the room.

Stella was asleep on the bed, the covers pulled up to her shoulders, her expression so still. But he could hear her breathing, knew she was okay.

Her long silvery braid stretched out on the bed, wisps around her pale face. Her skin was flushed with a healthy glow at least, not pale. Still, he didn't like how motionless she was.

Though he wanted to curl around her, to protect her, he pulled the two chairs by the window over to the edge of the bed and sat in one, then stretched his legs out on the other. It wasn't comfortable, but he wouldn't violate her space.

It felt wrong somehow.

True to her word, Greer sent up food not long after and he went ahead and ate because the healer was right. He needed to be in top form to keep Stella safe.

He ate the bowl of gumbo, something he'd had on a couple other occasions, the bread with it, and drank all of the water before he finally allowed himself to rest.

Scooted once again as close to the bed as possible, he laid his hand right next to Stella's over the covers, not touching her as he closed his eyes.

He would protect her while she couldn't protect herself. For as long as he could.

CHAPTER EIGHT

"I'm fine." Greer laughed lightly as Reaper pulled her covers up over her. He'd already fed her and was now insisting she sleep immediately. As if she'd had any other plans after such an intensive healing session. But she loved his overprotectiveness. "Just tired."

"I am allowed to worry about my mate." He stripped off all his clothing before getting in bed next to her, stretching out his powerful body with a sigh. He slept hot, rarely with any covers—unless her body counted.

She snuggled into him even as she wrapped her own blanket tighter about her. All that healing had drained the energy from her. "What do you think of the princess and her... I don't know what to call him," she murmured. The two had certainly made an interesting pair.

"I like the male."

She snuggled closer, needing all his warmth. "Really?"

He wrapped his big body around hers. "Yes. He fights like a beast. Why?"

"Normally you're a bit surly to other males. Especially unmated ones near me." It was a work in progress with the two of them.

"He wants that female more than his next breath. Something..." He leaned down, brushed his mouth over hers for a fleeting moment before he tightened his grip around her again. "…I can understand since you are my delicious mate."

A shiver rolled through her and she wished she weren't so exhausted. She'd be pinned against the mattress if she gave the slightest hint she wasn't too tired for sex. Sighing, she tried to steady her mind. Her body was ready for sleep, but the healer part of her sometimes simply couldn't shut off.

"What is bothering you, my love?" Reaper's voice was a low whisper, embracing all of her.

"I just worry for his heart," she murmured.

"Who? Rhodes?"

"Hmmm. He is very attached to Stella."

"So?"

"She's from a royal line, a realm we know little about. But…the realms I do have experience with can be unforgiving when it comes to mating if the mate is not…" She trailed off, not quite sure how to put her thoughts into words.

"A 'preferred' bloodline?" Reaper snorted softly. "I don't think Stella's family is like that. Her grandmother seems quite savage." And her mate definitely approved of savagery.

"I don't either. But…" She shrugged against him. It wasn't as if Greer truly knew Stella's family, not well. The way the male had looked at Stella had simply touched Greer. It was clear he cared for her.

"My sweet healer, always worried about others."

"I can't help it."

"I know." He kissed the top of her head oh so gently.

"Do you remember one of the first things you said to me?" she asked into the quiet.

He went very still next to her, the punch of lust rolling off him sharp. "I remember thinking you were offering to fuck my face and being very excited at the idea."

She smiled into his chest, biting back a laugh. He'd been so arrogant back then—was still arrogant. And he'd offered to let her sit on his face right in the middle of a kitchen a mere hour after meeting her. "Maybe when I wake up in a few hours I'll find your head between my legs," she murmured, sleep starting to take over.

"You can count on it."

Sighing against him, she closed her eyes and let her brain rest, knowing that all was well in this brief moment with her mate. The deadly mate she'd never seen coming.

CHAPTER NINE

Stella opened her eyes to find Rhodes hunched over in a chair, his hand laying on the bed right next to her thigh, but not quite touching her. He'd turned the chair so that he was facing her.

In the morning light streaming in from one of the window's blinds, he looked...not soft or gentle. Never that. But he looked younger, even with the wicked scar on his face. Less hard.

More than a bit of stubble had grown across his face, only adding to that whole sexy and brooding thing he'd nailed down. Goddess, the male was gorgeous. A warrior dragon she might never have met if not for this mission.

She wanted to reach out and touch him, to see if he was real, and must have made a move or maybe he'd just been alerted that she was awake.

He suddenly opened his eyes, his dragon looking at her for a second, then his eyes were human. He jolted upright. "Stella."

Whew, the way he said her name, ooohh, she felt it deep in a place that had never been touched. "Have you been here all night?" Or day? She wasn't even sure what day or time it was, hoped she hadn't lost much time.

"How are you feeling?" he asked, not answering her question. "Do you need the healer?" He'd gone from peaceful to tense, all his muscles bunched tight as he leaned toward her.

"I'm...good enough." Groaning, she sat up, not exactly surprised when he took over, helping her sit upright.

Her entire life she'd been smothered by her well-meaning family who'd been grieving the loss of so many of their dragonlings. So she'd accepted it even if it had started to grate on her lately.

With Rhodes, she found she didn't mind him caring for her at all. "I'm going to shower. Would you get me some food while I'm in there?" She also wanted to brush her teeth because yuck.

"Of course. There are toiletries and fresh new clothes already in the bathroom for you. Do you need any help in there?" He averted his gaze, his cheeks tinging a slight shade darker.

Well that was interesting.

She paused, thought about saying yes, but knew that was a bad idea. At least now. Because she couldn't deny her attraction to him. It was so raw, too bright a thing to ever ignore. "I don't think so."

Even so, he stood with her and walked her right to the shower, hovering a bit too much now. He smelled so damn good, that dark sensualness like candy. She wanted to bury her face against his chest and simply inhale all that goodness. When he continued standing there, she looked up at him. "Are you planning on washing my back?"

His eyes flared bright, but he swiveled, stalked out of the bathroom quickly.

And she could breathe again. The man was getting under her skin. She rolled her shoulders now that she was alone, took stock of herself as she stripped out of the tunic. She found she didn't want to wash it, which was silly. She'd sweated an insane amount when Greer had been pulling the poison from her. But Rhodes' scent was all over it too and she didn't want to lose it.

Maybe she'd steal something of his, tuck it away and smell him whenever she wanted. Hmm, her dragon liked that thought very much. It was very unbecoming of a princess but she cared little at the moment.

Wait...her dragon. She called on her beast, couldn't shift, couldn't reach her magic, but her dragon was there, deep, *deep* down.

Tears stung her eyes as joy flooded her. She could feel her beast much more clearly now.

Reaching for the shower knob, she turned it on with a sense of peace, enjoying even the blast of chilly water as she stepped fully inside the black and white tiled enclosure.

As it gradually turned from cold to scorching hot, she reveled in washing her hair, getting clean—and she had to actively not touch herself or think about the fact that Rhodes, the sexiest male she'd ever known, was so very close.

Because if she touched herself, gave in to what she wanted to do, he would scent it all over her. And that was just embarrassing.

When Stella stepped into the bedroom after her long shower, she found the bed had been stripped and remade with all new bedding and a tray of breads, nuts and meats waiting. Her stomach rumbled at the scents, her hunger nearly overpowering the need to see Rhodes again.

She really needed to get over whatever this weird obsession with him was. Unless she didn't? Unless she gave into it. But he was her guard, her escort, he wouldn't...want to break that informal rule of never touching a ward. Right?

Inwardly cursing herself, she sat by the window again, pulled the rolling cart toward her just as the door opened.

Rhodes strode in, a small tray in his big hands. His eyes heated for a moment as he raked his gaze over her, but then he was all professional as he shut the door behind him. "I got you fruit, cheese and juice. I thought you might want that instead of all the meat."

She blinked in surprise. Dragons were known for how much meat they consumed but in addition to being smaller than the average dragon, she also preferred far less meat than most of her kind. She wasn't sure if he knew that or had guessed. Either way, it was thoughtful. "Thank you. Have you had breakfast yet?"

He nodded as he set the tray on the cart next to the other tray.

"Did you truly eat or are you just saying that?"

"I did. The healer insisted," he murmured.

She giggled slightly. Healers tended to be very bossy and since they were usually right, it made sense. "Good then."

"How was your shower?"

She wasn't sure why the question felt sexual, probably her own projections, but she felt her face warm up all the same. "Wonderful, thank you. I feel much better." Which meant she could soon focus on the reason she'd been sent here. "I am a little tired still. How long did I sleep anyway?"

"Only seven hours. You need more rest." His jaw was set tight with disapproval.

She normally only needed a few hours of sleep a night—she was a dragon after all. But he was right, seven was the bare minimum. "I'll sleep later. What I really need is to eat and then we need to head to our accommodations." Her sister Juniper had sent ahead to request they stay with her new brothers-in-laws. "And I need something to secure my hair," she added as she scooped up a strawberry stuffed with clotted cream. Her mouth was already watering at the sight of it. She'd secured her long hair in a towel and needed to braid it while it was damp and pliable. But there had been nothing in the bathroom she could use.

"Your hair?"

She nodded, took a bite and couldn't stop a small moan from escaping. An explosion of flavor burst on her tongue, the sweetness amazing. Oh yeah, she was about to eat everything in sight.

Rhodes stood abruptly, moved to the window, giving her his back as he dug into the satchel he'd left there. When he turned back, he had a black tie in his hand. "Take your hair down. I will braid it as you eat."

She blinked at his words, at the *order*—and at the way her thighs clenched oh so tight at that order. She should not like anyone telling her what to do, never had in the past, but when he did it. Oh, yes. "You can braid hair?"

He nodded once, still all stiff and at attention as if expecting a threat at any moment.

"Okay." She pushed the tray forward slightly as she stood, pulled the towel off of her hair. Her silvery hair was ridiculously long, as was the style in the Nova realm, and she wondered if she might cut it while here. "Will you tell me why you know how to braid hair?" she asked as she sat back down.

He procured a comb from somewhere, because hers was still back in her bag in the forest of her realm. At that thought, she made a note to send a message to her family, to get progress on what had happened, to find out about those creepy fae who'd attacked her. She had no doubt that her family had started an investigation, had likely already dispatched warriors to hunt down whoever had sent the fae.

As he started to comb her hair, she picked up her fork again. The feel of him gently using the comb and his fingers to gather her hair was sending her senses into overdrive. He was so incredibly gentle. After she'd taken a couple bites, she thought he'd decided not to answer.

But then he said, "Over a century ago I lived with humans, in a small village. I did not actually live with them, but on the outskirts. The healer of the village had four girls, all under the age of ten. They taught me, told me I needed more useful skills than just fighting."

She laughed at the words even as she wondered why he'd lived with humans. "Useful indeed."

"The oldest said I could use it to impress any female." His voice had dropped low now.

Stella sucked in a breath, her fork paused midair. She swallowed hard, her brain freezing, but thankfully he continued.

"Your hair is beautiful." There was a touch of awe in his voice as he threaded his fingers through it.

She'd never had a male touch her hair like this. "Thank you."

Forcing herself to eat the wonderful food when all she could focus on was the sensation of his fingers combing through her hair, skating over her scalp, was a beautiful form of torture. It felt like ages had passed, but far too soon he was done and she felt like she could breathe steadily again.

"Did I miss anything while I was asleep?" She pulled her braid around, surreptitiously smelled the tie he'd used to secure her hair. It smelled like him so maybe she wouldn't have to steal something of his after all.

"Not much," he said as he rummaged around in his bag. "Though I think perhaps you should return to your realm—"

"No." That wasn't happening. "I was given a job and thanks to you, my family will now know about the fae who invaded our territory. There is nothing I can do to help them. They will send trackers far better trained than me to...wherever those fae came from." She'd only met a couple in her entire existence. Her realm had been so cut off before they'd found Juniper again. Now it was just opening up so it was not a huge shock that it had been invaded. Though the brazenness was surprising.

"You might still be in danger. Probably are still in danger."

"It's very likely they shot me down because I was an easy target." She'd been doing barrel rolls in the air, not using her natural camouflage at all. "And lucky for me, I'm a dragon."

"With no powers currently," he growled as he sat across from her, his mouth pulled into a frown. Not that it did anything to take away his attractiveness. Oh no. He was still a stunning male warrior very much in his prime. Even the scar on his cheek made him sexier.

And now that her dragon was starting to wake up, it was like all her senses were going into overdrive and focused solely on this male.

She bit back the sharp response on the tip of her tongue. She knew very well she didn't have her full dragon strength and didn't need him to remind her. She also knew how to get what she wanted. "Well then, luckily I have a very capable, strong dragon warrior on my side. Are you not up to the task of guarding me while I'm here?"

His dragon peered back at her then, fury in his gaze at the challenge. "Of course I'm capable."

She didn't smile, though she wanted to. "Then it's settled. We will stay in New Orleans and complete the job."

Instead of answering, he simply grumbled under his breath and started to do that pacing thing again.

She ran her hand down her braid before she started eating again. If she was going to do what she'd been tasked with, she'd need all the strength she could get.

And no dragon, no matter how sexy, was going to stand in her way.

CHAPTER TEN

Rhodes paused at the knock on the bedroom door. "It's open."
Greer stepped inside, smiled at the two of them.

Stella was still eating, was currently polishing off the last cup of fruit. It didn't seem like enough food to him, but he wouldn't push her on that. Not now anyway.

"You look wonderful." Greer's smile was genuine and she didn't have that drawn look as she'd had last night, so it seemed she'd rebounded from all her magic use.

"I am, thanks to you." Stella pushed the cart away, started to stand, but Greer waved her back down.

"Please don't get up," the healer said.

Rhodes hung back by the bed, feeling awkward as the healer approached Stella, then sat across from her, her expression gentle. "You have a visitor. It's Aurora. If you're not up to seeing her—"

"I'm up to it." Stella stood immediately, brushed her hands over her jeans. "I feel underdressed, however."

Rhodes knew the name Aurora, knew she was the new female Alpha of the region—had recently mated. He wasn't sure how that boded for him—Stella had assumed he was her bodyguard, sent by the palace. But there was a possibility he could be found out. He wasn't certain if the

Alpha couple would run a background check on him. Things were different now after The Fall so it might not be easy to do that.

Greer laughed lightly. "You're fine, I promise. She's wearing jeans too. We're not big on formality in this territory."

"That's a relief." Stella's bicolored eyes sparked as she looked at him and once again, he was struck with how much he simply liked this female. "Come with me?"

He would go anywhere with her.

He nodded, unable to find his voice for a moment. He wished things were different, that he hadn't met her under the worst circumstances, that he wasn't lying to her about who he was. Because a lie of omission was still a lie. He wished for a lot of things, but it wouldn't do any good.

She was ready in a few minutes, insisting she needed to brush her teeth and put on lip gloss. In reality she didn't need anything for her lips; they were perfect.

Downstairs, the female Alpha of the territory was sitting in the waiting room he'd seen when they'd first arrived yesterday. High ceilings, elegant furnishing, this was a well-kept healing center. Not all packs and territories had such places, especially after The Fall.

Aurora stepped forward, smiling at Stella, then nodded politely at Rhodes before she pulled Stella into a short hug. The scent of Aurora's mate was thick in the air; she'd been marked by the male for all supernaturals to know she was taken.

Once again Rhodes wished he could do the same to Stella.

"It's lovely to see you again." Stella's voice was soft, her words genuine.

"You as well."

Stella motioned next to her. "Ah, Aurora, this is Rhodes, he's with me, part of my territory."

He gave a polite nod to Aurora who smiled warmly at him. He didn't like Stella lying for him—when she had no idea that she even was lying. He hadn't thought all of this through, had thought only to protect her. He hadn't imagined she would introduce him as part of the Nova realm, hadn't thought she'd...introduce him at all. He was simply her bodyguard.

51

"First, let's sit." Aurora motioned to a cluster of delicate-looking furniture.

Rhodes sat next to Stella on a settee, his leg pressing up against hers, while Aurora sat across from them on a vintage-looking chair. He knew he should probably make himself invisible, step out of the room and give them the illusion of privacy. Probably what a real bodyguard would do.

But that wasn't happening. She was his to protect.

Greer had been right about the lack of formality. The other female wore a plain T-shirt that showed off strong arms and faded jeans with sturdy-looking boots. Her dark brown hair was pulled back into a loose coil at her neck. And she had flecks of paint on her fingernails—which made sense since she was an artist. The thing that made her stand out was the soft blue glow emanating from her—he'd heard that she was a phoenix, and knew that was part of her heritage. Though he knew phoenixes could cover their glow if they so choose. Clearly she wasn't hiding that part of herself.

"I'm sorry about what happened on your way here," Aurora said. "Do you have any news on who hurt you?"

"No, but my family should know by now." Stella glanced at Rhodes and he nodded.

Technically, they didn't know about the attack on her, simply that the realm had been invaded by a couple fae who had been killed by him —and he'd never introduced himself to the guards at the portal. They'd acted foolish when they'd left the portal door unguarded, had actually listened to his orders, but it had given him the ability to quickly transport Stella.

Unfortunately, he knew that eventually someone would come after her, come check on her.

His time with her was limited. He knew he should tell her the truth of who he was, but then she'd get rid of him. She wouldn't want a paid assassin with no known bloodline around her. Especially when he'd been paid to kidnap her by the same fae who'd shot her full of poison. Until then he would protect her as long as he could, until her family inevitably arrived.

"Do you think the threat has followed you here?" the Alpha continued.

"It is a possibility," Rhodes said before Stella could respond.

Aurora nodded, a frown pulling at her mouth. "King has already let our people know to be on the lookout for any unknown fae, so if we discover anything or anyone we believe is a threat, someone will alert you. He's also reached out to his father to see if he's heard of any potential threat against you from any fae."

Rhodes and Stella both nodded—he understood that King's father was fae, making the Alpha a powerful hybrid.

Aurora continued. "Do you have a means of communication while you're here?"

Stella shook her head. "Ah, not yet."

"I have a cell phone." Rhodes didn't often use it, but he'd purchased it from a witch after The Fall. Witches and other sorcerers were working with various humans to keep communication up and running. Many of the satellites had survived but communication was still spotty in places unless you had the right tech.

Stella looked at him in surprise, but didn't say anything.

"Good then. We'll make sure you have one as well," she said to Stella. "Our pack has more than enough to hand out. There's something else I need to talk to you about. I know you were supposed to be staying with Avery and Mikael, but they are out of town for a couple weeks on a construction project. I wanted to offer that you stay at my home...sort of former home," she said on a laugh. "I mostly stay at King's place— which is mine now too, it's just weird to say that. But sometimes we'll both crash with my OG pack as they refer to themselves. All my pack-mates live in a large mansion and there will be space for both of you."

"I've been there once," she said, smiling. "Juniper took me for a dinner over there along with Mikael, Avery and her brothers. I met some of your former roommates."

"Ah, that's wonderful then. I wanted to ask you before I asked them, but I already know they'll say yes. I think it would be better if you stayed there, especially if there is a threat still against you."

"Of course. It will be nice to see everyone again. How is Axel doing?"

Axel? That was a male name. Rhodes frowned.

Aurora simply lifted a shoulder, her mouth curving up. "He's always in some sort of trouble."

Stella laughed lightly and as they discussed people he didn't know, he focused on Stella's scent, the way it called to him.

And he questioned his dragon's sanity for falling for the most unattainable female on the planet. A princess far out of his league who would hate him once she knew the truth about who he was. What he was.

~

"ARE THE ROOMS TO YOUR ACCEPTANCE?" Bella, a petite shifter whose animal side he couldn't figure out yet, eyed Rhodes with a hint of a smile as he stepped out of the bedroom Stella would be sleeping in.

He'd inspected her potential room, making sure it was secure enough, and he was certain Bella was amused by his protectiveness. He didn't care.

Before he could respond, Stella said, "Of course they are." She was behind him on the stairs, nudged him once in the side.

Probably because he'd been obnoxious wanting to know about their security. Stella would be sleeping here, staying here; he had a right to know how secure the three-story mansion was. Especially since he knew the threat against her was very real. He didn't think the Domincary fae would venture after her this deep into King and Aurora's territory but it was a possibility.

"They're wonderful and we appreciate you allowing us to stay with you," Stella continued.

Bella grinned. "We're more than happy to house Juniper's sister. Though...our place might be different than your palace. A little rowdier at times. And we're not very formal."

"Good." Stella's vehement response startled a laugh from Bella.

"Stella will need a few things. Clothing mostly," Rhodes said quietly. He'd taken a few things from the healer's place, but most of the clothing there had been too large and too long for her. "Is there a place I might procure some things like that?"

"I wondered where your bags were," Stella said, looking between the two of them. "We're about the same size. What do you need?"

"Ah...everything really. My bag was lost when I was attacked."

Bella made a comforting sound and linked her arm through Stella's. "Let's raid my closet then. You can stay outside my room," she tossed over her shoulder to Rhodes.

He gritted his teeth. Of course he would not follow them into the other female's bedroom—but he would stand guard outside it.

As they entered a bedroom on the second floor, he crossed his arms and leaned against the wall to wait. Female laughter trailed out from the room and he tried not to think about Stella in any stage of undress. Would she...be trying on the clothing now? Or just picking things out?

Nope. He shut down the image of that fast.

Soft footfalls sounded on the stairs and a redheaded female, one he'd met earlier, stopped on the landing. Frowned at him.

"Who the hell are you?" she demanded.

He straightened, readying for a fight, all his muscles going taut at the deadly look in her eyes. The female with the double braids looked ready to do battle. "We met twenty minutes ago. Have you injured your brain?" Something was clearly wrong with this female.

"Oh." Her body language went a little less murder, though she still appeared primed to attack. In heavy boots, cargo-style pants and a skin-tight T-shirt, she looked like many warriors he'd met over the years. "You must have met my twin, Brielle. I'm Harlow."

Ah. That was when he scented the subtle difference. Barely there, but different all the same. "The tiger shifter. I did not realize she had a twin. I'm Rhodes and I'm with Stella."

"Right, I just got a text she was arriving today. Are you the only security? I thought a princess would have a whole brigade or whatever."

He scoffed slightly. "I am a dragon."

She let out a bark of laughter and turned toward the stairs. "I applaud your confidence, dragon. I'll catch you later." Then she hurried up the stairs and out of sight on quiet feet. Even if he hadn't known she was a tiger, he'd have guessed she was feline.

They all moved with a certain liquidity that seemed to defy physics.

The door behind him suddenly opened and Bella was there, a grin on her face. "I think I've found the perfect dress for her. I need your help."

Frowning, he followed after her only to stop and stare at Stella. In bare feet, she was standing in front of a long mirror wearing a skintight pale pink dress that shimmered.

It wrapped around her body as if it was truly a second skin and when she turned to him, he saw exactly how low cut it was. There was a deep V between her breasts, then a little scrap of fabric, then another keyhole below, showing even more skin, including an adorable bellybutton.

Bellybuttons shouldn't be adorable or sexy but he couldn't stop staring at hers, sweeping in every inch of her right down to her silver-painted toenails. Even her feet turned him on. She was beyond beautiful —but he didn't want any males to see her like this.

"She will not wear this," he barked, unable to stop the surge of possessiveness that pumped through him.

"Why not? She looks incredible." Bella shot him a dark look. "You were supposed to help! Axel," she called out. "Come to my room!" she shouted, making Rhodes wince at the decibel.

But he didn't take his gaze off Stella. She looked like walking sex and no one but him should see her like this.

"It doesn't look good?" There was a vulnerability in Stella's expression that took him off guard as she watched him, bit her bottom lip nervously.

"Of course it looks good. You are absolute perfection." She was the most beautiful female on the planet.

Feeling out of his mind, he stalked forward, not daring to touch her even as he wanted to point out exactly how little fabric she had on. Shifters got naked all the time but...this was unacceptable. "You will not be out in public like this!"

Her eyebrows rose. "Why not? Bella said this is appropriate for tonight, for the place we're going to."

That was something else he didn't want to think about. She'd secured a meeting with a vampire to talk about her family's stolen crown and afterward she wanted to go to a supernatural-run club. There would be far too many people around, too many scents—too many threats. Too many horny males. He didn't like any of it, especially when there was a very real threat somewhere out there—fae.

"What the hell, Bella," Axel muttered as he stepped into the entryway. The lion Rhodes had met briefly when they'd first arrived strode in wearing low-hanging sweatpants, no shirt, and his dark hair was pulled back into a bun. He was what some females would consider handsome. Pretty even.

Rhodes glared at him.

The male's eyebrows shot up as he spotted Stella. "Wow. You look stunning."

Stella looked back at Rhodes and a flicker of hurt flashed in her gaze before she turned away from him again and faced Bella. "It's perfect for later tonight. Thank you."

Bella nodded, then literally shooed Rhodes and Axel out.

"Where are you two going tonight?" Axel asked, yawning and stretching in a very feline way as Bella slammed the door in Rhodes' face.

"A meeting and then some nightclub," he growled, still annoyed.

"Is that a good idea?" Now Axel frowned, straightening. "Wasn't she just attacked?"

"That's exactly what I said." Maybe he didn't want to rip off this male's face after all.

"What is the level of the threat?" Axel demanded.

"This territory is secure. And it wasn't common knowledge before she left that she was coming to King's territory." He knew that much. He'd never told anyone about her schedule, her plans—he hadn't planned to give her over to the fae so he'd told them nothing. Clearly someone else had been watching out for an opportunity to grab her. "Taking her could have been a crime of opportunity." Doubtful. But he couldn't say anything with one hundred percent certainty. No one would have heard about their failure either. He hadn't checked in, never did until he was done with a job.

"It seems too dangerous." Axel crossed his arms over his chest, that frown firmly in place.

"She still does not have her dragon fully back either," he added, because he needed someone on his side.

"We can hear you!" Bella shouted from the bedroom "We're all going tonight. I've already told Cynara and she's giving us a secure area."

"Why is she going to a club?" Axel asked, ignoring Bella's shout.

"We are meeting with a vampire first about the reason she's in the territory. Then she wanted to experience a nightclub in the human realm. They don't have places like that in the Nova realm." And even if they had, she was a princess and he knew she wouldn't have been allowed to go with any sort of anonymity.

"Oh." The lion's expression softened slightly, then motioned for Rhodes to step away from the door and into a bedroom.

By the scent of it, it was Axel's. And...it was as if clothing had exploded everywhere. The sight of the clothing strewn all about gave Rhodes hives. How did this male live like this?

"I forgot how sheltered she's been. We'll all go tonight. The kids are all at Aurora and King's, completely safe for the weekend, and we've all got the night off. So we'll keep a tight circle around her, make sure she's safe."

He wanted to ask what kids the lion referred to, but didn't in case he was supposed to know already. Regardless, some of the tension in Rhodes' shoulders eased knowing that so many others would be there to help protect her. He was not used to depending on anyone. "Thank you."

The big male lifted a shoulder. "Of course. We look out for each other. What vampire are you meeting anyway?"

"A male named Christian. He is friends with her sister apparently."

Axel's expression darkened, his tawny-colored eyes flaring hot for the briefest of moments. "Will you do me a favor when you see him?"

"Of course." He found he liked this male.

"Punch him in his stupidly handsome face. Hard."

Rhodes blinked, but Axel had already turned away and was grumbling to himself about 'neat-freak vampires' while he started picking up all of his clothing.

Rhodes backed out of the doorway, closing it behind him. As he turned, he found Stella stepping out of Bella's bedroom, a small suitcase in hand.

"I think I have everything I'll need at least for a week." Her expression was more reserved than it had been earlier and he knew why. He was a giant dick. "Do you need anything? I'm sure we'll be able to get more clothes or whatever you need."

He was touched that she cared to ask. "I have everything I need. How are you feeling?"

"Honestly?" she said, picking up the suitcase.

He plucked it from her hands.

She gave him a small smile as she fell in step with him. "I'm tired," she continued. "I'd like to nap before we leave. I know the poison is out of me, but—"

"You don't have to make excuses, Stella. Sleep sounds like an excellent idea." And he needed to reach out to his contact—and lie about Stella's whereabouts. He wanted to throw the fae off her trail before he could figure out his next step.

"Thank you. I'm so used to being busy, to always doing something."

"You were just poisoned." He barely kept the grumble out of his voice.

Sighing, she simply nodded as they reached the next floor.

Once he was certain she was settled, he made his call.

CHAPTER ELEVEN

Stella stepped into her bedroom to find Rhodes already there, leaning against one of the big windows, looking out into the yard.

He met her with a heated gaze before a neutral mask fell in place, but he couldn't stop the sweep of her body from head to toe, then back up again.

A shiver rolled through her and even though she wanted to be annoyed at him for his behavior about her dress earlier—the one she now had on—it was difficult when she remembered how he'd called her 'absolute perfection'. Still, he'd been so angry about it.

But she'd had a nap and a shower and felt refreshed. And soon it would be time to go, though she was hoping to eat before they left. "So I guess everyone is meeting up with us after we speak to Christian?" He was a vampire her sister was friends with and had directed Stella to speak to—and Stella had briefly spoken to him at her sister's wedding festivities. So he wasn't a complete stranger.

Rhodes didn't respond. Instead, he pushed off the window frame with a liquid grace, watching her with the gaze of a predator as he stalked forward, his green-gold eyes glittering with… She was pretty sure it was lust. Which was a whole lot to deal with. He was making her crazy with all these new feelings.

"You look nice," she murmured, going to grab the clutch one of the women in the house had let her borrow. It felt weird not having any of her things but everyone had been so giving and accommodating. No one treated her like a princess who was 'less than' or breakable. She was just Stella, Juniper's sister. One of the crew, and she really, really liked it. "Your shirt is very human in style. Did you borrow clothes from Axel or—"

She turned when she felt the heat of him, realized Rhodes was crowding her up against the dresser where she'd laid out her few things. "What are you doing?"

He inhaled deeply as he leaned down against her neck and ooohh-hhh. Oh my, he was smelling her with the intensity she'd only ever witnessed in mates. He was all up in her personal space as he ran his nose along her jaw with absolutely *no* apologies.

She couldn't pretend to be unaffected, couldn't pretend not to care. She wanted this male desperately and he was acting nothing like the royal guards ever did. He was focused on her with an intensity that scared her in the best way.

And...no one from her clan was here. She could do whatever she wanted without any repercussion, any judgment. Maybe that was why he was into this too—there was no one from their clan around to know about any of this. They could just be themselves.

"So you're going with the dress?" he murmured, his mouth right at her ear, his voice a drug.

"What do you have against this dress?" Her heart was a wild beat in her ears. The only thing she was aware of was him, this larger-than-life dragon who'd awoken so many feelings inside her she couldn't contain them any longer.

"Forget the dress. I simply don't want anyone else to see that much of you," he growled. "I want you wearing my clothes, my scent all over you."

Oh. Hell. A punch of lust rolled through her at the possessiveness in his tone—and his words!—and not for the first time she wondered if she'd lost her mind in order to be okay with this. Was this what happened to people when they started having sex? They lost all sense?

She wasn't even having sex—yet. And she wanted more of this possessive talk from him, wanted to... She arched against him, pressing her body against his. She needed to be much closer to him.

As she pressed against him, she felt his very thick erection against her abdomen. "Too bad. I'm wearing it," she whispered, knowing it would trigger more possessiveness.

He pulled back to look at her. His dragon peered down at her for a moment and when she felt his big hands land on her waist, another rush of heat curled through her. He held her in place against him.

She loved the feel of his hands on her, and she really, really loved the feel of his physical reaction pressing right up against her. So far all his touches had been innocent enough, but the way he was holding onto her now... Whew. She tentatively placed her hands on his chest, watched in fascination as he sucked in a breath.

She had a certain amount of power over this male and the knowledge made her light-headed. The truth was, he had power over her too. Because if he pushed, she'd likely change the stupid dress and that scared her.

"What are you thinking right now?" she found herself saying. Because this was all new to her. She'd only ever had a few stolen kisses and they'd all been awkward, had left her feeling nothing at all other than relief when they'd been over.

Right now she felt as if she could combust. Her dragon was clawing at her deep inside, still muted while her body healed, but oh, her dragon liked this male too, wanted to get closer to him. Wanted to mark him, taste him, claim him. Devour him.

"That I want to taste you before we leave. I want my scent on you before we walk out that door." His words were a guttural growl, barely human as he flexed his fingers on her waist, held tight.

And *that* had been the right thing to say apparently. No male had ever talked to her like this before. It was freeing. Made her feel wild. Hungry. Desperate for more.

Going on instinct, she spread her legs slightly, hoping he meant what she thought he did. Because she wanted more than a simple kiss. "Okay. Taste me."

Raw heat flared in his eyes, combined with shock. But that surprise faded as he raised his hand, wrapped his fingers oh so gently around her throat and lowered his mouth to hers.

"I want more than your mouth." Another rough growl, his breath hot against her face.

"Good." She felt almost hollow now, desperate with a need to be filled by him. *This* was what people talked about when they discussed lust.

"Fuck." The savage word tore from him before he crushed his mouth to hers.

She lost all sense of time, of everything, as he plundered her mouth. She dug her fingers into his shoulders, trying to anchor herself as he teased his tongue against hers, invaded her mouth—claimed her.

And that was exactly what he was doing as he kept her pinned against the dresser and devoured her with his kisses.

Her nipples beaded tight against the built-in bra cups of the dress as she arched into him, the need to get closer instinctual. She wanted to wrap her legs around this male, to have him fill her even as she knew she was playing with fire.

They barely knew each other.

She simply didn't care. Her dragon cared even less.

She'd heard more than once that sex made you stupid and... Who cared? All she could focus on was the way he slid one of his hands lower, lower—and slipped it between her legs.

No one had ever touched her there before so when he cupped her mound, she jolted.

He pulled back slightly, his eyes dark as he stared down at her, his fingers still wrapped gently around her throat. "Is this okay?"

"Yes." She liked that he'd asked. It soothed her nerves, reinforced that this was the right decision. Not that she was actually doubting herself. She wanted this male with a desperation.

"I can't believe that you're not wearing anything under this dress," he murmured even as he oh so gently trailed a finger along her slickness.

Her throat tightened as she tried to process the pure pleasure of him

—then he slid a finger inside her. And her brain short-circuited for a moment.

"Rhodes," she gasped.

He growled soft and low, the sound a rumble that reverberated all around her. Then he slowly withdrew his finger, but before she could protest and demand he push deeper, add another one, he slid his finger into his mouth.

Tasting her.

Her mouth fell open as she stared at him.

"Fucking. Perfection," he growled.

Still staring, she swallowed hard as heat engulfed her. Not from her dragon, but from raw lust. This male had stripped her down to her barest self without undressing her and all she wanted was him.

His gaze still pinned on hers, he grasped the hem of her dress and shoved it up to her waist before he went down on his knees.

Okay, so this was happening.

Heat pooled low in her belly and her breath hitched as she watched him. He was huge, his shoulders broad as he knelt in front of her. The look of utter concentration on his hard face, the sharp scent of his arousal filling the air as he lifted one of her legs, eased it over his shoulder.

Impatient, she hopped up on the dresser and put her other leg over his shoulder as well.

His eyes darkened when she did that, looking nothing like the green-gold or even his dragon as he bent his head between her legs.

And as he did, she could barely breathe as pleasure punched through her. He slicked his tongue along her folds even as he slid his finger back inside her.

"Goddess," she murmured as she clasped onto his head, digging her heels into his back as she spread wider for him.

"Rhodes," he growled against her. "Say my name only." A quiet, heated demand.

Her inner walls tightened around his finger at the command. "Rhodes." She'd chant his name if he got her off, if he finished this in the way she was desperate for.

She'd only ever pleasured herself, always in private. This was a new experience for her and she already knew she was going to be addicted to him. She'd planned to let loose, was hoping to finally have sex with a hot male she liked.

But she should have known she wouldn't be able to separate physical intimacy and emotions. Because she was now hooked on this male, wanted all of his secrets. Wanted more than just sex.

When he added another finger, she jolted against his face.

And when he sucked on her clit, she cried out, unable to bite it back. Everyone was outside but they might still hear her. And sweet goddess above, she couldn't find it in her to care.

Then he did it again, thrusting his fingers inside her as he sucked on and teased her clit until the feeling building inside her finally crested.

All her muscles pulled tight, her back arching as she dug her fingers into his skull with the release punching through her. Pleasure poured out to all her nerve endings even as she tried to bite back another cry of pleasure, failed.

"Fuck," he growled against her as she came down from her high, her legs going lax as she half-stood.

He stood too, immediately grasping onto her hips as she plastered herself to him, covered her mouth with his.

He didn't seem to care that she was all over him. "Taste your pleasure." Another raw demand against her mouth that had more heat punching through her. She was pretty sure she might be able to come again, hoped she got to make him climax too.

The way this male talked to her was almost too much, got her hotter than she'd ever thought possible.

"I want to taste you too," she whispered against his mouth.

He went very still, his eyes darkening as he watched her. Instead of responding, he said, "Did you enjoy what I did?" There was a hint of vulnerability in his question, so faint she barely picked up on it. He *had* to know he was amazing.

"I don't have anything to compare it to," she confessed as she slid her arms around his waist, held him close. "But if I did, I'd still say that was the most erotic thing I've ever experienced." She was sure he'd been with countless females, of course he had. Something the darkest part of her didn't want to think about. Ever.

"Good," he growled out. "And for the record, I don't have anything to compare it to either."

Wait...what? Blinking, she stared up at him, not sure he meant what she thought he did. "You've never gone down on a female?"

He shook his head, his cheeks tinging the faintest shade of bronze. "I've never *been* with a female at all. With anyone."

Sweet goddess...how was that possible? "Well, you're a pro. But only for me," she snapped out, a sudden surge of possessiveness overtaking her. She wanted that very clear. "I don't share."

His eyes went almost obsidian for a moment as he leaned down, brushed his lips over hers. "I don't share either."

Then, he released a claw and quickly, expertly, sliced down the front of her dress so that it fell open, revealing all of her, the entire thing ruined.

"I guess you won't be wearing that dress tonight after all." Pure male satisfaction in his voice.

"Rhodes!"

But he'd turned away from her, stalked to the bathroom and shut the door with a resounding click. The shower started running a moment later and she...

What the hell had just happened? She'd wanted to pleasure him as well, to take him in her mouth and taste him as he'd tasted her. To watch him completely lose control. Then he'd gone all caveman dragon on her and... Damn it, she should not laugh. She would not laugh.

But she'd grown up in a castle full of obnoxious, arrogant and okay, wild and a little off-balance dragons. His behavior didn't surprise her one bit.

Sighing, she discarded the dress, grabbed a robe she'd tossed onto the bed and hurried out of the room to find Bella or Lola. If he didn't like that dress, he was going to hate whatever she decided to wear next.

There was one thing she'd learned from being raised by strong female dragons. No male would ever control her. Not even the sexiest dragon she'd ever met.

CHAPTER TWELVE

R hodes tried not to stare at Stella—and failed—as she paused at a row of shelves in the vampire's home they'd recently arrived at.

Christian was an older vampire, likely over five hundred years old if Rhodes had to guess. The male seemed nice enough, though he kept giving Rhodes odd looks. His dragon wanted to snarl at the male, but at least he didn't seem interested in Stella. He'd gone to get them 'refreshments' and Stella was giving Rhodes the silent treatment more or less while they waited.

After he'd brought her to orgasm in the best moment of his entire life, he'd gone with the impulse to destroy that scrap of a dress she'd been wearing.

He'd had no regrets.

Until she'd walked back out of the closet wearing some sort of sparkly little...*thing*. Two triangles covered in sparkles and sequins that barely covered her breasts. The back was connected by a sequined string. At least she had on black pants, though those might as well be a second skin. She'd left her long, silvery hair down and one of the females, Lola, had added sparkles to it somehow, and now Stella looked like a wet dream. He wanted to bury his face between her legs again. And again, and again. Fuuuck him.

She smells like you at least, simply bring her more pleasure, his dragon half snarled. *Chain her to your bed and keep her happy.*

While that idea didn't sound terrible, he ignored his beast, instead watching as Stella picked up small little trinkets and let out gasps at some of them. It reminded him that she hadn't seen much of the world. That much he knew from his prior intel on her and her family. The Nova clan had kept their realm shut off after a violent attack from another clan that had killed many of their kind, including many, many children.

He understood why they'd cut everyone out, but now he wanted to understand why the fae wanted Stella. They weren't getting her, but he still needed more intel.

"I can feel you watching me," she murmured without turning around —then she bent over, giving him the best view of her perfect, rounded ass.

"Of course I'm watching you. How long are you going to be angry at me?" He didn't like it, couldn't figure out a way to apologize that sounded sincere. "Because I'm not sorry about destroying your dress!" he snarled.

His dragon growled at him. *You need to work on your communication skills.*

"If that's your attempt at an apology," she snapped as she turned to face him. "It's terrible. And I'm not angry about the dress."

"You're not?"

"No. I mean, I am because it was Bella's, not mine. So you owe her for that. But..." She lowered her voice and for the first time since they'd arrived, she stepped closer to him until she was right up in his face. "You got to touch me, make me come, and then you just stomped away, didn't let me touch you."

He froze as her words registered. "That is why you're angry?" He'd been consumed with her, had been worried that if he'd let her touch him, he'd lose control. He'd already been on the precipice of it. If she'd put her mouth on him, he'd have likely embarrassed himself. That was unacceptable.

She gritted her teeth and started to respond when Christian stepped back inside, all elegant and handsome. His blond hair was thick and he had a sort of youthful face, adding to his charm.

Hmm, maybe that was why the lion did not like this vampire? He was very pretty and made Rhodes feel like a giant beast next to him. He looked at Stella, wondered if she thought the male was attractive. Then he dismissed the thought since he could still hear the echoes of her crying out her pleasure, could still taste her, *would* taste her again soon. And she'd told him that she wanted to taste him as well—he wanted to focus on that but knew if he did, he'd toss her over his shoulder and they would never go anywhere else tonight. He had restraint.

Hopefully. Probably.

"I prepared a few snacks I hope you'll enjoy. I must say, it's such a pleasure to see you again. How are Juniper and Zephyr?"

"Blissfully happy," Stella said on a laugh. "As they should be. And it's such a pleasure to see you as well. How were your travels back from our realm after the wedding?"

"Without issue thankfully. Please, sit. Be comfortable." He motioned for both of them to take a seat, the action regal, and Rhodes realized that the vampire was politely waiting for her to sit first.

His inner dragon sniffed slightly. *At least the vampire has manners.*

Once they were all seated on the expensive furnishings, Christian flicked a glance at Rhodes, his expression difficult to read. "So you two are staying with…Lola, Axel and the others?"

"Yes, they've been so accommodating. We ran into some trouble and they've let me borrow, well, everything." Stella said on a laugh, motioning to her clothes—or lack of them.

Rhodes nodded, motioning to his shirt. "The lion let me borrow this as well," he murmured, because for some reason, it seemed the vampire needed to know. It was in the way he'd said Axel's name. Maybe…he scented Axel on him because of the shirt and did not like it?

The vampire relaxed, leaning back against the Chesterfield. "I see. What kind of trouble?"

"The fae kind," Rhodes answered before Stella could because he knew that she wanted to talk about the stupid missing crown from her palace. But that was not what was important. He knew that it was to her, and he wanted to help her find it, but her safety was the only thing that mattered.

"Well, that's not why we are here," Stella said pointedly, her tone saccharine sweet.

Rhodes didn't like the fake edge to it, had to resist the urge to wince. He only wanted the real Stella. "Perhaps Christian will be able to offer information regardless," he said. "Stella was attacked by members of the Domincary fae."

"Wait, you know what type of fae they were?" Stella asked, surprise in her voice.

He simply nodded. "I recognized a couple tattoos before I cut off their heads." Plus, it was the same type of fae who'd hired him. He ruthlessly shoved down the guilt that wanted to overtake him. If he'd never taken that contract, he'd have never met her. That was the only thing that soothed him.

That and the scent of her still on him.

Christian cleared his throat gently. "Ah, I don't know much about fae, but I can put you in contact with someone who might be able to help you. She is half-fae and could possibly shed some light on some of the different houses or realms. And of course King's father is fae, but from a different realm. Still, it might be worth asking."

Stella shifted slightly against the couch, her knee touching Rhodes. "Aurora has already let us know that King reached out to his father. And thank you. I would appreciate an introduction to your half fae friend."

"Of course. And my home is open to both of you, should you need to move because of security issues," he said, looking between the two of them.

"We appreciate the offer," Rhodes murmured, surprised.

"Now what is this about a missing crown?" Christian asked, picking up a glass of what was definitely blood mixed with wine.

Rhodes was quiet as Stella filled him in on how someone had stolen from her family during her sister's wedding festivities. The thievery had been quick and had gone undiscovered for a couple weeks but unbeknownst to the thief, her clan had invisible security in place. Stella had the scent of the thief and, after a brief finding spell from one of the

Nova realm witches, knew that said thief was in New Orleans. But that was as much as she had.

"Do you know the name, gender…anything else about this thief?" Christian asked as he leaned back in his seat.

"Unfortunately no. Except our witch did give me a set of numbers she said kept coming up. She wasn't sure what they meant, however."

"Numbers?"

Rhodes frowned; she hadn't told him about that, hadn't told him much of anything other than about this meeting with this vampire.

Stella nodded and recited them to Christian. Then she added, "It stands to reason that whoever stole from my family was either invited or a guest of an invitee. As you know, we have a very strict vetting process for who is allowed in our realm but the wedding was chaos."

Christian nodded, a smile on his face. "I do remember. The numbers could be a phone number perhaps?"

"Oh…" She looked at Rhodes, who nodded.

"Ten numbers, it's a possibility."

"How would we even figure out who the number belonged to?" she asked.

"Ask Lola to help you," Christian said.

Now they both frowned. "Why?" Rhodes asked.

"She was a hacker before The Fall. At least that is my understanding, but I'm sure she would be happy to help you." He looked down at his cell phone, which had started buzzing. "I would normally ignore my phone but I'm helping King with something—"

Stella waved a brief hand. "Please, take it. We'll be fine here." Once they were alone again, she turned to Rhodes. "What's a hacker?"

His mouth curved up slightly. "Someone who can break into various types of technology for all sorts of purposes. If Lola is one, she might be able to track the thief using the phone number." He pulled out his phone, quickly texted Lola—the entire house had given them their phone numbers. "I just texted her."

"Thank you. The learning curve with phones is…steeper than I'd like to admit." Her cheeks flushed as if she was embarrassed. "I find texting frustrating."

On instinct, he reached out, gently cupped her cheek, rubbing his thumb across her soft skin.

The scent of her lust was instantaneous, punching through the air as she watched him, her eyes going heavy-lidded. Even if she was still annoyed with him, she wanted him regardless.

That soothed the most savage part of him.

"Why didn't you tell me about the fae?" she murmured, not making a move to pull back from him.

So he took another liberty, ran his thumb over her bottom lip. "Probably for the same reason you didn't tell me about the numbers. I didn't think of it, but I'm sorry for keeping you in the dark." He knew he needed to come clean with her, but he found that he couldn't force the words out. Because he wanted her too much, feared her rejection in a way he'd never feared anything.

Her lust was so potent now, his dragon was right at the surface, demanding he take her right here, right now.

"Are you sorry about earlier?" she whispered.

He swallowed hard when she gently nipped his thumb—taking him completely off guard with the sensual action. "I'm going to set that dress on fire."

She let out a startled laugh at his words and he dropped his hand, but didn't back up, didn't give her any space. "Not about the dress. Why did you...run away from me?"

"I wasn't running away. I was showing self-control." Barely.

At the sound of Christian clearing his throat, Stella jumped. Rhodes had heard him, he just hadn't cared about his approach. Other than to be annoyed.

"Apologies for my rudeness. I took the liberty of calling the half-fae you might want to speak to. Her name is Nyx and she is available to talk to you tonight. You'd have to go to Biloxi and you'd have to call the Alpha of the region when you enter his territory, as I'm sure you know. I can't make that call for you, or I'd have done so."

"I understand why Juniper adores you." Stella leaned forward to grab some grapes from the plate he'd laid out. "And thank you. I have Finn's number courtesy of my grandmother. I will go call him." She scowled down at her cell phone as she pulled it out and hurried from the room, clearly not a fan of the thing.

Once Rhodes and Christian were alone, Rhodes leaned back, tried to think of something polite to say. The male had been a font of information and was being helpful about the fae. Rhodes couldn't very well contact them himself and ask why they wanted Stella. They'd lied to him about her to begin with. He only ever took certain types of contracts; he killed or kidnapped certain types of individuals.

All violent monsters who deserved his brand of justice. And he'd been told that Stella of the Nova realm was one such monster. After watching her and being in her presence, however, it had been clear that was a lie. And he didn't work for liars. He was going to make them all pay for targeting her, for hurting her.

Christian cleared his throat, brushed off invisible pieces of lint on his jacket. "How are your accommodations?"

"Nice, thank you."

Another clearing of his throat. "How are...is Axel? Well, I hope?"

By now it was clear the two had a romantic history or something along those lines. "Ah... I don't know him well enough to say. But he's been welcoming, as have the others."

"Good, that's good." Now the vampire, who was impossibly polished, didn't seem to know what to do with his hands as he sat there.

"He was perhaps a bit down." Rhodes inwardly chastised himself. He should be keeping his mouth shut. But this vampire had been helpful and looked all lost right now. "Before we left we had dinner with everyone and he played a few melancholy songs on his guitar. The lion is talented." Though the melodies had been depressing. What Rhodes didn't say was that Harlow had thrown bread at him and told him to stop being a 'Johnny raincloud'.

Christian simply nodded, his expression distant for a moment before he straightened and stood at Stella's reentry.

Rhodes stood as well, could tell from her body language that they were leaving.

"We have entry into their territory. We can leave now if you'd like?" she said, looking at Rhodes.

"Whatever you wish." If she'd asked him to bring her to orgasm right then and there, he'd do it, the vampire be damned.

As if she read his mind, her cheeks flushed, but she nodded, then thanked and hugged Christian before they left.

Rhodes resisted the urge to knock the male's head off for touching Stella. Barely.

Once they stepped outside, he rolled his shoulders, ordering his dragon to behave—to not be a complete and utter barbarian.

It was going to be a monumental task.

CHAPTER THIRTEEN

Rhodes circled the location Stella had given him before they'd taken off, slowly eyeing the area from his dragon's-eye view and looking for threats. Down below them, he could scent many different supernaturals, mostly wolves.

There were a few vehicles in the parking lot of what had once been a hotel. He thought it was likely used as pack housing now or something similar. Once he was certain there wasn't a trap—not that he was truly expecting one—he descended to the far part of the parking lot with no vehicles at all.

Then he let his camouflage drop. He might not have to utilize his natural dragon camouflage in this new world but he didn't think he'd ever stop the protective measure. It was second nature, even if he hadn't been an assassin, and he imagined it was the same for most dragons.

As he stilled, he waited for Stella to climb off his back, took pleasure in feeling her hands all over his scales. Once she'd stepped away from him, he swished his tail, did a slow spin because he was truly gorgeous in this form. She needed to see all he had to offer and his dragon was shameless. Then he shifted to his human form, found her watching him with a hint of amusement as she handed over his clothing.

"What?" He frowned at her.

"Your dragon is very confident."

"Is there a reason he shouldn't be?" He knew what he looked like in human form, but his dragon was a wild, wonderful creature of darkness.

"No. You're the most beautiful dragon I've ever seen. I love your obsidian scales."

He blinked at her bluntness, the way she complimented him simply and thoroughly. It cut right through to the heart he was certain had turned to ice long ago. Turning away, he tugged on his clothing, unsure how to respond as he replayed her words over in his head. *The most beautiful dragon I've ever seen.*

"I'm impressed with how quickly we got here," she continued as he tugged on his boots.

Suddenly he scented at least six different wolves moving closer. It was clear she didn't scent them, likely because of the poison's lingering effects.

He pulled her close then shoved her behind him, ignoring her yelp as he said, "We are here with permission from Finn Stavros. I'm escorting Princess Stella of the Nova realm. If anyone makes a move against her, I will burn you all so thoroughly there will be no bones left."

At his words, a male and female stepped out of the darkness on the edge of the parking lot. Definitely wolf shifters.

The male stepped forward, nodded at them politely despite Rhodes' savage declaration. He had dark hair in a skull trim, dark eyes and was built in the lean way of wolves. "I'm Solon, a member of Finn's pack. He is unable to meet with you but we'll be escorting you to meet with Bo and his mate, Nyx."

The female hung back, only nodded at them, but there was a tenseness in the air, so thick Rhodes could almost choke on it. And he didn't think it was because of the threat he posed.

Stella must have sensed it too because she said, "Is everything okay? We would not have intruded in your territory if it's a bad time." Her tone was so kind and diplomatic. There was a reason she was a princess.

Solon glanced over his shoulder, his expression softening. "We've just been dealing with some random attacks from outsiders. Nothing we can't handle, but it's got tensions high right now."

"I'm sorry to hear that. If there's anything anyone from my realm can do, please convey that to Finn. I'm in this realm on a job but I'm also an emissary of my people."

Solon nodded, giving Stella an appreciative look as they walked. "I will, thank you. And he truly does send his apologies. He and his mate Lyra had planned to meet you here."

"It's no problem at all," she said as they reached the exterior doors to the hotel. A neon sign that was turned off, but still clearly spelled out Howlers, hung over the entrance to what appeared to be a restaurant. "Do people live here?" she asked, saying aloud what Rhodes was thinking.

"We've turned it into warrior housing mostly and what used to be Howlers is now our cafeteria. It's a solid spot to refuel and rest when we're out on patrol."

Rhodes had thought that as well when he'd been scoping out the area. "What kinds of threats have you been dealing with? Dragons? Or..."

Solon sighed, motioned behind them to the female that she could leave as he opened the glass door for them. "Humans mostly. But some fae as well—which is why Finn agreed to your entry into the territory. Well, one of the reasons," he said as he motioned off to the right into a huge space that had been indeed set up as a cafeteria. "He respects your family for what they did before."

Stella nodded, making it clear she knew what the male was talking about.

Rectangle tables were set in orderly rows and a few supernaturals were quietly eating and talking. A few tossed them curious looks but mostly the dozen individuals ignored them.

A male with light brown skin, a buzz cut and amber eyes sat at a table by the bank of windows overlooking the parking lot. Next to him was a smaller female with long black hair, ocean-blue eyes and a sort of ethereal quality to her. She had the scent of...fae, but not quite.

Ah, the half fae female they were meeting. Rhodes scented demon on the male, realized he was a hybrid of sorts. Interesting.

Solon veered off after he made quick introductions to Bo Broussard and Nyx, leaving the four of them to talk.

"Thank you for agreeing to speak with us." Stella's smile was genuine as she looked between the mated couple.

"Of course. Your grandmother and sister were instrumental in stopping that trafficking ring a few months ago. And your grandmother is quite impressive." Nyx's smile was soft and genuine.

Her mate just watched Rhodes as if he was a predator. Smart male.

Stella's smile grew. "Yes, they were happy to help end that awfulness. And my grandmother is a force of nature, that is certain."

"So...how can I help you exactly? Finn was fairly vague with details," Nyx asked.

"Honestly, I'm not sure." Stella cleared her throat, glanced at Rhodes.

"Stella was attacked by fae in her realm. Fae of the Domincary realm —they poisoned her but I believe it was to incapacitate her only. They wanted to kidnap her," Rhodes said.

Stella let out a small gasp. "How can you be sure? I thought they just wanted me dead."

He shot her a surprised look. "No. They wanted you alive, but incapacitated. If they'd wanted to kill you, they'd have shot you full of more of the poison." He'd thought she'd realized that. "There were spelled chains in their bags too," he ground out, shoving down his anger at the thought of them taking her, hurting her. He couldn't focus on that, however. She was with him now. He would keep her protected.

Nyx cleared her throat. "I don't know much about the Domincary realm, but I know they're aligned with my father. Which means they are very likely horrible beings with horrible intentions."

"Do you know why they would want a dragon female?" Rhodes asked, trying to keep his tone neutral when even the thought of Stella injured was making his dragon edgy.

"I can think of a few reasons," Bo finally spoke, his tone gravelly as he looked between the two of them. "None good."

Nyx's expression tensed as she nodded. "My father tried to force me into a marriage with another fae and the tactics he used were violent. And I am his own blood so..." She shook her head. "There could be any number of reasons. I've reached out to some contacts to see if they've heard anything. But with the world still rebuilding, communication is spotty sometimes."

"I understand. And I thank you for agreeing to meet with us on such short notice."

"It's our pleasure," Nyx said. "I don't have contact with any fae, but the ones I do know only care about one thing. Power. Above all else, power matters to the royal fae. Be careful if you have to deal with them."

Stella nodded her thanks again and Rhodes remained quiet. He knew that about the fae, had taken contracts from them before. Power and staying in control were of most importance to them. The contracts from the fae were almost always against other fae—usually to simply kill someone. And every fae he'd ever killed had deserved it. They'd all been murderers, rapists, traffickers. He had no guilt over ending them. Stella was the exact opposite of all his previous contracts—and he would never take out a light like her.

"I hate that you two had to fly all the way here. I can transport you back to New Orleans if you'd prefer."

It took Rhodes a moment to realize what Nyx meant—as a demigod, the female must have powers to transport to anywhere she wanted as long as she'd been there before. He looked to Stella and she nodded, so he did as well.

"Thank you," Stella said. "That would make things much easier on us."

Rhodes realized this would also allow them more time to track down the asshole who'd stolen from Stella's realm. He didn't relish the idea of chasing someone around New Orleans, but he couldn't argue with her. Not when he was supposedly here on her grandmother's orders.

~

"THAT WAS WILD." Stella's words were all breathy as Nyx and her mate disappeared as suddenly as they'd brought them to New Orleans.

In a shocking chaos of wind and sparkling stars.

Rhodes nodded, his expression neutral.

"What's wrong?" she asked, stepping closer to him. They'd been brought to a quiet park maybe a twenty-minute walk from the house they were staying at. Nyx had given Stella her phone number before leaving as well.

"Nothing." His gaze landed on her mouth, but he quickly looked away, his expression going hard. "I just don't like you out in the open."

She sighed, but then paused at a buzzing sound. "What is that?"

"Your cell phone."

"Oh!" She fished it out of her purse and after a couple tries, managed to swipe her finger across the screen properly. "Hello?"

"Hey, it's Lola. You free?"

"Yeah, just got back to the city. Everything okay?"

"I got a hit on that phone number you gave me."

"Hit?"

"Ah, I have its location."

"Oh wow, yes please!"

Rhodes gave her an interesting look, one she couldn't decipher as Lola continued, giving them the location.

"I take it you heard all that?" she said after she'd hung up.

"Yeah, and I know that area too."

"Good because I don't." She looked down at herself, frowned. "Should I change into something more...cat burglary?"

His lips twitched but he shook his head. "You'll be fine because we're not breaking in anywhere. And we can walk there."

Taking him at his word, she linked her arm through his as they headed down the sidewalk. She was going to trust that he knew what he was doing, and in that moment she realized she was glad that her family had sent him to look out for her.

Yes, because he'd saved her life. But it was also nice having a partner.

Sure, he was super possessive—which, okay, she didn't hate. And despite his weird response to her dress earlier, he didn't treat her like some fragile flower. He'd looked to her for confirmation when they'd been with Bo and Nyx, had treated her like an equal.

She...genuinely liked this male. This very mysterious dragon whose secrets she wanted.

And they had unfinished business because she wasn't done with this dragon. Not even close. Maybe she never would be.

CHAPTER FOURTEEN

For the eighteenth time, Christian questioned that he'd come to this club at all. This was not his scene—not for a long time. After hundreds of years, loud areas with too many sweaty bodies didn't appeal to him.

Unfortunately for him, one ridiculously handsome lion still did appeal to him.

"Christian, I'm so happy—and surprised—to see you!" Cynara, a half-vampire, half-demon kissed him on both cheeks, her smile genuine.

"Well, this is the only club worth going to," he murmured, knowing she'd hear him even above the music and laughter.

"True, true," she said, grinning, as they headed up the stairs toward the VIP section. "I'm going to send a bottle over on the house for the hot vampire who decided to get his ass out of the house for once," she said as they reached the top of the stairs.

He snorted. "Better not let Justus hear you say that."

"He's in the office," she said on a laugh. "I think he's at his limit with everyone except me tonight."

Christian understood that because he went through life the same way —though he hadn't always been so grumpy. After his mate had died centuries ago, depression, then ennui had set in. Some days...

Everything inside him stilled as he spotted Axel talking to a gorgeous female at the bar.

Feeling that irrational jealousy shove up inside him, he turned back to Cynara and faked a smile. "I might go see him later."

"No way, you stay out here and enjoy yourself." She kissed him again, a chaste peck on his cheek before pushing him toward the upstairs dance floor.

He ignored that and headed to a cluster of high-top tables, was glad when Harlow waved him over. Christian had behaved poorly at their house once, got into a brawl with Axel, but the others were always so kind to him, made him feel less alone.

It didn't seem Axel was hanging out with them anyway so that was good. Or that's what he told himself.

"My man." Harlow clapped him on the shoulder once. "I'm glad you're here," she murmured.

He looked at her in surprise, which just made her snicker.

"I swear you're one of the only sane supernaturals I know." She tilted her chin to a few tables over right next to the dance floor, where Lola was riding around on a unicycle in tight circles while Bella poured tequila down her throat straight from a bottle. Bella was standing on a chair as she did it, pumping her other fist in the air with the beat of the loud song playing.

"Some days I think I've seen it all and then I realize, no indeed."

Harlow just cackled. "Goddess, those two are out of control tonight."

"I'm scared to ask where they got the unicycle."

"No clue. I went to talk to someone on the rooftop bar and when I came back, utter chaos. I'm glad though, Bella's been wound pretty tight lately."

Alarm rolled through him. "Is everything okay?"

"Oh yeah, nothing bad. She's just been busy helping King and Aurora and tends to take on too much. She's always been like that, since we were kids."

Christian knew they were all in their forties, though they looked closer to early twenties. All varying types of supernaturals, their group had lived in an artists' compound as kids with their parents.

"How's work been going for you?" he asked, smiling politely as one of Cynara's employees dropped off a bottle of expensive red wine she must have been hiding somewhere.

Harlow let out a low whistle at the sight of the bottle so he passed one of the empty glasses to her. "You must join me."

"Okay, but only one. I'm not staying late. And to answer your question, good. We've been keeping the perimeter of the territory locked down fairly tight and we've found a lot of displaced humans we've been able to help get settled. I like being busy, makes it easy not to think sometimes," she said as she took the glass he slid her.

He paused in surprise, eyed her, since she was normally a closed book. "Think about what?"

Now *she* paused, looked down into her glass before she shrugged. "The past mainly. Loss."

Oof. "I understand that." He held out his own glass. The music and people talking and laughing around them was so over the top, he barely heard the clink of their glasses. "Do you wish to speak of your past?" he asked, watching the two snow leopards on the edge of the dance floor.

A small crowd had gathered around them—and now they'd switched places, with Bella on the unicycle and Lola pouring tequila down her throat.

"Just feeling melancholy over a male I once loved." She took a sip of her glass, stared out at the dance floor.

This was a very different side from the stoic Harlow he'd been slowly getting to know. "Once?"

"He's…gone. Dead. I killed him."

He blinked and she turned to him, her green eyes flashing tiger. "I probably should have just talked about the weather or something, huh?"

He snorted at her dry tone. "Not at all. I don't want just surface from you."

She gave him a small smile and clapped him on the shoulder once again in that 'soldier' way of hers. He'd seen her battle before, had heard stories from Axel about the tiger twins and their vicious fighting skills. "So, were you able to help out Stella and Rhodes?"

She was definitely changing the subject and he was *definitely* not turning around to look at Axel—who was still talking intently to the tall blonde female. Ugh. "Ah, yes, I hope. They've flown over to Finn's territory for a bit but I believe they'll be back tonight."

Harlow shot him a look he could only describe as mischievous. "Sooooo, were they all hot and heavy at your place?"

He raised his eyebrows. "Seriously?"

She snickered slightly. "I can't even be sorry, I haven't had any really juicy gossip for ages and holy Christmas, those two... He actually shredded her dress earlier because he didn't want her wearing it out in public. Man, Bella's not even mad, she thinks it's hilarious."

Christian blinked. "He shredded Bella's dress?"

"Oh, no, Stella was borrowing it and apparently, when he saw her in it, he wasn't having it." She snickered again before tossing back the rest of her wine. "I think I'd dick punch a male who did that to me but I can kinda get the appeal, I guess." She sighed wistfully and he wondered if she was thinking about the male she'd loved—the one she'd killed apparently.

"I...do not know how to respond to that." He surreptitiously glanced over his shoulder and saw Axel disappearing behind the door that led to the private rooms, his arm around the female. Aaaand, felt as if he'd been punched in the gut. He swallowed hard, and tried to keep on a happy enough expression but knew he was going to fail.

Clearing his throat, he slid off the stool. "Please enjoy the rest of the wine and give my felicitations to the others. It is a bit too loud for me, I'm going to head home."

She slid off her stool and grabbed the bottle of wine as she let out a loud whistle. Both Bella and Lola looked over then waved as Harlow motioned she was leaving.

"You don't have to leave," he said.

"This place is way too loud. But I'm taking this wine." She grinned as she fell in step with him and as they made their way out of the club, she avoided hugs from some bear shifters who apparently wanted to 'squeeze their favorite feline'.

"I swear," she said as they stepped out onto the street. "Moving here was the best thing we ever did."

He nodded as they ducked down a quieter side street away from the hustle of the main strip. "This place holds a special place in my heart." He'd been here for over a century.

"Axel wasn't hooking up with that female," Harlow said bluntly before taking a swig straight out of the very expensive bottle.

He cleared his throat. "Ah, what?"

"Come on, we're friends now. I saw you watching him. He's not hooking up with her, he was just walking her out the back so she didn't have to deal with her asshole ex, that's all. That was the only reason he was keeping her company."

Oh. Christian tried to ignore the relief that punched through him, but it was too vast. "I'm not sure why you're telling me."

Harlow shook her head as they stepped out onto a parallel street to the one with the majority of clubs. "All right, play it that way. I'm sure you two will figure shit out eventually. I will say, if you break his heart, I'll break your face."

"I thought we were friends now," he said dryly.

She lifted a casual shoulder. "I'm not saying I'll feel good about it, but it'll happen."

"What if he breaks *my* heart?"

She considered him for a moment. "Same goes."

"He's lucky to have a friend like you. And noted." He certainly wouldn't be breaking the lion's heart—they were, well, they weren't even friends. Christian wasn't certain what they were. All he knew was that the lion made him crazy—and Christian wasn't risking his heart ever again.

CHAPTER FIFTEEN

"What is this place?" Stella's eyes were wide, filled with fascination as she took everything in.

The restaurant on the far end of Bourbon Street had exposed brick walls and a long, skinny bar along one wall. Vintage-looking photos lined the brick behind the bar, as well as shelves with alcohol bottles on them. He'd been to multiple territories since The Fall and not all of them had fared this well. Though 'fared' wasn't the correct term. New Orleans had a strong Alpha couple determined to do things right for their people. The kind of Alpha that Rhodes could...see actually following.

Shaking *that* thought off, Rhodes wrapped his arm around Stella's shoulders as they stepped inside the small restaurant. "It used to be something humans called a speakeasy. Then a simple bar and restaurant. This one is supposed to be run by a friendly enough vampire."

She looked up at him in surprise. "How do you know that?"

"I have notes on many territories around the world," he murmured as he leaned in close to her ear, nipped her earlobe. Her eyes brightened, the scent of her lust spiking the air. "No more questions while we're here." He loved her curiosity but now wasn't the place for it. He didn't want to risk anyone overhearing them.

Even above the scents of the other thirty or so people inside, the punch of her lust wrapped around him as he pressed his teeth down on her earlobe again. Because he simply couldn't resist. He knew he was playing with fire; she'd figure the truth out soon enough.

Her family would come looking for her soon. Then he'd lose her for good.

But until then he'd keep her safe and pretend that in an alternate reality, she was his and he was hers. He knew that a male like him wasn't getting a happily ever after. But he'd pretend for as long as he was with her, and live on those memories for the rest of his life.

When she burrowed into him, wrapping her arm around him as they moved deeper into the place, his dragon settled. In that moment, everything felt right, because she was in his arms. She was his mate, of that he had no doubt. His dragon had recognized her at the most primal level, even before he had.

As he scanned the place, he saw that there were some humans listening to the Celtic band, but mainly it was vampires.

"What'll you have," the male behind the bar asked, his accent faintly tinged with Ireland. He was a vampire, his fangs clearly peeking out. But unlike many vamps Rhodes dealt with, this one had an easy demeanor, a quick smile. Rhodes didn't trust him for that alone.

He glanced at the menu behind the bar, but mainly looked at the mirror to see if anyone stuck out, was eyeing Stella. No one was paying attention to them, everyone's gaze on the female playing a fiddle on the small stage. Still, Lola had said the phone she'd tracked was here.

"What do you recommend?" Stella asked, that refreshing scent rolling off her.

He knew that as a princess she wouldn't have often been out at bars —or the Nova realm's equivalent of them. He liked how fascinating she thought everything was, liked basking in her joy.

"I'm going to make you something called Little Havana. It's sweet but not too sweet. I imagine that's perfect for a lass as attractive as you."

Rhodes kept his expression neutral enough, but knew his dragon flared in his gaze when the obnoxious bartender laughed.

"I'm not making a play for your female," he said as he started pulling bottles off the shelf behind him. "I'm taken and was just making an observation."

The sound of the fiddle player grew louder behind them and some of the patrons started clapping in a steady beat.

"Keep your observations to yourself," Rhodes murmured.

The male, who clearly had a death wish, just laughed lightly. "I haven't seen you two around here. New to the territory?"

"Sort of, but we've been in before. You must not work every night," Stella said.

Rhodes wondered what she was up to.

The male nodded. "Aye, true. So where are the two of you from?"

"Not this realm," she said, laughingly. "And I have a question. I left my cell phone in here last time we were in. I'm not used to the things and I'd hoped someone turned it in."

The vampire snorted softly. "I hate the things myself," he said as he slid the dark-colored drink with a garnish of pineapple over to Stella. Rhodes smelled it for poison, then handed it back to her.

The bartender reached under the bar, pulled out a small gray basket. "This is our unofficial lost and found. What's your phone look like?" he asked.

"It's a black phone with silver trim on the cover." Rhodes could see the contents from the mirror, but didn't bother looking at the vampire, pretending disinterest.

"I also lost some sequined pink panties," Stella added, her expression deadpan. "Thong. But I doubt they're in there."

Rhodes' dragon shoved to the surface as the bartender's eyes widened. Then the vampire let out a bark of laughter as he shoved the basket at them. "You must have had a grand time then. Grab whatever's yours," he murmured before moving on down the bar, a grin in place.

Rhodes lifted an eyebrow at her, but she just gave him a cheeky grin. He swiped the two cell phones in there, hoped the male didn't notice both were missing.

Stella took a sip of her drink, then turned to face the band, pure joy in her expression as they started up a livelier song. Rhodes didn't bother with a drink.

Instead, he guided her over to a small table in the back corner. As she sat on the little stool, he moved in behind her, wrapped an arm around her and set his chin on the top of her head.

It was the best position in the place to keep an eye on anyone who looked as if they might be up to no good, but he couldn't lie to himself. He simply wanted to pretend that he and Stella were here as a couple, that he had any sort of claim on her.

And in that moment, as he held her close, kept her back buffeted against his chest as the band played, he allowed himself to believe that alternate reality.

CHAPTER SIXTEEN

"That was smart saying you lost your phone," Rhodes said an hour later once they were blocks away from the little bar.

"Thanks." Stella was quite pleased with herself. "I'm hopeful that Lola can do something with one of them—if one of the phones even belongs to the thief."

He cleared his throat, looking at her with a certain kind of intensity she felt all the way to her core. "Why did you say you lost your panties?" He seemed to growl on that last word.

She grinned as she stepped off the curb onto a cobblestone street. It was close to one in the morning and while the others had messaged to say they were still out, she realized she didn't want to go to a loud, noisy club. The noise and the chaos of that little place had been enough for her. She'd thought partying would be fun but...maybe on a lower scale and only with people she was comfortable with. Everything was simply...overwhelming.

And if she was being honest with herself, she wanted to be alone with Rhodes right now. "I thought it would be funny and knock him off balance. My sister told me that was a useful tool when investigating stuff."

"She's not wrong," he murmured, eyeing their surroundings with that ever watchful, deadly gaze.

They'd turned onto a side street that had a decent amount of people, but nothing like where the clubs and bars were on the main strip. She knew from Aurora that the clubs were only open two nights a week. The Alpha couple wanted to make sure people didn't lose sight of the rebuilding of the territory.

Stella missed Rhodes' arm around her shoulders, had loved the way he'd possessively held her at that little 'speakeasy'. She was going to look that word up later because it was difficult to discern what it was from context. And she hadn't wanted to ask Rhodes because she didn't want to remind him how little she understood the nuance of the English language.

But, she was still feeling bold so she reached out and linked her fingers with his.

He jolted and she thought he'd pull his hand back, but instead he gave her a searing look as he squeezed her hand, tugged her even closer to his side. She loved the idea of being his, of being able to make a claim on him.

The two males on the sidewalk coming toward them veered to the side, giving him a wide berth, both avoiding eye contact.

It made Stella's inner dragon smile. Rhodes really was a gorgeous, dangerous dragon and it seemed even other supernaturals sensed that.

The rest of the walk back to the house was silent, uneventful, but she found she liked the scents of the city. All the noises. The whole place was fascinating and she enjoyed being around so many different types of beings. But just not in a crowded club.

The Nova realm was her home, always would be, but getting to experience something new—even with the awful poisoning—made her feel alive. Wild. As if anything could happen.

And her dragon was getting closer to the surface. Not quite there yet, but she was working her way up, would soon be ready to fly free.

Right now she felt safe and protected with Rhodes—she had no doubt he would defend her against anything. And very soon…she hoped they picked up where they'd left off earlier.

~

RHODES STEPPED into the pack's kitchen on his way back from the security check he'd just finished, and found one of the tiger twins—Harlow, he scented—sitting at the island top, making tea. He nodded politely at her. He was surprised to see her since he knew she'd gone out with the others.

There was a deadly glint in her eyes, but he understood it wasn't directed at him. That was just the way she was. "Any luck tonight?" she asked, blowing on her tea. Her pajama pants had little dragons on them, which made him blink.

"A bit. Found a couple phones where Lola sent us, might be from the thief." The whole house knew why Stella was here. "I've left them for Lola outside her door."

"I'll let her know if I see her. I think they're going to be out late." She rolled her eyes. "They were still going strong when I left."

He simply nodded his thanks, then said, "I did a perimeter check, everything looks good." He knew they also had spells and charms in place to ward the home and property, but he wasn't taking anything for granted with Stella's safety.

"Thanks. I did one too…and I checked in with some of the wolves running security for the borders. No one's scented any unknown fae or heard any rumblings. The territory is locked down fairly tight."

The tension in his chest eased a fraction. "That's good to know."

Now he could be with his female.

As he made his way up the stairs to the third floor, the scent of Stella called to him, a siren's song he couldn't resist. When they'd returned half an hour ago, she'd gone to change and get ready for bed, but he had too much energy simmering underneath the surface. He'd done an aerial recon in dragon form, then checked the whole perimeter on foot and that restlessness was still there.

Keeping her safe was a compulsion, one he didn't care to keep in check. Even if he was getting too attached.

Once he was inside her room, he shut the door behind him, breathed in deeply. He could hear the sound of water running in the bathroom, imagined she was washing her face or...whatever females did. Perhaps she was naked? That sounded a thousand times better.

He wanted to discuss what had happened earlier with her. He wasn't sorry about destroying the dress, but she'd said she wanted to touch him. And then she'd held his hand on the way back to the house.

He...did not know how to process that. What to think of it. The only thing he knew was that their time was limited and he couldn't waste it.

He looked around the room, that compulsion to keep her safe riding him hard—battling the need inside him to claim her forever. There were two windows, both overlooking the yard and beyond. But filmy cream-colored drapes had been pulled into place for privacy. The bed itself was king-sized, but still not as big as he'd prefer to do all the things he wanted.

The covers were cream and pale pink, feminine and airy. The rest of the furniture was the same, in whites, the build delicate. Little lights had been strung up around the two windows and they were the only ones she'd left on.

He rubbed the back of his neck, studiously not looking at the dresser where he'd pinned her up against earlier and then tasted between her legs. He hadn't been lying—he'd never pleasured a female before. He'd never let his guard down enough to be with any female.

Stella had been everything he'd ever imagined and more.

How should he bring up the topic of...getting naked with her? He'd acted like a barbarian earlier. To be fair, she hadn't seemed to mind, but she was a princess. He needed to be better for her, even if he knew he'd never deserve her.

Turning at the sound of the bathroom door opening, he froze as she stepped out, a lightweight robe cinched around her waist. Smiling, she shut off the light behind her and stepped into the room. "Is everything all right with the house?"

"Secure," he rasped out, trying not to stare.

Her silvery hair was down, long and lush and it fell around her in soft waves. Her bicolored eyes glinted with something he couldn't quite read as she stepped closer to him, her steps sinuous. Sensual. "I've come to a decision." There was a seriousness to her tone he hadn't been expecting.

He tensed, preparing for the worst. "What?"

"I wish to have sex tonight. Right now. With you."

Hell. Yeah. His dragon was done holding back.

CHAPTER SEVENTEEN

"Stella..." He couldn't get out much past her name as he digested her words. She'd all but told him she was a virgin. Now she wanted to have sex? His dragon roared to the surface, ready to claim her, devour her. But... "Is this because your clan isn't here?" He knew he shouldn't care, that he should just take what she was offering, but he found he very much did care if she wanted him specifically.

Or if she just wanted him because no one from her clan was here to find out about them. Maybe she thought of him as a dirty secret?

She frowned as she stepped closer, the pale pink robe loosening slightly, the sweet scent of her making it hard to think. "What do you mean?"

"Do you want me because no one will see you with the bodyguard?"

She blinked, then fury popped off her. "I want you because I want *you* and only you! Some random dragon or other shifter would not do."

"You don't know everything about me," he growled, some part of him wanting her to stop this. Because he sure as hell wasn't going to. But he might be able to push her away. He wasn't a good enough male to stop once they crossed that line. He would claim her fully, make sure she felt every inch of him inside her.

"I don't need to! I know what you make me feel. And I want this.

Want *you*. And I know you want me too!" Even with the fire in her voice, there was a hint of vulnerability that flashed in her eyes, as if she doubted he wanted her.

Hell no. He couldn't have her doubting that. Ever. "I want you more than I've ever wanted anything. More than I will *ever* want anything. You consume my waking thoughts—I was watching you before this trip to New Orleans. And I'm. Fucking. *Obsessed*." His dragon prowled beneath the surface, ready to pin her to the bed, claim her forever.

She stared, her eyes wide now. He expected revulsion, but the sharpest, sweetest scent filled the air. Raw lust. "You watched me? Like...around the castle?" The question came out all breathy, her pupils dilating slightly.

"Yes." She'd consumed his days and then his thoughts at night.

Her gaze fell to his mouth and then she slid her robe off, letting it pool on the floor beneath her as she took a step closer, completely naked now. Aaaand, he forgot to breathe as she pressed herself up against him. "This isn't just about sex for me," she whispered. "I know I shouldn't admit that, but I really like you, Rhodes."

He'd all but admitted he'd been stalking her and she still wanted him. He grasped onto her hips, a shudder rolling through him as he held her close. The deepest part of him was afraid she'd change her mind and leave. Because he wanted her too much, and that terrified him. But she didn't know the truth. And if she did, she would reject him.

When she reached up, traced her finger along his bottom lip, his cock swelled even harder.

He nipped her fingertip, sucked it into his mouth as he kept his gaze pinned to hers.

Her eyes brightened, some of her dragon's essence returning.

"I want to taste you again," he growled as she withdrew her finger. Once hadn't been nearly enough. Not even close.

That sweet scent of her lust punched through the air as she stared at him, a slightly dazed expression. "Then I get to taste you too. No running away."

Her words almost sent him to his knees, the thought of her pleasuring him that way making his head spin. He nodded because he didn't trust his voice, even as he scooped her up and deposited her onto the fluffy bed.

Her silver hair splayed out everywhere, a fan around her lean, strong body. She might be petite, but he could see strength in every line and muscle. He'd seen her training once, knew she could fight, defend herself.

He kept his clothes on, not trusting himself to be naked yet as he pinned her beneath him.

When she spread her legs to accommodate him, he cupped the back of her head as he teased his tongue against hers.

She made little moaning sounds as they tasted each other, her hips rolling up to meet his with abandon.

But he couldn't focus when she was grinding on him, could barely think straight. He grasped onto her hip, squeezed to keep her in place.

She wiggled against him, let out a frustrated groan.

"Stop moving or I'll tie you up," he murmured against her mouth, wondering where the words had come from.

She sucked in a breath, her lust wild in the air, sharper now. "That sounds more appealing than it should." Her cheeks flushed at the admission.

He groaned, brushed his lips against hers briefly. "Not this first time."

"There will be more than one time?"

"Many, many more." There was no way he could stop at one time. Not with her.

He nipped at her jaw, letting instinct guide him as he moved lower. He might not have been with a female before, but she'd liked what he'd done earlier.

And he'd simply gone with what felt right. Instinct. Now he would do the same, kissing and teasing all over her body, listening to the sounds she made. "If you don't like something, tell me." A soft order.

She slid her fingers through his short hair, clutched onto his head as he reached one full breast. "I think I'll like everything," she breathed out unsteadily, then yelped as he sucked one hard nipple into his mouth.

She tightened her grip. "More, more." A desperate plea as he flicked his tongue around her nipple, bit down on the sensitive bud.

His erection was thick and heavy in his pants and he was glad he'd kept them on, even if he was desperate to feel her against him, to feel the skin-to-skin sensation he craved. To slide between her legs.

He alternated between her breasts, feeling as if time was moving too fast. He knew things wouldn't last, knew he didn't have a real chance with her, but he would remember all of this. Every single moment.

She spread her fingers over his shoulders, tugging at his shirt—not gently. "At least take your shirt off," she demanded as he began moving even lower.

His erection kicked against his pants at her desperation, because it mirrored his own. Wordlessly, he sat up, tugged his shirt over his head. And when he saw the pleasure in her eyes as her gaze raked over him, he felt invincible in that moment.

"You are beautiful," she whispered, sitting up to run her hands all over him. And that was when he noticed the dark smoke swirling around the bottom of the bed, surrounding them. It took him a moment to realize what it was—his mating manifestation.

He might have no clan, no experience with females, but he knew what this was. When a dragon claimed a mate, it manifested in a very visible or audible way. Since he didn't know where he came from, he'd had no idea what his might be. But this was definitely it. No doubt in his mind, because he wanted Stella with a desperation he could barely control.

She didn't seem to notice, likely because it was so dark in the room. He ignored the fact that she wasn't exuding any manifestation in turn. No fire or lights...screw it. It didn't matter.

He couldn't find his voice as he dipped his head lower, lower, until his face was between her legs again. "Perfection," he murmured before he zeroed in on her clit.

She'd seemed to enjoy that so he planned to do exactly what he'd done before. Only this time he slid two, then three fingers inside her as he began teasing her.

She jolted off the bed, her hips rolling up to meet his face as he

KATIE REUS

licked and teased her, drawing more moans of pleasure from her. Drinking them in.

Her inner walls clenched around his fingers and though he was desperate for her to come around his cock, he wanted to give her an orgasm before then. At least one.

Forcing himself to slow down, he eased off the pressure on her clit even as he pulled his fingers out.

Going on instinct, he moved one of his slick fingers back farther, farther, teased her small rosette with one. She tensed as he began to push inside her. His finger was slick from her wetness, would slide in easily. But her whole body went tense as she looked down at him.

Her eyes widened. "What are you doing?"

"I thought you might like it."

Her breathing was shallow as she watched him, then she nodded, a sensual smile on her face. "Let's try it."

Thank the goddess. As he slid his finger inside her, knuckle deep, her eyes rolled back as a moan tore from her and in that moment, he knew he'd do anything she asked of him. Always and forever.

Those tight muscles started contracting around his digit and he knew it wouldn't be long before she climaxed.

So he returned to teasing her clit, sucked hard even as he slid his thumb inside her slick folds.

The action set her off, her orgasm punching through her as he continued pleasuring her. She trembled with the force of it, her thighs squeezing against his head as she rode through it.

"Too much," she finally rasped out, her legs falling open.

He sucked on her clit once more, earning a yelp of surprise before he withdrew his fingers and climbed back up her body.

She stared up at him, a small grin on her face as she cupped his cheek. "I understand why sex makes people stupid."

He let out a bark of surprised laughter at her words, his stomach muscles tightening as he laughed. He never knew what was going to come out of her mouth, and he loved that.

She took over then, not waiting a moment as she reached between their bodies and rubbed her hand over his covered erection. "I want to see all of you now. Please undress." A soft demand, but a demand none-theless.

Throat tight, he eased back so he could slide his pants off. He'd never been harder in his life and for the first time, he wished his dick was slightly smaller. It jutted out from between his legs, hard and angry looking.

She was up on her knees, however, watching him with interest and lust. "Will you lay on your back?" The question came out tentatively.

"I'll do anything you ask." Something she should know by now.

As he stretched out on the bed, she crawled up his body, her eyes drinking him in and yeah, he really did feel invincible. And yet completely vulnerable in a way he'd never experienced. Never even thought possible.

Her silvery hair swished over him as she straddled his thighs. She trailed her fingers up them, stopping right on his hips, but not moving any closer to his erection.

"You can touch me," he rasped out. Tried not to beg.

Her gaze snapped to his and he could see the nervousness there.

"You can't hurt me," he added in case that was what she was worried about. Not physically anyway.

She grasped onto his erection and stroked once, the feel of her soft hand on him nearly enough to make him lose it. But no way in hell would he embarrass himself like that. Hopefully.

Her strokes were light, gentle, so he covered her hand with his and squeezed, showed her what pressure he liked.

Then she batted his hand away as she started stroking him hard now. "I want you to come for me. Do you want my mouth on you?"

He nearly choked. "Anything you want." Goddess, all his words were coming out in rasps. Of course he wanted her mouth on him.

Still stroking him, she leaned down and took the head of him in her mouth. She sucked the tip in, her tongue teasing against him oh so gently and, sweet goddess, he wanted to come in her mouth.

To his surprise, she sucked on him hard, working his cock with her hand in a fast rhythm. Not as hard as he normally jerked himself off but this was so much better.

He threaded his fingers through her hair, cupped the back of her head gently. No pressure though, because he didn't want her to feel forced. Fuuuck. He wanted this to be perfect for her. But he still needed to touch her, to be anchored to her.

"I'm gonna come soon, princess," he murmured. "Pull back."

But she only gripped him tighter and he wasn't going to stop her. He lost all thought process as she stayed bent over him, her hair surrounding them, her mouth pure and utter heaven.

He finally came with a shout, unable to hold back her name as his climax overtook him in hard, long strokes.

She kept going until he was done, though not fully sated—he didn't think he ever would be where she was concerned.

As she sat up, she gave him a very satisfied smile, her dragon flickering in her gaze for just a moment.

"That was perfect," he growled, reaching for her, tugging her onto him because he needed to feel her lithe, naked body on his.

"It really was," she agreed as she splayed over him. "I think we'll be good at sex."

Laughing, he buried his face against her neck and simply inhaled as he wrapped his arms around her. Already thinking about what it would be like to slide inside her slick heat and truly make her his...if only for a little while.

"If you fit," she added, her tone breathy.

Now he laughed even harder, feeling rusty as he did. It had been years since anything had made him truly laugh. "I'll fit, princess. Trust me."

CHAPTER EIGHTEEN

"I feel like I might be overreacting." Juniper hefted up her bag, but Zephyr plucked it from her immediately.

It didn't matter that they were both strong dragon shifters, he simply couldn't help himself sometimes.

And she loved it—and him, more than life itself.

"She's your sister. It's not overreacting."

She'd sent a messenger to New Orleans—to Aurora—with a quick note checking in on Stella. The response she'd received had been brief—Stella had settled in fine. That should make her feel better, but something was pushing Juniper to go to her sister.

As they descended the stone steps, she slipped her hand into Zephyr's, grateful she had him. "It'll be good to see my crew," she murmured.

"I do wonder what they've gotten up to, especially Hyacinth." There was laughter in his voice as he squeezed her hand. "Are you thinking about moving there?" His tone was neutral enough.

She shot him a surprised look. "Seriously?" They'd just had an official mating ceremony and had made the decision to stay in the Nova realm.

He lifted a shoulder. "Just checking. I don't want you to feel trapped in a decision you made before."

"I don't feel trapped at all. I feel...like all this is too good to be true," she whispered as they reached the bottom floor. A huge tapestry hung on the wall in front of them—a long-ago image of her grandparents raining fire down on screaming enemies. "Which is why I want to go see Stella. Because what if—"

"Nope." He leaned over, took her mouth in a hard kiss. "No what ifs. That's a game of utter madness, my love. We've heard back that she is there and your grandmother has already sent scouts to different realms to gain additional intel on the Domincary fae."

She knew all that, but it didn't stop that insistent buzz at the back of the skull—her *instinct* that had never let her down.

"Do you have everything you need?" Soleil appeared out of nowhere, striding toward them in dark pants and a dark tunic, her silvery hair in a tight braid.

"We do, thank you."

"I've had food packed up for you so you won't need to stop and hunt."

Juniper suppressed a smile. It wasn't an overtly long trip. Yes, there was a decent bit of flying but it wasn't obnoxiously long. And if they didn't stop, she wasn't even worried about food. But she understood this was her mother's way of telling her that she loved her and wanted to take care of her. "Thank you."

"The offer to go with you still stands."

"I think you're more needed here." That was far more diplomatic than saying Soleil might piss off Stella if she showed up suddenly. Juniper could play the big sister card and get away with it.

Soleil watched her carefully, then nodded and changed the subject. "Ares is in the bailey and would like to say goodbye before you leave."

"Of course."

"Also, Milana and Andre will be arriving soon but I swear on my honor as a Nova dragon that they will be safe and protected—"

"Mother! I know you will take care of them. I'm not worried." Milana and Andre, her adoptive parents, the two wolf shifters she called

Mom and Dad with ease. Soleil and Ares had been so welcoming of the two, so grateful that they'd raised Juniper in a happy, safe environment when she'd been thought dead by her people. But she knew it was difficult on Soleil to call them her parents.

Tension seemed to drain from Soleil at her words. Then she cleared her throat. "Will…ah, do you think…" She cleared her throat, tried again. "If you do not wish to call me Mother when Milana is around, I will understand." Her words were as stiff as her posture.

Juniper stepped forward, pulled her into a big hug because it was clear Soleil needed it and okay, she needed one too. Right now she was worried about her sister. "Milana will be thrilled to hear me call you Mother. Her heart is bigger than both of ours combined."

Soleil squeezed her tight, then thumped her hard on the back. "Go. Find Stella, make sure she is safe."

"Watching you two is like watching a master class in awkwardness," Zephyr murmured as they stepped outside, cool air wrapping around her.

It hadn't taken long to get used to the chilly weather here in the Nova realm and she found she enjoyed it. "Shut it," she grumbled.

But he just snickered. "I'm so glad Milana and Andre are coming, it gets even worse when they're around."

"You just love to be babied by her."

"Uh, yeah." He shot her a sideways glance. "It's awesome. Plus she promised to bring me baked goods." He patted his flat stomach, grinned mischievously.

She simply shook her head. "Shameless."

"You love it."

"My daughter." Ares, much like Soleil, appeared out of seemingly nowhere, an old magic running through his veins as he approached her across the nearly empty bailey. He must have told everyone else to get lost. Or, maybe because it was after midnight, people were simply sleeping. But somehow it seemed eerily quiet tonight, as if he'd made it clear that no one was to interrupt them.

Her shoulders stiffened as he reached them, preparing for more awkwardness, but he simply embraced her. "Give Stella my love and tell her I'm proud of her for standing up to all of us, for spreading her wings."

Juniper blinked in surprise, but nodded. "I will."

He nodded back, then did that whole warrior style hand thing with Zephyr before he shoved a pack into Zephyr's hand. "Put this away and make sure you take care of Juniper. Make sure she eats."

Instead of telling her father that she could very well take care of herself, Zephyr nodded. "Of course. Be well."

Ares grunted, then hugged her again before hurrying away.

"Master class, my love. Master. Class," Zephyr said.

"Just hush," she muttered even as a smile spread across her face. "You ready?"

He nodded and stripped down to his birthday suit—her very favorite look on him. She didn't have to take off her clothes, she simply called on her magic and let the change overcome her.

Magic exploded in the air as her dragon took form, her wings stretching wider until they collided with her mate's wings. He leaned in close, nuzzled at her neck for a moment before he turned and took to the skies.

She stretched out, embracing her animal side, savoring it, before she plucked up her pack and followed him into the air.

It was time to go see her sister, to make sure everything was okay.

Which of course it was. It had to be.

CHAPTER NINETEEN

S tella yawned as she opened her eyes, paused as she realized she was alone. A weird sense of panic slammed into her until she heard the shower running in the bathroom.

The door was cracked open with steam billowing out.

Instead of second-guessing herself eighteen hundred times, she jumped out of bed, and crept into the bathroom. Rhodes probably heard or scented her, but whatever.

She hurriedly brushed her teeth, rinsed out her mouth, then tiptoed toward the shower. "You want some company?"

Rhodes' big arm shot out from behind the shower curtain and tugged her in with him.

Laughing, she found herself plastered against him—and his very large erection. There was a little circular window high above them, letting in natural light, the sun highlighting all of Rhodes'...assets. And there were so many.

Seeing him in the bright light of day, she drank in every inch of him. She knew he had broad shoulders, but in the shower, they seemed even more defined—this had definitely been built with smaller humans in mind. She traced her fingers over his biceps, forearms, as she said, "I slept so good last night."

"Me too." He clasped onto her hips before he wrapped his big arms around her, held her close.

She liked the intimacy of the moment, plastered herself to him as water pounded down around them. She felt so safe with him and found herself wondering if they might have a future. A real one. Something more than just sex. "Can I ask you something?"

"Anything." His gaze was on her mouth, hot and hungry.

"How did you get this?" She traced a gentle finger over the scar on his cheek, had the urge to hunt down whoever had done it and destroy them.

His mouth quirked up slightly as he covered her hand with his bigger one. "A very savage fight with another dragon who thought I was encroaching on his territory."

"Is he dead?"

"No, but he flew away in as bad a shape as I did. It happened decades ago and I've never seen the male again."

"Well if I find out who did that—"

He cut her off with a quick kiss, his tongue searching, teasing, before he pulled back. "You will do nothing."

"I don't like the thought of someone hurting you."

He simply ran his hands down her hips, up her back, as if he couldn't get enough of her. And she found herself a little flustered even though they'd been very intimate last night. And then again a couple hours later. Two more times. But it was as if he was holding back from her.

"I'm going to check in with Lola this morning." She needed to ask her if she'd found out anything about that phone. "And Christian." He'd texted her some time earlier in the morning but she'd been in such a deep sleep she must have not heard it. His message had simply said 'please call when you can'.

Rhodes made a hmming sound as he continued to run his hands down her back, over her ass, and back up again, as if he was just touching her everywhere because he wanted to.

Oooh, she liked the idea of that, being able to touch him anywhere. This was so new to her and she wondered if there were…rules. Apparently there didn't seem to be any in the bedroom. When he'd pressed his finger inside her last night... A shudder of pleasure rolled through her as she remembered how amazing her orgasm had felt. That one and the ones later.

She trailed her fingers down his back, felt grooves that might be scars. Maybe like the one on his face. She wanted to know who had dared to hurt him. "Will you help me wash my hair?" she whispered, wondering if that was okay to ask a dragon to do. It felt sort of intimate in a different way.

She had no clue what they were at this point. There had been no promises or anything between them. Just a lot of lust. But he had braided her hair before.

"I would love to," he murmured, his voice deep and soothing. "Turn around."

As she did as he said, she heard a little snapping sound, then scented coconut and rose. Her dragon senses were coming back even more, the teasing of her beast under the surface, so much closer now. And it wanted Rhodes.

"Will you tell me more about yourself? Maybe about the human village you lived in before. I'm curious about why you lived with humans and how you came to live in the Nova realm."

He was quiet as he massaged his fingers into her scalp. She couldn't bite back the moan of pleasure as he washed her hair, worked her scalp so expertly she was close to melting. This should not be as much of a turn-on as it was.

Finally he said, "I never knew my family. My earliest memory is when I was a dragonling. I was perhaps eight or nine in human years. I...was simply alone. It was easy enough to take care of myself, to find food. But I was curious about humans."

"You were born in the human realm?" she asked, even though she'd told herself to be quiet once he started sharing.

"I must have been."

So he didn't even know? She hated that for him. Her own sister had been stuck in the human realm but she'd been lucky enough to be taken in by kind wolf shifters. It seemed that Rhodes hadn't been so lucky—he seemed too alone at times.

"I discovered other realms later...discovered a lot later. But when I was young, I watched humans. I used to guard a small winter village that was in a sort of...no man's land. They dealt with random raiders from a neighboring country who liked to abduct their women. I put a stop to that."

Her heart warmed at his savage words. It didn't matter how young he'd been, he'd known that some things were very wrong.

"So they took you in?"

"Sort of. I was never one of them. They offered to let me live with them, but I preferred the forest, preferred being in my dragon form. It always felt safer. When I was older, some of the village males tried to marry me off to their daughters."

Stella stiffened, which just made him laugh lightly.

He pinched her butt. "I obviously did not. You are the only female I've ever touched intimately," he murmured, close to her ear now.

"Well, you're very skilled." It had made her wonder at his level of experience, despite what he'd said. But...she'd gone with her instinct and he'd seem to love what she'd done with her mouth as well.

"So what happened then?"

"I lived with the humans for a while, had grown to care for many of them. I went on a hunting expedition with some of the males and when we returned..."

"You don't have to continue." She reached behind herself, grabbed onto his hip to comfort him.

He cleared his throat. "The village had been wiped out by an avalanche. They never stood a chance. If it had been human raiders or even supernaturals, I could have hunted down the culprits, could have done something. As it was... That kind of loss was so overwhelming, so devastating, it was difficult to deal with."

His voice was a raw, open wound now. She couldn't believe he was sharing so much with her, but she drank in his words, even as she ached for him. "I'm so sorry," she whispered.

"I helped the males find all the bodies. We buried everyone and then... Once I knew they were settled in new villages, I left. I flew far, far away and inadvertently discovered supernaturals. Fae."

"Ugh."

He snorted softly. "Ugh, indeed. They were my first introduction to the supernatural world."

"That is unfortunate."

He continued working his fingers through her hair, all the way down to her butt, his fingers skating over her skin, sending shivers through her as he briefly cupped her there.

"There are ways to find out where you came from. If you want," she added. "I'm sure you've thought of it, but my sister said that there are things called databases that help displaced shifters. I don't know about dragons though." Her own realm certainly didn't have anything like that; they'd been shut off from the rest of the world for so long until recently.

"How is it having your sister back?" He sounded curious, but it felt like a deflection.

One she would respect. If he didn't want to talk more about his past, she could understand that. "Simply amazing. She was my rock when I was young. Then she was just...gone. It's still hard to believe she's back. And mated." Stella smiled as she thought of Juniper and Zephyr, two dragons perfectly made for each other.

He shifted slightly, guided her under the water, letting it rush over her as he moved to stand in front of her. A slight frown marred his expression.

"What?" she asked, raising her hands to finger comb through her hair. Normally she combed her hair while showering but had forgotten it on the countertop earlier.

"You're not resentful of your sister coming back now? She's next in line to be queen."

Stella snorted. "I could never be resentful of her. I love her. And she can *have* that role. If she'll take it." Juniper had been resistant to the idea, but Stella had never wanted it. "I'm just glad she's home. She used to read me stories at night and never cared when I snuck into her room— which was mostly every night."

"You're lucky," he murmured.

"I know." Her gaze fell to his mouth and she thought of the little boy who'd been lost in a wild human world with no clan. She hated that he'd had no one and hoped... Well, she hoped that maybe they could have a future. That he would let her in, maybe consider creating a family with her.

She wasn't sure if it was too soon to be thinking of that, wished she could read his mind. Because she was consumed with him. "Can I touch you?" she asked, meeting his gaze.

Raw lust burned bright, his eyes a shining green-gold. "I said before that you may touch me anywhere and anyway you wish. That's a standing invitation."

"Standing, huh?" She grinned up at him.

"From now until eternity."

Oooooh. She sucked in a breath as his words and heat wrapped around her—and feeling bold, she reached out and wrapped her fingers around his thick erection.

He sucked in a breath, braced a hand on the tiled wall. His dark hair was damp against his head. "May I touch you as well?"

"No," she whispered, feeling mischievous.

"No?"

"Not right now." She gripped him hard, remembering how he liked to be stroked. Even her hard strokes hadn't seemed to be enough, but he clearly liked what she was doing now.

His neck muscles were pulled taut, his forearm muscles flexing as he kept his hand on the wall—as she stroked him harder and faster.

His breathing grew raspier, harsher, the faster she went.

Until he suddenly groaned. "I'm coming." His words were a hard growl and then, he did just that, came all over her hand and his stomach.

He rubbed his hands over his come and...spread it over her stomach. "I know it'll wash off, I just want my scent on you," he growled.

Her inner walls tightened at the possessiveness in his voice, at his action. It was so honest, so...everything. "You can touch me now."

He moved lightning fast, pinning her up against the wall, the tile a cool contrast with the hot water. "I haven't even kissed you properly this morning," he murmured, slowly lowering his head to hers even as he kept her in place.

He'd brushed his lips over hers, but it was clear he meant something deeper. She arched up to meet him, her nipples already hard with want, brushing against his chest. The slight stimulation sent a wave of heat through her, which was intensified when he reached between her legs, cupped her mound.

"Mine," he growled against her mouth.

Oh yes, all yours. This male had so much power over her and it should scare her more than it did. She rolled her hips against his hold, was rewarded when he slid a finger inside her.

The finger wasn't enough, that much she knew. Not between them. She wanted so much more.

As he teased his tongue against hers, she savored his taste, the simple feel of him keeping her pinned in place. She'd never wanted anything like she wanted him. "I want to feel you inside me," she murmured into his mouth.

He stilled, slid another thick finger inside her.

She swallowed hard. "More than your fingers."

His eyes went pure dragon for a moment. "Stella—"

"No. It's *not* too soon." Her entire life people had been telling her what was good for her or what wasn't. But she knew her own mind, her body. And she wanted Rhodes.

"I was simply going to ask if you wanted to take this to the bed."

"You're not going to stop this?" she whispered.

"No." A one-word growl she felt all the way to her core. "I don't deserve you, however. Just know that."

She grabbed his face in her hands, ignoring the stupid statement and pulled him back to her, needing his mouth on hers. "I don't need a bed," she managed to get out against his mouth. She just needed him.

The following sound he made was so primal, so purely Rhodes, she felt it reverberate all the way to her core in a shockwave.

His hands on her hips tightened as he lifted her up against the tile, the show of power impressive. Of course he was a dragon, so she wasn't surprised. Just turned on.

So, so, turned on.

She spread her legs, wrapped them around him as he slowly, so slowly, settled her slick opening over his thick erection.

She sucked in a breath as he began to push inside her, the sensation of being filled by him like nothing she'd ever experienced before. Even as she had the thought, a black fog-like smoke started to surround them in the shower. Panic bled through her rising pleasure. There was no scent to it, but—

"It's just me," he murmured, nibbling at her bottom lip.

Immediately she settled, though she was still tense as he slid deeper, deeper until... "Goddess." She let her head fall back as he filled her to the hilt.

"Rhodes. Say my name," he growled as he buried his face against her neck.

She clenched her inner walls around him, savored how thick he was, the sensation as he hit a spot deep inside her she'd heard talked about before. But feeling it was something else altogether.

"Now." He nipped at her earlobe, bit down.

She sucked in another breath, clenched around him again, smiled as he hissed in a breath. "Rhodes." His name came out as a whisper, a prayer.

"You feel amazing." His words were gravelly as he slowly pulled out, the smallest fraction, eased back inside her.

Hitting that spot again. She'd expected pain. Instead all she felt was...pure pleasure. The whispered talks she'd heard over the years hadn't prepared her for this wonderfulness. She couldn't find her voice, could only dig her fingers into his back as she rolled her hips against him.

"Rhodes," she gasped out again, realizing she could easily come.

"Ride me, use me for your pleasure." Another order, one she wanted to follow.

Those words set something off inside her and she started rolling her hips, basking in the raw pleasure of his thick cock hitting that spot, over and over.

She was so wet, hadn't imagined she could actually get so turned on.

Then he reached between their bodies even as he kept her pinned in place, and rubbed his thumb over her clit.

She bucked against him, crushed her mouth to his as she tightened her legs around him. Even as he kept her pinned against the wall, she rode him. Something about the position kept her spread wide open for him and—when he gently pinched her clit, she surged into orgasm, a dual sensation of pleasure punching through her.

She came with her entire body, a ragged cry tearing from her. "Please come in me." This first time, she wanted everything from him.

As the black fog grew thicker, all she could see was his beautiful face, feel the water pounding down over them as he found his own pleasure.

His thrusts grew harder, faster, and she heard a cracking sound, ignored it as he came inside her in long, hard strokes.

Feeling weak, she was glad when he slowly eased her off him— though she immediately missed him filling her—and set her on her feet. But he kept his steady hold on her, wrapping his arms gently around her as he kissed her again.

This time soft and sweet, his kisses almost chaste. "How do you feel?"

"Amazing." Even if she'd wanted to, and she didn't, she couldn't have held back her smile as she looked up at him. "That was exquisite pleasure and I would like to do it again soon."

"We will do this many, many times." His green-gold eyes had turned almost obsidian again as the black fog dissipated around them.

She wanted to ask him if it was his mating manifestation but found the words stuck in her throat. Because if it wasn't... She didn't even want to think about that.

Much like she didn't want to think about the fact that her mating manifestation hadn't shown up at all.

So she wrapped her arms around him even as the water had started to turn tepid and simply held onto him, enjoying the feel of his arms securely around her.

For just now, she was going to take this time with him and not worry about the future.

CHAPTER TWENTY

"You have broken tile in the bathroom and destroyed Bella's dress. I think you have a problem," Stella said around a snicker as she pulled her borrowed jeans on. After finally experiencing sex—with a male she was quickly becoming obsessed with—she was starving.

Rhodes' lips twitched slightly as he stood by the window, eyeing the yard below.

"What's wrong?"

"Nothing. I have an errand to run and I need you to stay here."

"I'll go with you." She needed to talk to Lola and was hoping the snow leopard shifter had worked her 'hacking' magic, even if she wasn't quite sure what that was.

He pushed away from the window, his movements economical, lithe, especially for someone so large. He was in a tunic and loose pants, choosing to wear his own clothing instead of the more modern style that Axel had let him borrow.

Stella found that she liked him best in nothing at all.

"I wish you could." His expression was sincere as he grasped onto her hips in that deliciously possessive way that made her squirm. "But I need you to remain here. Safe. Not that you are not capable," he tacked on.

As if he was soothing her frayed edges. Which, okay, he was clearly trying to. "Where are you going?" She didn't want to be separated from him, not even for a moment, and the realization was sharp. She slid her arms around him, held tight.

"I can't tell you. And I don't want to lie to you."

She blinked at his forthrightness, even as frustration boiled inside her. He was being honest at least. "Will it be dangerous?"

"Anything could be considered dangerous."

She glared up at him but didn't release her grip. "You're being intentionally frustrating."

"Yes." He leaned down, captured her mouth in a sweet, sensual kiss that sent heat curling through her.

Sighing, she stepped back. "You're not getting away with it because of that kiss, but because I trust you. Just be safe and let me know if you need help. And I promise to stay put."

The look he gave her, she couldn't even begin to read. But then he kissed her again, this time more thoroughly.

She clutched onto his shoulders, needing the anchor as he practically devoured her. When he finally pulled back, she wanted to beg him to stay, to get naked again.

But she had pride. Sort of. Maybe not so much where he was concerned.

Then he groaned, laid his forehead against hers. "I really have to go, but I don't want to. I'd rather be naked in bed with you."

"I'd rather that too," she whispered.

Sighing, he stepped back, his expression promising she'd get her wish later at least. And that would have to do. She was beyond frustrated he was just leaving but...she trusted him.

Once he left, she made her way downstairs and found one of the tiger twins in the kitchen making coffee. It would have to be Harlow, she realized, because Brielle was off on a short mission. Even if she hadn't known that, she'd have recognized Harlow's eyes. Both tigers were clearly deadly, given what her sister had told her, but Harlow simply had a lethal look about her.

But the tiger smiled at her as she said, "Coffee?"

"Yes, please. I'd never had it until Juniper brought some to our realm. Now I'm obsessed."

Harlow snickered and grabbed a mug for her. "Yeah, I'm glad coffee survived The Fall."

"This whole territory seems to be doing well."

She nodded, her long auburn braid sliding back over her shoulder when she turned to grab a small bowl. "Would you like sugar?"

"Yes, and cream if you have it."

"Milk. We just had a delivery yesterday. One of the local farms provides milk to the city and we got a couple cartons."

"Thank you for sharing all your things with me. And Rhodes," she added, still disappointed that he'd left without giving her many details. What was he hiding? Why couldn't he tell her?

"Of course. We love having people visit." She doctored her own coffee while Stella did the same to hers.

"So...is Lola still asleep?" She wanted to ask her about the phones they'd found, felt almost useless now with no real leads. Just waiting for information was quite frustrating. She wasn't cut out for the 'private investigator' life. Really, she was just glad to be away from her realm. And getting to spend time with Rhodes.

Harlow snickered. "Oh yeah. She won't be up for a few hours."

Stella took a sip of her coffee, sighed in appreciation. "What do you normally do on a Sunday morning then?" She often had plenty of tasks at the castle. Her work was never ending. Not that she minded, she preferred to stay busy. But she realized she didn't have any plans right now and it was odd.

"If I'm not on a patrol shift, which I'm currently not, just depends really. Might go visit with friends, go running, ah...spar with my psycho sister."

She stared in alarm. "Your sister is psycho?"

She laughed, the sound infectious. "No more so than me. And I'm just playing. Sometimes we spar with each other because we're evenly matched and need the practice. But Brielle is on that out-of-town thing for King. So." Harlow shrugged.

"Would you like to spar with me? I'm not up to full speed but I can feel my dragon under the surface." And it might be good to work out some of her energy. She thought sex was supposed to make you tired, but instead she simply wanted more from Rhodes. So. Much. More.

"You sure you're up to it?"

She shrugged. "We can find out."

"I like your style, princess. All right, let's eat breakfast first because I'm starving."

"Can I help with anything?"

"I'm good. Just relax and drink your coffee. It'll be nice to cook for someone anyway, and I'm not waking up any of those freaking degenerates," she grumbled, love clear in her voice. "The kids are gone this weekend so the others have devolved into acting worse than children."

"What kids? Aurora mentioned them before."

"Oh right. They weren't here last time you visited, I don't think. We've adopted three shifters who lost their family during The Fall. One teenage girl and twin boys who are balls of energy." More love and adoration colored the tiger's voice. "You should get to meet them soon."

Which made Stella smile. She liked everyone in this house, they were so warm and friendly and didn't treat her the way she was often treated back home. It ranged from being sheltered by her family to others who saw her as defective because of how small in stature she was. And she knew it wasn't all of the realm, just a few assholes, but it still hurt. It was one of the reasons she'd never complained that her family had pushed her so hard to train. She liked being strong. Out here, she felt like she could be her real self.

"I broke a tile in the bathroom," she blurted. "And I will of course replace it or pay for the damages."

Harlow just snorted. "Don't worry about it. That's not the first time it's happened and probably won't be the last. We tend to break shit at a shocking rate. Luckily we know people who can help fix it if we can't ourselves. Or we have a witch friend who can repair the really, really broken stuff."

"You think she could fix a dress?"

Harlow let out a real laugh now. "I heard about that. Man, males are just bonkers, I swear."

"I don't know what bonkers means."

That just made her laugh more as she cracked eggs into a bowl. "I should have asked, are eggs okay?"

"Perfect, thank you." She turned as Axel stumbled in, bleary-eyed, heading for the coffee and mumbling about stupid drinking games.

She wished Rhodes was there with them for so many reasons. She thought he would enjoy the banter—and something told her that he hadn't had much laughter in his life.

She wanted to change that.

CHAPTER TWENTY-ONE

R hodes kept his natural camouflage around him as he waited in the shadows of the oak trees. He'd arrived to the graveyard early for his meeting with the fae male who'd contacted him an hour ago with a simple text demanding his presence. Because of course the fae would demand, not ask.

The location for the meeting was just outside King's territory, not really claimed by anyone, though Rhodes figured King would eventually expand and claim it. A human graveyard worked out well because Rhodes had seen it from the sky. He liked easy visual markers instead of meeting in random places.

The oaks were thick, some of them probably older than him, and helped with his camouflage. Unlike most dragons he knew, he exuded shadows, was able to keep himself cloaked even with his clothes on. As long as there was enough darkness around him, he could pull it to him, use it as a protective barrier. He'd heard of some wolves who could do it too.

Right now he wanted to be back with Stella, naked in that fluffy bed. Where he could splay her out, enjoy her for hours. Feast on her. He still couldn't believe what they'd done only hours ago. That she'd allowed him in her body, *still* seemed to want him.

Because the goddess knew he wanted her with an obsession that bordered insanity.

But the fae, Julius, had requested a meeting and Rhodes had to take it. It could be a trap—he usually assumed it was when it came to the fae. Either way, Rhodes needed to know what the fae wanted and how many trackers they'd sent after Stella. He needed to gauge how widespread this threat was. Then make a decision on how to proceed.

In the end he might have to send her back to her realm—or just escape somewhere, the two of them. Things he didn't want to think about.

A sweet scent wafted on the air and he straightened, scanning the overgrown field beyond. Surrounding the graveyard were unused fields, and two farmhouses in the distance. Long fallen into disrepair. The entire area had been abandoned, with most people moving to King's or another Alpha's territory. No one wanted to be on their own now, not with the world uncivilized in so many territories.

There. He spotted a tall male moving across the field in quick, supernatural strides. He'd have transportation nearby, likely a horse. The fae loved their equines.

As the male reached the edge of the graveyard, the barrier only a rusted chain-link fence, he jumped it in one stride.

Rhodes paused, waited for anyone else to appear, then dropped his camouflage and stepped out into the sunlight, taking pleasure when the fae paused in surprise. It was slight, but he liked the fear he saw in the male's pale blue eyes, even if it disappeared quickly.

That's right, his dragon purred beneath the surface. *Be afraid.*

Julius kept walking toward him, his boots crunching over the grass and other foliage. "Where is the female?" he demanded, his tone all snooty.

Obnoxious fae, he thought to himself. And this male in particular was overly insufferable for a male with a name linked to a fruit drink.

"How many individuals did you hire to take her?" he asked instead of answering. "And do not lie." He let his dragon bleed into his gaze, wanting his beast right at the forefront.

"I did not hire anyone else." He paused, flicked off an imaginary piece of lint from his richly dark blue tunic. "But I did send two of my warriors to her realm."

"I know. They're dead."

The male's eyes flared with rage. "Killed by who?"

"Me. They poisoned the female, would have killed her. And my job was to bring her in alive." He made a tsking sound. "And you fae love to get technical. I wasn't going to allow you to welch on our contract because one of your people killed her."

Julius gritted his teeth, but didn't break his gaze. Some fae kept their hair long, well past their shoulders. This male's hair was slightly shorter, but long enough that he'd pulled it back right at his nape. "They would not have killed her, just incapacitated her. I take it she is still alive then?"

He nodded.

The male shoved out a sigh of relief. "Good. When do you plan on delivering her?"

"You still haven't fully answered me. Did you send anyone else?"

"No. For now. But I expect results."

"You'll have her soon." A lie he loathed telling, his dragon clawing him up even as he spoke the words. He would never let this male or anyone else have her. "But I am curious, I was told the female was a monster accused of many crimes against your people. I've watched her for weeks and it is difficult to believe she could harm anything."

The male rolled his eyes, slightly relaxing. "Why do you care?"

"I'm a dragon. I'm curious by nature. Why do your people want her?"

The male let out a long-suffering sigh. "Why else? Revenge. My father, *the king*, has a long-standing grudge against her grandmother." He shrugged. "So he's going to take it out on the weak one. Make an example out of her."

"Weak?" Stella was kind, but not weak.

Julius looked at him as if he was stupid. "The small dragon female. Everyone knows she's not built like the rest of her clan, *your* kind. He might even breed her, I don't know. She is a princess. And I don't care either way. I don't like being out in the human realm," he said absently, looking around as if the entire place offended him.

It took all of Rhodes' self-control not to rip this male's head from his body. To simply burn him to ash where he stood. What he was saying his father wanted to do to Stella had his dragon ready to burn their entire realm to nothing. "That's not how my contracts work. I only deliver or dispatch those who deserve it. Something your people know —or you'd have told me from the start about her." He also hadn't mentioned his father being involved.

"Ah, I see." Julius watched him, calculating. "How much more money do you want?"

He paused, as if considering. Of course the fae assumed he simply wanted more payment. "A bag of gold should do it." He kept his tone neutral while inside he was screaming, ready to murder this male where he stood. But that would be foolish, if satisfying.

The fae male nodded. "You have three days to bring her to the portal to our realm. If you don't, the contract is void and we'll expect repayment for what we've already given you."

"I will be there." More lies. But he wanted this male to assume he'd follow through, let his guard down—and not hire anyone else.

The male nodded, looked ready to leave, then paused. "If you have her or know where she is, why haven't you brought her to us? You'll not get more gold for taking your time—and wasting mine."

Rhodes lifted a shoulder. "I befriended her. I'm helping her with something. Once she has what she came to the human realm for, we'll return to her realm. Or she believes we will. I intend on knocking her out at the portal, then transporting her to yours." All lies. Thankfully the fae didn't have the same scent capability that shifters did. He would not scent anything off with Rhodes' words.

The male nodded his approval. "I'd heard you were ruthless. If your schedule changes, contact me. I would prefer to leave this realm sooner than later."

As the male stalked off, Rhodes moved back into the shadows, allowing his rage to surface. This male wasn't going to make it through the day.

But Rhodes had to be patient, had to follow him, to see who else was with him. Because a royal prince from any fae realm would not travel alone.

Anyone who had come with Julius today, would die. Anyone who intended to harm his female, was going to die bathing in his fire.

RHODES FOLLOWED ABOVE, keeping his camouflage in place and flying high enough so that the sound of his wings wouldn't carry. The fae might not be as sensitive as shifters, but it was a quiet day.

And Julius was riding farther outside the territory into what looked like abandoned neighborhoods. Rhodes could scent a few humans nearby, but not many. And he definitely scented fae.

Julius rode his horse for longer than Rhodes had expected—hours—the sun shifting in the sky by a good bit. He wanted to contact Stella, but couldn't while he was flying and he couldn't risk losing the fae male.

Finally. The male slowed by a cluster of cabins in what had potentially been a campsite at one time. A sparkling lake glistened beyond the cabins and he could see what appeared to be homes on the other side of it.

The male rode into the middle of the cabins—four total.

Immediately three males strode out of a cabin.

Rhodes swooped lower, but used the air to keep him aloft as he glided, listening to their conversation.

"The dragon has her. And he killed my men," Julius said without any preamble.

"Stupid savage," one snarled.

"You shouldn't have sent them to the Nova realm anyway," another said, and from Rhodes' view, he could see the male had a similar coloring and hairstyle to Julius. Gold glinted off the male's hand. So maybe another royal if that was a ring on his finger? It would explain why he spoke so boldly to Julius.

"Thank you for pointing out the obvious."

The male gave an obnoxious, mocking bow. "I'm here to help."

Julius growled something too low for Rhodes to hear as the wind shifted.

But then another male riding a horse appeared out of a nearby thicket of trees, with something rolling behind him. A large, sparkling cage of sorts. Not from this realm.

Rhodes found himself annoyed at the interruption because all conversation about Stella ceased and he still needed more details.

The male on the horse let out a whooping sound and the four other fae hurried toward him as he jerked to a halt.

His horse whinnied slightly but didn't move as the male strode back to the large cage. "I have found entertainment while we wait on the savage dragon to deliver the goods."

Fae loved to call dragons and other shifters savage, as if it was an insult. Rhodes swooped out, then back in, moving even lower on the chilly winds.

His blood iced over as he watched the male drag out a bound and gagged human female. Then two more.

Oh hell no.

Apparently he would not be able to wait out the fae because he would not allow them to hurt these females. If possible, he would leave one alive to gain more intel later.

A female screamed as one of the males ripped her gag off.

The fae slapped her across the face hard, the sound echoing. "Scream all you want, stupid human whore. We'll just like it even more."

All the males laughed, even the high and mighty Julius chuckled darkly.

Rhodes wanted to roar in rage but kept very, very quiet as he arrowed down toward the other side of the cabins. He wanted to simply blast them with fire but he might hurt the humans if he did.

And knowing the fae, they'd have some sort of ward to protect them from dragon fire. At least temporarily, because spells and wards only lasted so long before the raw power of dragon fire broke it down.

Once he shifted to his human form, he pulled out a spelled necklace from his pack and slipped it over his head. It had been created specifically for him and would only work for him—to protect him against poison. He'd had this created long ago because of all the work he did with the fae. They loved poisons in a way other supernaturals didn't, and could never be trusted.

Then he slipped on loose pants and picked up two short swords. It had taken maybe sixty seconds but the screaming of the females grated against his senses, had fire tickling at the back of his throat.

Hurrying around the small cabin, he didn't even bother to pause as he lifted one sword, hauled back and threw it at the fae who was straddling a cowering human.

It cut straight through his chest and all noise stopped as the male flew back through the air.

Rhodes didn't stop moving, instead raced at the nearest fae with supernatural speed—the one with a similar build to Julius—and sliced across his throat in seconds.

As blood arched through the air, the other males jumped into action, Julius screaming in rage as he withdrew a sword of his own.

The others did the same, lunging at him.

Rhodes let loose a stream of fire at the fae, the humans now to his right and slightly behind him. Out of the danger zone.

One of the fae males screamed oh so briefly as his body erupted in flames, but Julius and the other one kept running at him.

Rhodes ducked and rolled between them, slicing out with his blade at the other male's left leg, and ignored the pain burning through his back as someone hit him with a blade.

As he jumped back up and turned, he saw blood pouring out of the other male's leg.

Rhodes stepped on the fallen fae's chest, yanked his other sword out and faced the two males.

Julius pulled out a weapon, shot a dart at him.

The spelled necklace made the dart fall to the ground, harmless. Instead of having a charm that would ward off everything—and therefore weaken its power and length of usefulness—this was very specific.

Julius growled in frustration but didn't back down. "Leave, contact our realm," he ordered the other male instead. "Tell them the dragon is a traitor."

The other male limped off toward the horse, jumped on it even as Julius stalked forward.

Rhodes needed to stop the male, wasn't sure how far the portal was to their realm. But he'd have to kill Julius first.

"I'm surprised by your treachery," Julius spat.

"I don't know why." Rhodes' voice was butter smooth as he pushed out his senses, searching for any more threats. Nope. Just Julius as the other male rode off. And the scared humans, who were slowly crawling away from them. Good, they needed to get back from this mess. He didn't want them getting caught in the crossfire.

"You had such a solid reputation. Never failed in a contract."

Rhodes simply bared his teeth, his dragon in his eyes. He had to make this quick, had to hunt down the other one. "You lied when you offered the contract. So you broke it, which makes it null." By stating that Stella was a monster who deserved to be kidnapped, they'd voided everything. Not that it mattered, he'd have never taken her in. "And you're stalling," he snarled, calling on the magic of his shadows as he rushed forward.

He could see Julius swivel in confusion as the darkness wrapped around him.

Rhodes struck, shoved his sword straight through the male's chest, yanked upward, cleaving him in half. "I'll be back to help," he shouted to the humans right before he shifted to dragon form, took to the skies.

They screamed again, but their cries soon grew distant as he chased after the trail of the running fae.

He had him chased down in less than ten minutes, the scent of his blood a powerful beacon through the woods. As the male emerged through a thicket of trees, glanced behind him, Rhodes' dragon smiled to himself.

The male might be spelled against dragon fire, but it wouldn't stop him from getting eaten by one.

On a silent descent, he ripped the fae's head off his body in one fell swoop as he rode.

The horse reared up on his back two legs, tossing the body clear before racing off.

Rhodes scooped the body up in his mouth and crunched down on it with his jaws, flew it back to the rest of the bodies. As he'd suspected, before he returned, the humans had run.

No surprise. But he would still find them, attempt to help them.

After gathering all the fae remains, he incinerated them until their ash lifted on the wind. Then he scooped up all their belongings that might be of use and put everything into one bag.

Only then did he go searching for the humans who'd left a scent trail of fear so wide, a human could have hunted them down.

CHAPTER TWENTY-TWO

As Stella stared out the glass panes of the big window overlooking the backyard, she frowned at... everything. Herself. Rhodes. *His absence.*

Stella had promised Rhodes she would stay at the house—but that had been hours ago. That morning in fact.

She'd spent the day sparring with Harlow, then helping with their garden, which had been wildly therapeutic, then she'd helped gather eggs from their chickens. Then Lola had finally woken up and was looking into the history of the cell phones Stella and Rhodes had taken. And Stella was trying not to obsess about Rhodes and where he was.

Who he was with.

Because in an hour and a half, Stella was leaving to meet with Christian whether Rhodes returned or not. Part of her was worried that something had happened to him but he was so strong and capable, it was difficult to imagine that. Another part of her was fighting anger that he'd just left her here.

She was a mess. Her dragon was starting to claw under the surface, so close to being out but not quite there.

"Hey, Stella, you busy?"

She turned at the sound of Lola's voice to find the female stepping through the doorway of the little library. "No, everything good?" she asked.

Lola lifted a shoulder, her rainbow-colored hair shimmering slightly with the movement. "So-so. Look, before The Fall I would have been able to dig deeper for you, look at call histories and...never mind, doesn't really matter," she said on a laugh. "But I did a deep search on both phones and long story short, they were both purchased together. From the same batch. There were some texts I was able to recover as well. It looks like whoever used these was communicating about stolen goods. I mean, they're using code, but it's not great." She handed both devices over and continued. "There's no code on them anymore. You can read what's there, though I don't know that it'll be helpful."

"Thank you for all you've done." She pocketed the phones, planning to look at them when she was alone.

"I wish I could've helped more." A frown played across the pretty female's face.

"This is a help. And I have a lead I'm following up on in a little over an hour. Seems as if someone might have put the crown up for auction or is thinking about it."

"Oh yeah, Harlow said something about that. Where's your big bodyguard? I thought he'd be back by now." Frowning, she looked past Stella into the library as if Rhodes was hiding in the shadows.

"I don't know where he is but I'm leaving with or without him." She kept her tone neutral, but inside she was beyond annoyed.

Lola nodded, her rainbow-colored hair moving like liquid around her shoulders. "Let me know if you want company."

"I will, thank you."

Once she was alone upstairs in her room—definitely not stretched out on her sheets because they smelled like Rhodes—she read over the texts and Lola was right. Not very subtle code, talking about packages and deliveries. But nothing specific, because of course it wouldn't be that easy. At least Christian seemed to think tonight would garner something real.

Frustrated, she tossed the phones onto the nearby dresser but froze when the bedroom door swung open and Rhodes strode in, his expression neutral.

"You're okay," she breathed out, her fear winning out over her anger.

Until he simply nodded. "I'm good, but I need a shower. I'm sorry I'm so late, I won't be long."

She blinked as he headed straight for the bathroom without so much as touching her and yep, anger took over, swift and sharp. She moved like lightning, following him into the bathroom. "Where have you been that you couldn't call me? Were you with another female? Is that why you need a shower?" Oh sweet goddess, she sounded wild and jealous but…why *did* he need a shower? All these stupid lustful feelings were making her crazy.

He swiveled back to look at her, surprise in his green-gold eyes. "You can seriously ask me that after all we've shared?"

"That's not an answer," she growled, her dragon prowling closer to the surface as she glared up at him. And that was when she scented… dragon fire. And blood. "Wait, are you bleeding?"

"The blood's not mine. And I need a shower because I don't want to touch you while I'm covered in fae blood. And human blood," he sighed.

"Wait, what? I need an explanation *now*."

"I killed a handful of fae who wanted to hurt you. Kidnap you. Bring you back to their realm."

She could scent the truth rolling off him, realized the effects of the poison must almost be fully out of her system now. Getting her senses back made everything feel brighter. "You're…sure they wanted me?" What was going on? Maybe he had been right and they should return to her realm. She'd never wanted him or anyone else to be in danger.

"They definitely wanted you—one of them was very vocal about why." He sighed, scrubbing a hand over his face. "And I don't want to talk about it."

She lifted her chin, refusing to back down. "Well too bad. I don't know what we are right now but you don't get to treat me like some fragile flower. I need details that pertain to my own safety. Who were the fae and what did they say about me?"

He turned away from her—infuriating her dragon. Then he stripped off his clothes and stepped into the shower.

So, she got naked and followed right after him. She slid in behind him and wrapped her arms around him. She was angry but she still wanted to comfort him, touch him. She wasn't going to let him block her out and she realized that with the way he'd grown up, maybe he wasn't used to opening up to anyone?

Immediately, he covered her arms with his as water pounded him in the face.

She tucked her face against his back as it turned from cold to warm, then scorching. It didn't matter that she was annoyed with him, the feel of his naked body against hers had heat spiraling through her.

"I don't think you're a fragile flower," he finally growled. "I just don't want to repeat what that asshole said because it makes me want to kill them all over again."

She simply grabbed a stick of soap and began washing his back, savoring the feel of rubbing it and her hands over his back. Over each muscle and indentation. "I don't need full details, just general intentions."

"The father of the male I killed, Julius Domincary, apparently has a grudge against your grandmother and wants you as a way to get back at her. His plans for you..." A low growl rumbled out of him, so she stopped washing him and wrapped her arms around him again.

"I'm still here," she whispered against his back. "No one has me."

He turned suddenly, his eyes shifting to that unique obsidian as he looked down at her. "And you're not going anywhere. I won't let anyone take you." His voice was gravelly, unsteady.

She pressed her breasts against him, arching into him. She'd thought he was shutting her out because he thought she was weak, but she could see the real fear in his eyes.

"I'm a dragon," she murmured. "And I almost have all my powers back. No one will get the jump on me again."

The fear was still there as he crushed his mouth to hers. She had more questions but shelved them as he wrapped his arms around her, pinned her against the tile. It was difficult to focus on anything other than Rhodes as he ground himself against her.

His erection was thick between them and the energy rolling off him was too raw, unsteady. Yes, her questions would wait a teeny bit longer.

She slid her hands up his chest, back down again, then around him, wanting to touch him everywhere. To ease his fears. Goddess, was this what happened when you fell for someone...

Oh, no.

This was *exactly* what happened. Because if the roles had been reversed, and someone was threatening him, she'd go pure raging dragon on anyone.

"I missed you today," she whispered against his mouth, her words garbled.

He simply growled against her mouth as he reached between her legs. "I need in you."

She was already wet, something he quickly found as he slid a finger inside her. Her need for him had started the moment he'd stripped off his clothes, her body's reaction instantaneous. It hadn't mattered that she'd been angry—she was turned on by this huge male no matter what, she realized.

"I'm yours," she told him.

"You are mine." He slid another finger inside her. "Say it again." His body was vibrating with need.

"I'm yours." Goddess, this thing between them should be too soon, but she didn't care. Dragons weren't like humans and as her dragon half was starting to emerge again, all she wanted was to stake her claim on him.

That same fog-like darkness appeared and she leaned into it now, not afraid as he lifted her up, heat spearing through her as he slowly, torturously lowered her down onto his thick cock.

He wasn't kissing her now, instead was watching her intently, fire in his gaze as he slid deeper, deeper...

"Rhodes," she rasped out, the word shoving from her in a gasp of air as he hit that oh so special spot. The one that made her entire body shake as his thick erection dragged over it.

Holding her hips tight, keeping her in place, he did it again, pulled back, thrust up, then did it again.

Pleasure started low in her belly as he thrust harder the next time. Everything about this moment had her emotions wide open as they stared at each other. They'd barely even kissed and he was simply watching her with a wild hunger as he slid inside her over and over.

She still needed... Reaching between her legs, she started rubbing her clit.

"Oh yeah, rub yourself, princess." His voice was gravel now. "You're the most beautiful thing I've ever seen. Later, I want to splay you out on the bed and eat you until you scream my name."

Her inner walls tightened around him at his words.

Which just made him grin, the sight beautiful and wicked as he looked down at her. She could barely feel the water anymore, could only focus on him as he pulled his hips back, slammed home again.

"You like the thought of me doing that?" he whispered.

"Yes." Desperately so. *Please*, she thought, just a little faster. That new sensation was building inside her at the feel of him moving and she wanted more of it, wanted all the pleasure.

As if he read her mind, his thrusts grew wilder as he began pounding into her.

She clutched onto him, wrapping her entire body around him as he lost himself inside her. And when her climax hit, she bit down on his neck. Not hard enough to break the skin, but it was close. She wanted to claim him, wanted to bite him, draw blood and let the entire world— every single realm—know that he was hers.

But she wouldn't take what he hadn't offered even if she wanted it more than her next breath.

"Fuck," he growled right as he let go, his entire body shaking as he came inside her in hard thrusts. "Next time I'll be slower," he murmured before he took her mouth, softer than before, sweeter.

"I liked that," she said against his mouth, wondering if he'd say anything about her biting him.

Dragons only did that when they were close to mating and...she wanted to be embarrassed, but she wasn't. She was desperate for him. A groan escaped as he eased her off him and like before, she felt hollow without him inside her.

As her feet hit the shower floor, she was careful not to step on the fallen tile. "Crouch down," she ordered as she took the shampoo bottle.

He did as she said and as she started washing his hair, he spoke again, his words surprising her. "There were some humans the fae took, hurt. Not irreparably, thankfully. But they planned to abuse them before they killed them. I took them back to their little home and offered to bring them to King's territory. I spent a while trying to convince them, but they declined. And by the time I was heading back, I realized my phone had died. I am sorry you worried, that I wasn't able to contact you."

"Oh, Rhodes, I'm sorry. Do you think they'll be okay?" She loved that he'd helped random humans.

"I don't know. I didn't scent any other supernaturals nearby. I think the fae stumbled on them by chance but it was mainly females. And I know females are just as capable as males, but...these ones are human, soft, and I don't like the thought of them out there alone. I sent a message to King about their location when I got back."

Of course he had. Oh, Stella had fallen for this male so hard and so fast and it was no wonder. "King will send people to help them, I'm sure." He was a fair Alpha, one who'd kept his territory from devolving into chaos after The Fall. If anything, it was better run now than it had been when humans were in charge.

Rhodes turned and held her close, burying his face against the top of her hair and inhaling. "I didn't mean to close you out," he finally said. "I'm not used to...feeling like this. To having anyone." The last part was said so quietly, it cracked her heart open.

"I'm not used to feeling like this either." He'd come out of nowhere and just stolen her heart. She didn't want it back either. She'd always had her family. Even when they'd lost so many of her people, she'd still had family. A core that anchored her. It seemed Rhodes had no one.

The very thought of that made her ache. She squeezed tighter, burying her face against his chest. "I hate to do this now, but we do need to leave soon. Christian has a lead for us."

"I don't like you saying another male's name while we're naked."

Despite the seriousness of his words, she snickered against him. "I don't think you like it whether I have clothes on or not."

He grumbled in answer.

CHAPTER TWENTY-THREE

"Turn around and face the mirror." Rhodes had just slowly towel dried Stella and he knew they needed to leave. But...he wasn't done with her. He would *never* be done, but at the moment, the mating frenzy was riding him hard.

She hadn't deeply questioned the dark fog that surrounded them whenever they were intimate and she had to know what it was. The mating manifestation. Right? Yet she hadn't...exuded anything in return, something he was definitely choosing to ignore.

"Wh..." Trailing off, she stared up at him, her bicolored eyes curious, but she did as he said.

"Place your hands on the countertop." He ran his palm down her spine, cupped her perfect ass.

She did as he said, watching him in the mirror as he slid his arms around her, cupped her breasts, pressed his cock against her as he leaned down and nuzzled her neck.

When she shuddered, the scent of her lust spiking in the air, he nipped at her skin. He didn't break it, though he wanted to. Hell, he still couldn't believe she'd bit him before—and he wished she'd broken his skin.

He hadn't meant to keep walls between them before, but he was still coming to terms with his feelings for her, still barely processing them. He'd never had anyone to take care of, not truly. When he'd lived with humans, sure, he'd helped them out. But this was different.

He'd been thinking of that fae's words, his intentions, on repeat in his brain since he'd killed the lot of them. Just the thought of Stella being vulnerable, of anything happening to her... He finally understood why matings with dragons were so intense.

Why if one mated dragon died, so did the other. Dragons had the ability to destroy the world, and if he lost her...

Nope. He nipped her again, forced his mind to focus on the female in front of him.

That dark fog surrounded them now but he could see her clearly in the mirror, watched as her eyes dilated, her breathing grew erratic.

He ran his hands down her sides, over her hips, back up again before he cupped her breasts. Her nipples were already beaded tight but he gently rolled them between his finger and thumb, enjoying the way she shuddered under his touch.

"I love your hands on me," she whispered, her words cutting right through to his core.

He couldn't find his voice so he slid one hand lower, down her stomach, lower still until he cupped her mound. Then he lazily dragged his middle finger over her clit, began slowly teasing the sensitive little bundle of nerves.

She shoved back against him, her ass grinding against his erection as she sucked in a breath. He hadn't given her any foreplay in the shower and right now he hoped he could give her some.

He was definitely going to make her climax again. And he wanted to mark her, wanted his come on her, in her skin. He didn't care how primal that was, the need was riding him to mark her.

To let everyone with a supernatural ability know that she was off limits.

That she was his.

Mine, mine, mine, his dragon purred.

When she reached behind herself, ran her palm over his cock, his whole body jerked against the gentle touch. He'd planned to take her from behind but...

Grasping her hips, he turned her around and set her on the countertop.

"I like it when you manhandle me," she whispered, the words sounding a lot like a confession.

He was such a goner. He claimed her mouth as he guided his erection to her slick opening, teasing the entrance with the head.

His balls pulled up tight at just that bare touch. She was so damn wet, all for him.

It was no wonder he was addicted to her.

She wiggled against the countertop, trying to get closer so he grasped her hips again, held her in place. He didn't want her to be able to move just yet. "Tease your clit while I push inside you."

Another spike of lust filled the air as she reached between their bodies and began slowly touching herself.

He looked between them, watching as his cock disappeared inside her, as her long, delicate finger pleasured herself. Fuuuuck.

Her breathing grew shallow as he pulled out, slowly thrust in her again. And her inner walls were already starting to pulse around him, to grip him hard. Oh, it wouldn't take his princess long to come.

He rolled his hips into her, thrusting harder even as he kept her in place.

She instinctively tried to move but he remained firm, the scent of her lust telling him everything he needed to know.

"Goddess," she murmured. "I'm going to come again." And she sounded surprised by it.

So he let go of his tight hold and she immediately bucked against him, meeting him stroke for stroke now with wild abandon.

He crushed his mouth to hers as he pumped into her and when she bit down on his lip, crying out his name, a shudder of pleasure spiraled through him.

He held back from coming, enjoying the way her inner walls clenched harder and harder right before her climax hit.

She arched her back, sucked in air as she clutched onto him, grounding herself as she came. Only then did he thrust harder, harder... He pulled out at the last moment and came all over her stomach and breasts, covering her with himself.

A growl rose up in his throat as he rubbed himself into her skin, and when she placed her hand over his as he did, helping him, something inside him cracked open.

He needed to tell her the truth about who he was, had to find the damn words. He was just so terrified of losing her.

He'd barely known her for a few days, but the thought of his world without her in it? No.

CHAPTER TWENTY-FOUR

S tella enjoyed the feel of Rhodes' hand at her back as they strolled through the posh open room of the mansion and looked at the various art, sculptures and paintings. Christian had invited them to an auction—supernaturals only.

It seemed odd that this was even a thing after The Fall but Christian said vampires and supernaturals had held onto their things for centuries and now was no different. When they wanted something, they would trade for it or pay with gold, art, whatever. Things they'd hidden away.

She wasn't impressed with some of the 'art', but there was a cluster of wildly colorful paintings of men and women in different stages of dancing. They were so erotic even though everyone in the paintings were clothed. And all around the dancers, shadows crept in and around the various scenes. It almost looked as if dragons were rising out of the shadows, but if she shifted on her feet, looked at the images from a different angle, they were just shadows. Whoever had painted these was wildly talented.

"Stunning, aren't they?" A male in a three-piece suit approached her and Rhodes, his haughty tone reminding her of some members from her clan's court.

"They really are." No need to hide her awe. "Who's the artist?"

"A human." The male, definitely a vampire, sniffed. "She's the only human allowed here tonight, in fact." He nodded behind them. "Hopefully she'll allow herself to be changed into one of us because this kind of talent needs to live on and grow."

Stella looked where he'd indicated, saw a female with auburn hair talking to whom she assumed were two vampires. The two males were way too close in her personal space, but then suddenly Aurora was there, sidling up to the human in the slightly large dress, and the two males smoothly stepped back.

"Her name is Mia," the vampire continued. "And I know you're Stella, a visiting princess, correct?"

"Who the fuck are you?" Rhodes growled, taking her by surprise.

But when she looked up at him, she realized he must not like this male so close to her.

Thankfully the vampire just snorted. "My name is Claude. No need to be so rude." He sniffed slightly, took a sip of what looked like champagne.

Stella placed a gentle hand on Rhodes' forearm as she smiled at the vampire. "This is Rhodes and yes, I'm Princess Stella of the Nova realm. We're guests tonight of Christian, who thought we might enjoy this auction. My family loves to collect rare items. What about yourself?" she asked, wanting to focus on him—so Rhodes wouldn't bite the guy's head off. Perhaps literally. He seemed edgier than normal tonight. "What are you hoping to purchase tonight?"

The male's demeanor eased slightly as he started talking about a vase from some past century. Stella tuned most of it out, but nodded politely as she scanned the room. Her family's stolen crown was nowhere to be seen but Christian had promised her that there was almost always an exclusive, smaller gathering at these things that happened after most people had left. He'd said they needed to be patient.

After a few minutes of chatting, Christian appeared, his expression charming as he slid up next to Claude. "Are you talking their ears off about Greek antiquities?"

The vampire laughed, the sound genuine as he nodded. He seemed more real now, less haughty. "Of course."

Stella took the opportunity to murmur a polite goodbye and ease away with Rhodes. "Why were you so rude to him?" she whispered as she picked up a glass of champagne from a passing tray.

There weren't too many people here tonight, only about a hundred, so the three connected rooms, where the prospective buyers were milling in and out of, weren't too crowded.

Rhodes lifted a shoulder, sniffed her champagne once before he nodded his approval that it was poison free. "I didn't like how close he was to you."

"You can't bark rudely at people because they're too close to me," she murmured as they approached Aurora, who was now talking to the human female alone.

"I can indeed." He looked all haughty dragon in that moment.

"Rhodes."

His mouth curved up ever so slightly, a hint of wicked in his eyes. "Apologies, princess. I'll try to be polite tonight."

Goddess, the deep tone of his voice sent a shiver of delight down her spine. Right about then, she wanted to be back in her room with him, naked and... She shut that thought down as she felt her cheeks heat up. "Will you give me a moment?" she whispered.

Nodding, he stepped back as she approached Aurora and the human.

Aurora immediately embraced her. "I'm delighted to see you here tonight."

"Thank you. It's a pleasure to see all this wonderful talent on display...and I'm hoping for an official introduction to you," she said, smiling at Mia, who had her hands clasped nervously in front of her. This close, it was clear she'd borrowed the dress from someone and was feeling very out of place. She looked as if she'd rather be anywhere than at this auction. "I've only seen a handful of your paintings and they're stunning."

"Stella, this is Mia," Aurora said. "I'm mentoring her, but if I'm honest, she's going to outpace me soon."

"Aurora," Mia gasped, shaking her head. "That's not true," she said as she looked at Stella, her expression almost horrified. "I have so much to learn."

144

"Then I can only imagine how incredible your later paintings will be because what I've seen so far makes my heart happy. I'm hoping I'll be able to buy one from your collection." Or all of them.

"Mia wants to travel to another realm so if you offer her a long enough trip to yours, I imagine she'd give you the entire collection on display in exchange for safe passage and lodging." Aurora's voice was smooth, her expression neutral, as she negotiated for the human.

The excitement on Mia's face, however, was bright. "You're from another realm?"

"I am." Stella smiled at the human, realizing how young she must be. Maybe in her late twenties—it was too difficult for her to gauge human ages. Until recently she'd barely had any contact with humans at all. "And Aurora is correct. In exchange for your collection, I would love to offer you a place to stay in my realm for as long as you'd like. You could paint and work or just enjoy yourself. But we have a few artists I know would welcome you into their little enclave with joy. They've never met humans and would enjoy having someone new visit. I'm sure you could all learn from each other."

Mia looked between Aurora and Stella, her green eyes wide. "Yes. You can have the entire collection. Thank you. I...that's amazing. Could I...go soon?"

"Of course. As soon as I'm done with my business here, I will happily set something up."

"Thank you," she said, looking between the two of them, pure joy in her expression. Oh, this little butterfly would fit right in with the artists in the Nova realm.

"Thank you," Stella said. "And we will definitely talk later," she murmured as a male and female approached Aurora and Mia, clearly wanting to talk to Aurora.

It was also clear that Aurora was keeping an eye on the human, who needed to work on her bargaining skills. Mia could have asked for more and Stella would have given it to her—likely would still give her more. The human wouldn't have to worry about a thing while she visited her realm. Her gaze drew back to the collection of paintings even as Rhodes moved in behind her, his presence solid, anchoring her. In the one closest, she loved the way the male and female were embracing mid-dance, the colorful feathers of the woman's dress flaring out, looking so real.

"They're so beautiful," she murmured.

"Hmm." He placed his hand at the small of her back as he leaned down. "*You* are beautiful," he growled. "And I can't wait to have you stretched out on my bed later."

A shiver rolled down her spine at his words, his dark, sensual tone. "We can't talk about that here." Or she'd combust. She had to stay focused on her task—even if she found herself caring less and less about the stolen crown.

She just wanted more naked time with Rhodes. She would make a terrible spy or investigator, she realized.

Suddenly she straightened as she saw someone familiar. "Hey, that looks like the bartender from that place last night," she murmured, indicating the male who was talking to someone from catering. "Is it weird that he had those phones and is here now?" The guy had simply given them the phones—well, access to the lost and found. Was it simply a coincidence he was here tonight? It had to be. She just found it jarring to see him when they were hunting down her stolen crown. He didn't look like a guest, though, was dressed casually in jeans and a T-shirt when everyone else was more formal.

Rhodes gripped her hip and moved her so that they were standing behind a big sculpture of a dragon. She couldn't see but he clearly could.

"So?" she asked.

"He's talking to a male fairly intently... He's heading into another room. Stay put. I'm going to follow him. Keep an eye out for anything suspicious." He gave her a quick kiss then moved *so* quickly she couldn't protest or call out without drawing any attention to herself.

"Stay put my ass," she muttered to herself and followed after him. That wasn't how this worked.

CHAPTER TWENTY-FIVE

"Breathe, my love." Zephyr's voice grounded Juniper in a way no one else could.

Because her new mate understood her at a deeper level. "I just want to see her, hug her." She missed her baby sister and they should have already been reunited.

But she and Zephyr had gone to Zephyr's brothers' place—and discovered that Stella was with Aurora's crew. She knew her sister was in New Orleans, but still, Juniper was still edgy. "And I don't even have a way to contact her."

Zephyr took her hand in his as they hurried down the long driveway to where Stella was supposed to be staying. Juniper could faintly scent Stella on the air, which told her that at least Stella had been here recently. So that was something. She was being ridiculous, she chided herself. She'd received confirmation from Aurora herself that Stella had arrived in New Orleans.

Laughter rose up from behind the mansion so they hurried around the side to find a cluster of people gathered, laughing and eating—Lola, Bella, Axel, Harlow and... Hyacinth! Joy rose in Juniper at the sight of one of her best friends.

Who happened to be sitting in the lap of the Magic Man, a human.

Juniper still didn't understand why her vampire bestie was getting her heart tangled with a human but it wasn't something she was going to worry about. Not now anyway.

"Juniper!" Hyacinth saw her before anyone else and jumped up, raced at Juniper with vampiric speed, literally jumping on her and wrapping her arms and legs around her as she noisily kissed her cheek.

Laughing, Juniper stumbled back under the impact. "I've missed you too!"

Hyacinth squeezed tight before she leaned back, dropped her legs from around Juniper. Her short, tight curls were pulled back with a shimmery red headband that matched her ruby-red lips. Tears glittered in her amber eyes. "I can't believe you didn't send a message! I've missed you so much."

"We're here to check up on Stella," she confessed, her big sister mode coming on strong. But she couldn't help it. Juniper hadn't been there for most of Stella's life and while she had encouraged her sister to come to New Orleans to spread her wings, she was still worried for her. That was her big sister right and she wasn't going to feel guilty about it.

"You just missed her," Harlow called out. "They left about an hour ago. Headed to that auction."

Juniper frowned at the use of 'they' but realized not everyone was present so maybe Stella had taken backup.

"Yeah, come sit, eat. They shouldn't be gone all night." Axel stood and motioned to his chair, pulled up another for Zephyr. "I'll grab you two drinks."

"Told you all was fine," Zephyr murmured, kissing her temple before he strode over to where Axel was, followed him as he headed inside, presumably into the kitchen.

"How is she?" Juniper asked Hyacinth. "And how are you? And Ren and Griff?" She missed all of her old crew so much and seeing Hyacinth in person was driving that point home.

"I actually haven't seen her at all. We just stopped by tonight for drinks before heading back home." A wicked glint sparkled in her eyes as she glanced back at Thurman—aka, the Magic Man of New Orleans. He was an older human, a seer, who was fascinating. He could see beneath shifters' auras, knew what kind of animal they were. "And Ren and Griff are on a rescue op—Grace is with them. I think Ren might finally make his move on her." Hyacinth grinned at that.

Before Juniper could respond, Lola jumped in.

"Your sister is doing great," Lola said, her hair rainbow colored once again. Last time it had been purple. "They've got a lead on the missing crown, hopefully. Christian heard through the vampire grapevine that someone might be trying to auction off something that sounds very similar to what she's looking for."

Oh, Christian. Relief punched through Juniper. He was an older, very capable vampire Juniper had been friends with for decades. If Stella was with him, she felt much better. "Goddess," she murmured. "I've just been so worried about her and now I feel foolish."

Harlow gave her a sympathetic look as Juniper sat next to the tall redheaded tiger shifter. "It's not foolish to worry about your sister, especially after her poisoning. But she's fine—"

"Poisoning?" She jerked upright in her chair.

Everyone grew quiet as she looked between Bella, Harlow and Lola.

"Ah… Stella was poisoned in the Nova realm," Harlow finally said. "Greer pulled all the poison from her but she's still sort of recovering. She's in good health, just can't call on her dragon yet. But she's fine! That big bodyguard won't let anything happen to her."

Bella, Lola and then Axel—who was just getting back to the table with Zephyr—all snickered.

"Definitely not," Bella said on a laugh. "That fool isn't allowed to destroy anything else though."

She wasn't sure what the heck they were referring to. "Wait, what bodyguard?"

Everyone went quiet again, watching her in surprise.

"Uh…the hulking dragon who's been following her around everywhere? The one who's totally smitten with her?" Harlow said, though it came out more like a question. "He saved her from the fae who poisoned her—"

"Wait, the *fae* poisoned her?" What the ever-loving fuck was going on! Their realm had been infiltrated by a couple fae but one of the realm guards had killed them and delivered them to the guards at the portal. There'd been no mention of Stella being poisoned. "Someone better tell me where she is right now."

"She's with her...not-bodyguard and Christian, at an auction," Harlow murmured. "His name is Rhodes."

"You're sure he's not her bodyguard?" Axel asked. "Maybe your grandmother or mother sent someone after her? He's very protective of her and she said he was from your realm."

"No, they did not. They wanted to but I convinced them to allow her to go alone. They wouldn't have lied to me." She looked over at Zephyr, whose expression was grim, then back at the others. "I need more details and we need to get to her now." Stella was sheltered and if some male had lied about being her bodyguard, who knew what else he was lying about.

"I'm going to call Christian," Axel said, already pulling his phone out. "To let him know there might be an issue."

Juniper nodded, even though it was clear Axel wasn't asking.

"All his stuff is here," Lola said, standing with the others. "If he's not who he says he is, then—"

Juniper was already moving, heading into the house, Zephyr right with her. "Tell me what you know," she said to Lola and Harlow, who were hurrying after them.

She listened as the females recapped the last couple days but when she got to the bedrooms on the third floor, she saw red.

Because the scent of sex filled the air, thick and heavy.

She was going to kill whoever that male was. Rip him limb from limb if he'd been lying to her sister.

CHAPTER TWENTY-SIX

Rhodes scented sweet strawberries before he heard Stella duck into the hallway behind him, not listening to anything he'd said about staying put. He'd followed the bartender up a set of stairs and the male had disappeared into a doorway at the end of the hallway. Perhaps the male was supposed to be here, but Rhodes' sense was telling him the guy was shifty. He'd been far too charming last night—and screw it, Rhodes didn't need a reason not to trust the guy.

Rhodes had used his natural camouflage and hoped Stella had managed to sneak up here without being seen. "What are you doing here?"

She simply raised an eyebrow at him.

Gritting his teeth, he nodded to the end of the hallway. "He's in there."

She bit her bottom lip, then glared at the door. "I wish I could use my natural camouflage," she ground out. Then she paused, looked as if she wanted to curse when it was clear she still couldn't call on her dragon, her magic.

He hated that she'd been poisoned, that it was still affecting her.

He eased closer to the nearest door, opened it. Inside was an empty bedroom so he tugged her in with him. As he pulled his tunic off, he said, "I'm going to go into full camouflage from the outside of the mansion, see if I can hear or see what that male is doing. But I need to know you're safe. Will you stay here? I'm only asking because you can't shift right now," he added, even though he was a giant liar. He never wanted her in any potential danger, ever.

"I'll stay here," she finally agreed, hands on hips, looking fierce and...adorable.

Goddess, she was perfection.

He moved quickly, stripping off his clothes and bundling them up before he went to the nearest window and called on his natural camo. Once it was in place, he barely eased the window open, looked down.

A few vampires were on the lawn below, talking, but no one looked up as he climbed out onto the ledge. The way the exterior was bricked made it easy enough to climb along the outside, moving from window to window using his natural supernatural strength and balance.

The first two windows were bedrooms—and one was occupied with a group of four having an orgy. The third window had blackout curtains pulled over it but he could hear a muffled conversation. Something about not having the proper champagne?

Rhodes rolled his eyes and started to move to the next window, which should be the correct room, but he paused when Christian stepped outside, talking on his cell phone below.

"He's not who he says he is? You're sure?"

Oh, hell. Rhodes paused, gripping the brick tightly as he focused on the conversation below.

"I don't know, they disappeared." A pause. Then, "I doubt he's going to hurt her." Another pause. "Of course I'm safe. I'm capable of taking care of myself," he said in a haughty tone. Then, "Fine, I will find them, but I don't think she's in danger. That male cares for her. They're probably off shagging somewhere." Another pause. "I imagine this is simply some misunderstanding." Another pause, then a sigh. "I'll see you soon."

After more back and forth, Christian sighed and hung up the phone, muttering to himself about an overbearing lion before he stalked back inside.

As panic hit him hard, Rhodes hurried back the way he'd come, completely abandoning his current job. Someone, likely one of Stella's relatives, was in New Orleans and his time with her was up unless he came clean.

He should have done it sooner, not waited until he was forced into a corner. Because now it was likely too late. He wanted to hope she would forgive him, but that wasn't likely to happen. Still, he had to try.

As he slipped back into the room and let his camouflage drop, Stella pushed up from the bed she'd been leaning on. "Did you find him?"

"No, but we need to leave. Now."

She blinked in surprise, her gaze snapping up from where she'd been staring between his legs to his face. "Why?"

"Do you trust me?"

"Yes." She didn't even pause and he knew he didn't deserve her.

"Then we need to leave. I need to talk to you about something important. But not here." He wanted to get her somewhere private and then he'd do what he had to. What he should have done before.

"Okay, let's go." She held out his clothes, the trust in her eyes clawing at him.

~

"You're starting to worry me a little." Stella sat on the park bench with Rhodes, not liking the wild energy buzzing off him.

He'd practically dragged her from the auction—they hadn't even told Christian they were leaving—and they'd finally stopped at a park. No one was here because it was well after dark but the place had decent lighting.

Rhodes was a pent-up ball of energy crouched down in front of her, worry etched deep in his face, his scar seeming even more pronounced than normal as he watched her.

"Why don't you sit next to me?" she finally murmured when he remained crouched, like a predator ready to strike. Not that she was worried he would hurt her. But his anxiety was starting to rub off on her. "Oh goddess, it's the poison isn't it." Reality slammed into her. "You heard from Greer and I'm not—"

"No, you're fine!" He slid onto the bench then, tugged her right onto his lap. "I just have to confess something to you. Something...big."

"Okay. So tell me."

He watched her warily. "I...don't know how to say this, Stella. But I've fallen for you. Harder than I ever imagined, ever thought possible."

Okay, this didn't sound like a confession. Well, not a bad one anyway. Was he...going to tell her wanted to officially mate with her? Her dragon punched to the surface at the thought, very pleased at the idea. "I've fallen for you too." She cupped his face gently, trying to soothe whatever was going on with him.

"You might not say that in a moment." His expression was haunted as he met her gaze.

"Stella!" She turned at the sound of her sister's voice, stared in shock as Juniper, Zephyr and most of the crew from Aurora's house strode across the grassy lawn of the park. "Get away from my sister," Juniper snarled as she raced at them.

"Fuck," Rhodes growled.

Stella turned to look at him in shock, then the others, worry crawling up her spine. "Why are you guys here?"

"We didn't send him. He is not your bodyguard. And if he doesn't take his hands off you right now, I'm going to remove his head from his body." Juniper's magical glowing chains were out, whipping around her ankles, lightly, with a snake-like fluidity.

Stella called on her own chains, only got a flicker of feeling. "Wait... what?" She turned to Rhodes, ignoring the others. "Are you not one of my grandmother's soldiers?"

His jaw flexed. "No. I was not sent to guard you. I was sent to kidnap you."

She sucked in a breath, hearing the truth in his words. "You said...oh goddess, you never actually said you were sent to guard me, did you?" She'd made assumptions. So many of them.

Looking miserable, he shook his head.

She shoved away from him, stood and stared, but didn't move back as agony punched through her. "So what was this, some sick game?" He probably hadn't been a virgin either. She was such a fool. A stupid, stupid fool!

"No!" he snarled, standing, but he kept his palms up when some of the others growled behind her.

"Everyone back up," Stella snapped without turning around. She hated that she had an audience for this, but she was going to get answers.

"I was hired by the Domincary fae to kidnap you. I'd been led to believe that you were guilty of heinous crimes but after watching you, I realized it was all lies. I was following you the night they attacked you and... I knew I had to keep you safe. So when you assumed I was sent by your family, I didn't correct you. And I did kill those fae to protect you —everything I told you I learned from them was true."

When they'd been intimate, he'd actually told her that he'd been watching her before they'd met—and she'd thought it was hot. Of course she hadn't realized he'd been hired to kidnap her. "I can't believe anything you say," she snapped.

"Believe it or not, but I love you." Raw agony laced his words. "I didn't expect you, Stella. I would never have taken you back to them."

"Then what was the plan!"

"I...was just trying to keep you safe. I knew who the threat was and thought..." He rubbed his hand over his face before he met her gaze again. "I don't know. I knew I was on borrowed time with you."

"Everything you said about the Domincary fae?"

"That is true. They have a grudge against your clan... I didn't realize what they intended to do with you until I killed the fae I followed today. That was true too."

She took a step back as pain settled into her bones, as his betrayal scraped against her senses. He'd lied to her. Lied and made her fall in love with him. Made her believe that he'd fallen for her too. "So is this what you do? You...kidnap people?"

"Mostly I kill them. The fae specifically. I'm a paid assassin." He spoke quietly, his expression almost blank now.

And she wanted to scream at him for making her want him, care about him. "I wish I'd never met you," she whispered.

He looked away, but not before she saw the pain in his gaze. "I'm still glad I met you, princess. And I'll never stop loving you. I wasn't lying about that. You are the best thing that ever happened to me, even if I'm the worst that happened to you."

Tears stung her eyes as she turned away from him, his words pouring over her in an avalanche of agony. But she quickly swiped at the wetness on her cheeks, beyond embarrassed that everyone was seeing this play out. More than that, she was just...heartbroken.

Goddess, she'd fallen for a male who'd been hired to kidnap her, turn her over to the fae as part of some contract. "No one is going to hurt him," she said, her gaze on her sister.

Juniper's magical chains slashed out at the air, clearly in protest.

"I'm serious." It didn't matter how angry she was, how hurt, she couldn't bear the thought of anyone hurting Rhodes. "You either," she said, glaring at Zephyr, who'd been suspiciously quiet. "Swear it!"

They both finally nodded. So she looked at the others. She just wanted Rhodes to go so she wouldn't have the agony of seeing his face. "And no weird loopholes either, Juniper. No one here will hurt him, or go after him. And no one from our clan or realm will either."

"Fine. Unless it's in self-defense," Juniper finally agreed. "No one will attack him—but I don't want to see your face again," she snarled at Rhodes.

Stella couldn't make herself turn around, couldn't look at him again.

She just wanted to be alone with her pain. Far, far away from him. She didn't care about the stupid missing crown, didn't care about anything other than getting away from Rhodes as fast as possible.

Without another word, she ran away from all of them.

CHAPTER TWENTY-SEVEN

"Why are you still here?" Rhodes snarled at the darkness, the scent of the handsome vampire light in the air. He wanted to be alone in his misery, wallow in everything he'd lost.

Christian stepped out of the shadows, casually approached Rhodes and sat on the opposite side of the bench, stretching his legs out as if he didn't have a care in the world. "You certainly botched things up good and proper." His British accent was slightly stronger tonight.

Rhodes just growled at him. He knew that, didn't need some vampire rubbing salt in the wound.

"I heard what you said to her," Christian continued.

"You and everyone else." He scrubbed a hand over his face, wanting to drown in his pain. The way Stella had looked at him, with such betrayal... Goddess, he wanted to erase that from his memory forever. Instead it would play back over and over on repeat. Because that was how shitty life was. He knew he wasn't going to get a happy ever after with her, had known it in his soul from the start, but that hadn't stopped him from wanting her. Hungering for her. Imagining a future with the two of them together.

"You really love her."

"Of course I love her," he snapped. "But it would have never worked out anyway. I'm such an idiot for ever thinking it might."

"Jesus, I hope I don't sound this whiny." The vampire stood suddenly. "Come on then."

Rhodes stared up at the male, found himself irrationally annoyed with how good-looking the guy was. At least Stella had never seemed to think so...not that it mattered anymore. She wasn't his, never had been. Not truly. Now she never would be. And that made him want to howl in agony. "What?"

"Stand. Now. We're going to see King. You need to get squared away with him before you do anything else. He's the Alpha of the territory and he's a fair leader. But you were here under false pretenses and now you need to explain to him why. Otherwise, you're going to find your-self facing down King and his pack. And you can't win back Stella if you're dead."

Rhodes continued staring at the vampire, who was watching him carefully, his expression neutral. "First of all, I can take on some wolves. Second, why do you even care?" He was a dragon and this male was a vampire, they had nothing in common.

"Well, *first* of all," Christian snapped. "You can't take on the whole territory unless you've got a death wish. And the reason I'm helping you is because you are the saddest sad sack I've ever seen and I know you love her. And...I'm old and grumpy but apparently I still believe in love. So get off your dragon ass if you want to actually fight for the female you love. If you don't, you can rot on this bench for all I care."

Growling, Rhodes stood and fell in step with the vampire. If this was a trap...hell, Rhodes deserved it.

～

RHODES HUNG BACK while Christian and the Alpha, King, talked by an Olympic-sized pool. They were speaking quietly, but Rhodes overheard a few words like 'vouch for him'...and he wasn't sure why the vamp was vouching for him at all.

He leaned against an oak tree in the massive yard of the Alpha's pack residence. He was surprised that he'd even been allowed on the property.

And now he definitely owed the male because Christian was right, Rhodes needed to fight for Stella. He just wasn't sure how. He knew nothing about females or relationships or even courting. He could bring Stella all the pleasure she wanted, but...not if she wouldn't talk to him.

He replayed the way she'd ordered the others not to hurt him—not that he was worried about his ability to take care of himself. But still, she hadn't *wanted* them to hurt him.

That had to mean something, right?

A soft rustling above him sounded before a dragonling suddenly burst through the leaves straight at him. Surprise punched into him right before the baby dragon did, not slowing down in time.

Despite everything, a laugh escaped as the dragonling rammed into him, knocking him onto the ground. The baby dragon chirped and babbled and batted at him with his wings as if to say 'I'm sorry'.

"It's okay," he murmured, sitting up as the gray dragonling jumped off him. "You've gotta work on your landings though, slow down a little. If you cup your wings more, it'll help."

The dragonling continued chirping its head off, then pointing upward with one of his wings.

"His name's Hunter. And he can land just fine—he wanted to get your attention. One of his cats is stuck in the tree," King called out, not bothering to look in his direction.

But Rhodes was under no illusion that the powerful Alpha wasn't paying attention. He definitely was.

"You want me to get your cat?"

Hunter chirped loudly, once.

Okay then. Why the hell not? Rhodes scaled the tree quickly, and found an orange tabby with faint white stripes along its back and tail far up in the tree. It hissed wildly at Rhodes as he moved out onto the same branch it was on.

"Yeah, I feel you," he murmured. "But you're gonna have to come with me unless you want that dragonling down there to knock the whole tree down."

It hissed again in warning.

Rhodes moved quickly, not giving it time to try to jump to another branch, using his supernatural speed to move along the branch and pick it up by the scruff.

It hissed and dug its claws into Rhodes' forearm as he climbed down. The pain in his chest was a billion times worse than the little needles digging into him.

And the moment he reached the ground, the cat let go and raced over to Hunter, scaling one of its outstretched wings before it climbed up onto the dragonling's back. Then it hissed at Rhodes.

"That's the thanks I get?" he murmured to the cat.

Hunter, however, bowed at him, as if thanking him. And...okay, the dragonling was one of the cutest things Rhodes had ever seen.

"You're welcome," he murmured.

"The cats are all demonic assholes," King said as he approached. "But Hunter will now love you forever for saving one of his babies." The big male shook his head as Hunter scurried off toward a cluster of cats gathered on a corner of the lawn. "I think he's starting an army of them."

The Alpha assessed him with eerie blue eyes. "So. You've been lying to me."

Rhodes straightened. "I never lied."

"You just let Stella lie for you."

"No," he snapped out, his dragon in his eyes. "She truly thought I was her bodyguard; she never would have lied knowingly. She is an honest, worthy female. I take all the blame and punishment for my actions and hers—inadvertent though they were."

The wolf was in King's eyes, watching Rhodes. The male was about the same height as him, ice-blue eyes bright against his dark skin. Subtle waves of power rolled off him as he stood there. Finally he said, "We found the humans you saved. They are very grateful. They said you were gentle with them when they screamed and shouted at you and told you to leave."

He blinked in surprise at the change in subject. "They were just afraid. Are they doing well?"

"They are and they agreed to come with my wolves. We're going to be bringing their small group back into our territory over the next week. They've been fighting to survive and I think they'll integrate well here. All because of you."

He shrugged, feeling awkward.

"They also said you didn't have to go after them. You'd killed the fae, you could have just returned to Stella. Why didn't you?"

He shrugged again. "I...didn't like the thought of soft humans out in the wild by themselves. The world can be cruel."

"Is it true that you are an assassin?"

"It is."

"Why?"

"What do you mean, why?" He was good at it, that was why.

"Why do you do what you do?"

He blinked. No one had ever asked him that before. "I...fell into it, I guess. I don't have family and it pays well. And I'm good at it." Might as well be brutally honest. He was who he was and wouldn't deny it.

"What kind of contracts do you take?"

"Usually for the fae—they have a strong hatred of everyone. Including other fae. I am always particular about the people I kill. I don't kill innocents."

King watched him for a long time, then said, "If given the chance to stay here, what will you do?"

"Try to win Stella back." He didn't even have to think about it.

"And if she doesn't want you?"

The male's words were like a dagger to his chest. Rhodes didn't want to even think about that possibility. "Then... I do not know. But I will let her go, if that's what you're asking."

Again, King watched him with those pale eyes, the intelligent wolf peering out at him. "You have my permission to stay in my territory as long as you follow all the basic rules of supernaturals."

"I will."

"You said you have no family. Have you ever had an Alpha?"

"No." He'd never had anyone. Until Stella. Now he was alone again.

"If things between you and Stella do not work out, and you find you'd like to stay here, we will talk again. I think you would do well here."

He blinked in surprise, watching the Alpha warily, not sure why the male was being so accommodating.

"My dragonling likes you," he said as if reading Rhodes' mind. "And I'm a really good judge of character. So's my mate and she's seen you with Stella, says you'll die before you hurt her. And I trust my mate more than anyone. That combined with what the humans told me—what your *actions* with them showed me—means I'm going on instinct here. So as long as you don't screw up while you're in my territory, you're welcome to stay as long as you want—and if you see or hear any more fae, I want to know."

"Of course. Thank you for allowing me to stay here." This had gone far better than he'd expected.

King nodded once. "I believe in second chances. Don't ruin yours."

Christian approached then, nodded once at King. "He'll be staying at my house if you need him. Thank you for this."

King nodded at the two of them before he stalked away toward his dragonling—who was now letting a menagerie of cats climb all over him.

"Now that you've gotten that out of the way," Christian said once they were alone on the sidewalk outside the Alpha's compound, "you've got to figure out how to win your female back."

He'd been wracking his brain about it since Stella walked away from him. "It is probably useless to try. She is a worthy female and I don't deserve her." He'd done nothing but lie to her.

"That's the winning spirit." The vampire's tone was dry.

Rhodes snorted, realizing that he might like this vampire after all.

CHAPTER TWENTY-EIGHT

"Go away," Stella called out, not bothering to get out from under the covers.

She'd barely slept last night, just tossed and turned all night while inhaling the scent of her and Rhodes' sex. Goddess, her dragon was back, right under the surface now, which meant all her sensory abilities were back too.

She was drowning in Rhodes' dark, sensual scent and wanted more of it. More of him, even after he'd lied to and betrayed her. She was so pathetic.

Her bedroom door opened, then closed. "I'm not leaving you to wallow," Juniper said.

"I'll do what I want," she grumbled, keeping the sheet and comforter firmly over her head. "I'm pathetic and will not be facing anyone right now. I'm a princess and that is my right."

Juniper snorted then suddenly the covers were lifted and she got in next to her. "I see you're still wearing your pajamas and smell like him." Her tone was only a little dry, but not judgmental.

"I feel like such a fool." She turned away from her sister, buried her face in a pillow. Of course it smelled like him. It was like he'd imprinted himself on the whole room. On her actual soul. She squeezed back the rush of tears that wanted to fall again as her chest ached with a pain that wouldn't ease. She had to stop crying, had to stop thinking about him somehow. An impossibility, she knew.

Her sister's gentle hand rubbed down her spine. "You're not a fool. You had no reason to disbelieve him. He killed those fae."

"Well I'm a fool for having sex with him!" For still wanting him so badly she ached with it.

Juniper's hand only paused for a moment. "My sister is not a fool. And if you hadn't made me promise, he'd be dead now." A deadly vow.

"I don't want him hurt." The very idea of something happening to him had both her and her dragon in a panic. And that was just…ugh. Pathetic.

"It seems as if he was at least telling the truth about the fae. The clothing from the dead ones in our realm are from the Domincary realm."

"I just don't know what he gained from lying to me. From…" She couldn't even voice it. Maybe he'd just been using her for sex. But that seemed so stupid. A male like that could get sex anywhere. Aaaand at that thought, her dragon got really, really cranky. He better not be getting it anywhere else. "When he told me he loved me, it sounded and scented like the truth." Closing her eyes, she buried her face against the pillow again as stupid tears leaked out.

"Yeah…it really did." Juniper's words were carefully spoken.

Stella rolled over, shoved the covers off both of them as she faced her sister. "Really?" She'd been so distraught last night, her emotions so chaotic and wild that she hadn't been sure if she'd been projecting her own feelings.

"Well…yeah," Juniper finally grumbled. "He was telling the truth about loving you. Stupid jackass. Goddess, I want to punch his face so bad."

Stella's magical chains burst free from her wrists, snapping out so fast, she barely processed it as they wrapped around Rhodes' bag on the floor.

Juniper blinked. "I take it your dragon is back."

She could feel her dragon in her gaze, peering out as she answered.

"Yes. Oh sweet goddess, yes." She looked down at what was in her hands —a bag of his stuff. She brought it up to her face and inhaled deeply. "Don't judge me," she growled as Juniper stared.

"I'm not judging. I'm stupid where Zephyr is concerned too."

At a knock on her door, they both turned.

"Come in," Juniper called out before she could.

Zephyr poked his head in cautiously. "I just heard from King. It's about Rhodes."

Stella sat up straight, still holding onto his things like a security blanket. "Is he okay?"

"Yes. He's staying with Christian and...King has allowed him to stay in the territory for the time being. He did say that if you wish him gone, then he would arrange it but he apparently believes the male is sincere about you."

Ooooh. Her heart twisted. Goddess, she must be all kinds of stupid since those words dried up her tears. "Why is he staying?"

He flicked a glance at his mate, then back at Stella. "To win you back. Says he loves you."

Her dragon half wanted to preen—he did love her!

"He...could have taken you at any time," Juniper said into the silence. "Especially after you were poisoned. And he didn't have to kill all those fae or save those humans. I mean, he could have been running a long con, but I can't see to what end."

"I thought you wanted to kill him," Stella said. She couldn't even think about a world without him in it, liar or not.

"I still kinda do." Juniper shrugged. "Or at least rearrange his face. But the pain rolling off him last night when he was losing you was enough to make me choke, it was so thick."

Stella turned away, shoved off the covers, her emotions a riotous mess. "I'm going to go flying for a while. I need to be in touch with my dragon." It had been too long and she needed to think, to consider...everything.

"Do you want any company?"

"Not really, but thank you. I'll stay in camouflage mode." If she'd been in camo mode the night she'd been attacked, it was unlikely the fae would have even seen her. But then, she might not have met Rhodes. And…she was so glad that she had, even now.

"Okay, well we'll be here when you get back."

She stayed turned away from them, waiting until they left the room before she fell back on the bed again.

How could she have fallen for the male who'd been hired to kidnap her, deliver her to the fae? Even if he really did love her…how could she ever trust him?

CHAPTER TWENTY-NINE

"I do not have unlimited paper." Christian's tone was dry as he stepped back into his library.

Rhodes looked up at him, frowned. "What?"

The vampire motioned to the balls of paper littered around Rhodes.

"Oh, apologies. I will reimburse you."

Christian simply snorted.

And Rhodes went back to writing, scratching out various lines. *Stella, you are the most beautiful dragon to ever live. Your eyes are like...* Ugh. This was all utter trash. He sounded like a fool, talking about her eyes. He needed to convey how sorry he was, not tell her how beautiful she was. He crumped the sheet into another tight ball.

He was trying to figure out what he wanted to say, attempting to write down his feelings, his apologies to Stella. "Everything I say sounds stupid," he muttered. He wasn't a poet. Not even close.

"Just speak from your heart." Christian had his back to him as he studied a bookshelf, appeared to be choosing one of the thick tomes.

"What would you say? If you were writing to...the lion maybe?"

Christian swiveled, his eyes narrowed. "What do you know about him?"

Rhodes shrugged, glad to not be talking about himself or focusing on his epic mistake. "There is a chemistry between the two of you, I believe. The lion said your face was handsome." He'd also wanted Rhodes to punch him, but Rhodes left that part out.

Christian simply sniffed haughtily. "He flirts with everyone."

Rhodes lifted a shoulder. "My mistake. I thought there was something between the two of you." He looked back down at his new sheet of paper, frowned at the emptiness.

"Why do you love her?" Christian asked on a sigh, sitting down on a chaise near one of the bookshelves.

"She's kind, gentle, cares for those around her. And she sees me, the real me. She makes me want to be a better dragon."

"Then say that."

He looked up at Christian. "That sounds…"

"Honest?"

He frowned and started scribbling, his dragon cringing at making himself so baldly vulnerable on the page.

"Now why did you lie to her?" Christian asked.

He froze, looked up again. "Because I didn't want to lose her. I was afraid that if I told her the truth, she'd kick me out of her life and I wouldn't be around her to protect her. And…because I'm a selfish male and I wanted to spend all my time with her." Because he'd known it was limited. He looked away, out the nearby French doors. Darkness had fallen an hour ago but Christian's backyard was lit up, showing a big pool and expensive-looking furniture around it.

"Then tell her that. Tell her every single thing you didn't get to say last night. Lay it all out there and if she rejects you after this, then you know. You'll be able to move on."

"I'll never be able to move on," he finally said, but he started writing anyway.

"Hell, say that too," Christian murmured.

Rhodes didn't look up. He poured out everything in his heart, even though it was beyond uncomfortable to make himself so vulnerable, to admit that he'd been so painfully lonely until her.

She was a bright ray of sunshine he wanted to bask in, to orbit around. She was his north star and even though he was pretty sure this letter wouldn't make a difference, at least he was trying.

If he didn't, he couldn't live with himself. She was worth fighting for. She was worth everything.

"Did you see that?" Christian asked sometime later.

Rhodes had lost track of time as he continued writing, was on his third page now. "What?"

Christian had just started to rise from his seat when glass exploded, the French doors shattering inward in a whoosh of noise and flames.

Rhodes whipped up, blasted fire at the opening and whatever enemy this might be.

A blade flew past his head even as Christian grabbed a pistol and sharp-looking knife from beneath the chaise.

"Go to her!" Rhodes shouted at the vampire. "Make sure she's safe! Call and warn them. Now," he growled before he blasted fire again to clear his way, then raced out the doors. He didn't need to specify who, this had to be the fae and they must want Stella. As he called on his shadows to hide him, he eased outside, scented the fae before he saw them...

There.

Three shadows were up on the side of the house. He called on his dragon, started to shift—

Thud, thud, thud, thud, thud, thud, thud, thud... Darts slammed into his chest so fast, poison pumping through him, slowing his movements... Oh, hell, he hadn't worn his necklace. Hadn't put it on after his last shower.

He fell to his knees on the grass, was vaguely aware of Christian firing his pistol at one of the fae.

Rhodes could barely hear the gunshot as blood rushed in his ears, as the poison numbed him.

A fae male dropped to the ground from a nearby tree and Rhodes blasted out fire at another.

The male incinerated right in front of him, but the one with a cloak and crossbow reached him, said something he couldn't hear over the ocean of waves sounding in his ears.

Then light blasted all around them as the shadowy male transported them away...

Stella, please be safe.

CHAPTER THIRTY

Stella landed in Christian's backyard, shifted to her human form immediately, worry coursing through her. Now that she had her magic back, she was able to clothe herself through the shift, didn't have to worry about carrying clothes with her.

Not that she was worried about anything but Rhodes.

She was aware of her sister and Zephyr landing behind her as she hurried toward Christian—who was crouched over a very dead fae male. Blood covered his chest and half his head was gone. "Where is he? What's happened? And what are you doing?"

"A group of fae attacked my house," he said without looking up, as he scraped under the fingernails of the dead male. "They hit Rhodes with darts but he still managed to kill a couple of them, one after he'd been hit. I shot this male and I'm taking samples of his DNA for King in case he needs it to prove an attack on his territory," he said, finally standing, his expression grim. "A fae male transported Rhodes out of here in a blast of light and noise. I don't know if he is part demigod or something else, but I'm betting he used a transport spell. He chanted something and demigods don't need to do that."

"Goddess," she breathed out as ice snaked down her spine. "He didn't deliver me to them. They are...likely going to kill him."

Christian simply nodded. "That is what I thought as well. The only positive thing is that the fae will..." He cleared his throat. "They won't make it quick, so we will have time to get to him, rescue him. Unfortunately, they will hurt him."

Her stomach lurched at the thought of Rhodes being tortured. "We?"

"Are you going to leave him to his fate?"

"No!" How dare he ask her that! Her chains whipped out in anger, but she paused as her sister placed a gentle hand on her upper arm.

"That's why I said we," Christian said. "I'm going with you, that is all I meant. He ran right out at them, his only concern your safety. I will not leave a male like that to die."

Unexpected tears stung her eyes as she swung on her sister and Zephyr. "I don't care what you say, I'm going after him."

"This could be a trap," Juniper said.

"Not by Rhodes," Christian said before Stella could snap at her own sister.

Fear raced through her and she wanted to raze everything to the ground to get to him. She didn't care that he'd lied to her, had been hired to kidnap her. She loved him and yes, she was still angry. Beyond angry that he'd deceived her, but she didn't want him to die. Even the thought had her dragon shoving at the surface, ready to start destroying everything in her path.

Before Juniper could respond, Christian shoved a handful of papers at Stella. "He was working on this before we were attacked."

"Are you injured?" Juniper asked Christian as Stella started reading over the papers.

A letter to her from Rhodes. Her breath caught in her throat as she scanned his very blunt, honest words—oooohhh. Her heart twisted as she finished the first page, tears blurring her vision.

Unable to read all of the pages, she folded them up and tucked them into her jeans pocket as Axel, Lola, Bella and Harlow arrived, all in animal form. They quickly shifted and started putting on clothes.

"Oh Jesus." Axel's voice was filled with worry as he hurried over to Christian. "Are you okay?"

The two males stood in front of one another all awkward, but Stella didn't have time for any of that. They'd worry about Christian's house later.

"I'm guessing they took Rhodes to the Domincary realm. I need to figure out how to get there," Stella said, looking at Juniper. "Your friend Hyacinth—her Magic Man should be able to help us, right?"

"He probably can," Christian answered. "But Nyx—"

"Nyx!" Stella said, interrupting him. *Of course.* She fished out her phone, now glad to have the blasted piece of human technology. "She gave me her phone number when we met."

As the others talked quietly, she tuned them out, dialed Nyx with a trembling finger. She had to get to Rhodes. Had to save him from those monstrous fae.

"Stella, hello," Nyx said.

"I'm sorry to call and ask for a favor, but I'm desperate. The Domincary fae have taken Rhodes and I need a transport to their realm. I will be in your debt and my kingdom will owe you a favor if you help get me there." Anything for Rhodes. Anything at all.

"It has only been ten minutes." Juniper's voice was gentle as she stepped through the demolished entryway into Christian's library.

Stella simply nodded as she inhaled around the desk where Rhodes had been sitting. His scent was strongest there and she couldn't believe he'd been taken, didn't want to think about what might be happening to him right now. "I know." Nyx had agreed to help her, had said she needed to make arrangements first—likely to talk to her mate and Alpha about taking them to the Domincary realm.

Because breaching another realm could be an act of war. One Stella was most willing to do considering the Domincary had breached her realm first.

But Nyx wouldn't be able to make that decision so lightly.

"I don't expect you to come with me—"

Juniper's eyes went supernova for a moment. "I'm going to pretend you didn't say that, let alone think that," she growled as she stalked toward her. "You're my baby sister. I go where you go."

"I know," she whispered. "I'm just scared for him. What if we're too late?" The words she didn't want to say aloud came tumbling out. "Or what if we go to the wrong place?"

"I wouldn't worry about that," Zephyr said as he stalked through the busted-out entryway, kicking a piece of doorframe and plaster out of his way. "Thurman, ah, the Magic Man is working on a finding spell that should work well with Nyx's transport. He'll get us within a few miles of Rhodes at least."

She shoved out a breath and nodded. That close, her dragon should be able to scent him and save him. "Thank you. Who is coming with us? Not that I expect the others to," she added quickly. "But I want all this settled before we leave. I'm not waiting for anyone once Nyx gets here."

"We're obviously in," Juniper said, nodding to her mate. "And Christian is insisting on going," she added. "Don't let that charming, youthful face fool you. He's deadly. And he can fly short distances as well."

Stella raised an eyebrow. She'd known vampires who could do that, but they were rare.

"I also contacted my old boss. He's sending someone to help us. The twin of his...female. She's been to the Domincary realm before, long ago. She'll be able to help."

"What is she?"

"Dragon."

Stella nodded. "Okay then."

"We're going too," Lola said as she stalked through the mess. "In case you heifers think you're leaving without us."

"Yep." Hyacinth looked fierce as she stalked inside. "Thurman isn't coming because he's human, but my man's given us all protection wards that should help in our fight." She held out an armful of necklaces—leather strips with little gems on the end of each, clearly hastily made.

Juniper frowned at her best friend and it was clear she was going to tell Hyacinth to stay put. But all Hyacinth did was lift a hand. "Don't even. You've been my ride or die for decades, that's not stopping now."

"Fine. But the rest of you have kids to worry about," Stella said, stepping forward. She hadn't even met them yet, but knew their household had just adopted three young shifters.

"And they're fine," Harlow said, the quiet tiger slipping into the room without a sound. "Marley just got back from her mission and she's going to be staying with all of them. Brielle should be back soon too. We're going."

"Thank you, guys," she whispered, overcome with far too many emotions. They all clogged her throat as she tried to shove her feelings down.

She needed to keep her shit together. She could lose it once they'd saved Rhodes.

At a whoosh of sound outside, she hurried out into the yard—to see Christian and Axel arguing.

And a large dragon female in the yard. As Stella started to shift, Nyx and Bo suddenly arrived in a rush of wind, the demigod's hair wind-blown as her mate gripped her hips tight.

"Is everyone ready?" Nyx asked, her expression tense. "Because I've got a lock on a place we can transport to. But it's got to be now and it's got to be fast."

"Yes. Everyone who wants to go, gather around now," Stella snapped, not bothering to look at anyone as she hurried to Nyx and Bo. They were going to save Rhodes. And if he was...gone...

No, she refused to let her mind go there. Outright refused.

CHAPTER THIRTY-ONE

S tella glanced up at the violet sky with two faint moons illuminating the snow-covered countryside and the mountains in the distance. She wasn't sure how some realms were so vastly different than others and didn't much care at the moment.

She just wished it was darker here, but unfortunately, the moons lit up the night sky in various shades of purple, the white snowy fields stretching out in front of them seeming to glow.

"Thank you for bringing us this far," Stella murmured to Nyx and Bo, who would not be joining them on the mission to rescue Rhodes and destroy anyone who got in their way.

Nyx and Bo would be their ride out of here and this wasn't their fight. She was simply grateful they'd given them transport. Otherwise, who knew how long it might have taken to get here.

"According to the finding spell," Juniper said, holding out the square piece of parchment she'd brought, "we're only a couple miles away."

Prima, the dragon Juniper's boss had asked to join them, stepped forward. The female reminded Stella of her grandmother—she looked to be maybe in her forties by human standards, but her eyes held thousands of years of knowledge. But more than that, it was the power that rolled off the female. Ancient and terrifying, the kind you couldn't mute. It seemed to pour out of her in waves.

"August sent me because I've been here before," she said to Juniper, before turning to Stella. "If your male is in this realm, he'll be in the castle's dungeon. It's far underground—under the castle. I know a way in, a secret entrance, but there are far too many of us to use it. If you want my opinion, I suggest that Juniper, Zephyr and I attack from the air, creating chaos high enough above them that they will be distracted, desperate to bring us down. They won't, of course, as this current king is much weaker than his predecessors. This place has devolved, I've heard." She cleared her throat, continued when no one said anything. "I would prefer to be the one to rescue the male, but—"

Stella's chains were out in a flash. "I'm going in."

The ancient female nodded once. "That is what I thought. So while Stella sneaks in through the secret entrance—and takes one person for backup—I suggest the others attack around the castle where possible, but only to the point where you will keep the fae distracted," she said, looking at Axel, Harlow and the others. "The objective isn't taking their castle or even destroying it. We simply need to rescue the dragon. Once that's done, I imagine that your realm will be back to finish the job later since the Domincary realm has clearly declared war on your people. So right now we must focus on one job—rescuing him."

Stella looked at Juniper, raised her eyebrows. She might have been sheltered, but she'd been raised to fight, to kill. Her mother and grandmother had trained her. Even if she'd been protected her entire life, she understood what she had to do and had no qualms about killing anyone. But as far as battle tactics? That was not her specialty. What Prima said sounded good to her, but she didn't have enough experience to know for certain.

"Excellent plan," Juniper said, with both Axel and Hyacinth nodding in approval.

Harlow also nodded, her expression one of respect as she watched Prima. Then she looked at Stella. "I'll be your backup in the castle. I'm good at getting into small places—and ripping out the hearts of my enemies."

Stella blinked at the dead calm of the tiger's voice. "Okay then. Let's do this." Stella was desperate to get to Rhodes, was doing her very best not to think about how he might be suffering, or worse, if he might be... gone. No, she couldn't think like that.

And when he was safe, they were going to work things out between them. Sure he'd lied to her, but she loved him. Simple as that. And the male she'd spent all that time with loved her too, she had no doubt. "How will we get into the dungeon?"

CHAPTER THIRTY-TWO

R hodes bit back a groan, refusing to let out a sound as the fae torturer shoved a knife between his ribs. They were not happy he'd welched on his deal to deliver the princess.

And oh yeah, killed two of the royal princes—in addition to the other fae he'd killed.

The current ruling king didn't care so much about his sons, just that Rhodes had backed out of his deal more than anything.

They'd pumped him full of poison but he'd built up such a tolerance to it over the years from self-injection that they'd had to shackle him with spelled chains. He was still cursing himself for not remembering to put his spelled ward on. He wouldn't be in this mess if he'd been thinking clearly. And if they'd stop torturing him for just a few minutes, he might be able to get out of this mess.

But they hadn't stopped since they'd brought him here. He wasn't sure how much time had passed, but his internal clock was telling him that it was still dark out. It had been maybe an hour—even if it felt a hell of a lot longer.

"You've only made things worse on the princess now," the male said, pulling out another thin blade.

It wasn't a knife, was more of an ice pick. Slim, perfect for—yep, sliding right between his ribs.

He choked back a cry of pain as the male treated him like a pin cushion.

"Once we find her, our king will make you watch as he defiles her. You should have just done what you were ordered, you savage beast." The male backhanded him, but Rhodes barely felt it.

They didn't have Stella, the stupid male had confirmed it with his disgusting words. She was safe. Her sister was with her—no one would touch her.

No matter what happened to him, she would be safe.

The sound of footsteps pounding down the wet floors echoed and moments later, a female guard appeared in front of his cell.

Or he thought she might be female, it was difficult to see through his swollen eyes.

She spoke in a different language, an ancient version of the Domincary realm, but he caught a few words—dragon and attack.

Wait...an attack here? At the castle?

Oooh, noooo. Goddess no, it couldn't be Stella. No way would she have come for him.

But perhaps her family had come as retribution for the fae attack in the Nova realm. He hoped that was it because he couldn't stand the thought of Stella here.

No. She wouldn't have come for him. Even as that thought pierced him far deeper than the blade embedded in his chest, he was glad for it.

His female needed to be back in New Orleans. Or in the Nova realm. Safe. Cherished. Anywhere but here.

The fae male, his torturer, growled out what was definitely a curse, stalked back to Rhodes and slammed a blade into his inner thigh.

Fuuuuuccck!

He couldn't cry out, couldn't even breathe.

"I'll return soon," the male whispered in his ear before stalking away, slamming the door shut behind him.

When he heard the other door—the sole one into the dungeon— slam in the distance, he growled as he tried to straighten.

But the bastards had chained his wrists up high enough that his toes barely touched the concrete. It was impossible to get purchase, especially when he could barely draw in a breath. Not with the blades embedded in his lungs, with the poison making him stupid.

If he'd been human, he'd have already been dead. But his dragon genes were keeping him alive.

He wasn't sure if that was a good or bad thing.

He wasn't sure he even deserved to live.

It wasn't as if he was a good male, though he'd never claimed to be.

But Stella made him want to be more, to be better, to be everything for her. And he very much regretted ruining his chance with her.

Using what little strength he had left, he tried to reach up, to wrap his fingers around the chains above his wrist, the ones secured to the ceiling above him.

But he couldn't get a good grip.

Pain lanced through his chest when he dragged in a breath. He paused, made his body stay still as he gathered strength again. This was going to hurt like a mother—he paused at a low creaking sound, a door opening.

Great, the bastard was back. Maybe the whole thing about the dragon attack was a lie, a con to make him think he was getting a reprieve. Then they'd come back in here and...

Wait, what?

He blinked, trying to process what he was seeing as Stella and Harlow stepped into sight behind the cell door.

Stella gasped, her hand flying to her mouth right before magical chains shot out of her other wrist, yanked the prison door off its hinges. She tossed the door away as if it weighed nothing, the huge metal thing skidding across the stone.

Goddess, she was amazing. But she shouldn't be here. "What the hell are you doing here?" he rasped out, eyeing Stella and Harlow, his vision red from the blood covering his eyes. "Get her out of here," he snarled at the tiger shifter.

They both ignored him.

Stella strode forward, an avenging dragon female, whipped her chains upward, snapped both his restraints.

Before he fell on his face like a pathetic fool, Harlow caught him, even as Stella said, "We must hurry, they'll realize it's a distraction soon."

"This is gonna hurt," Harlow murmured, right before—

He sucked in a breath, the searing agony making his vision go hazy.

She withdrew the blade from his leg while Stella took out the ones in his chest.

Instead of bleeding out like a human would have, immediately he could feel his dragon taking over, healing him. Now that the poison-tipped blades weren't inside him anymore, his strength was returning. "Gotta get—"

Stella snapped off the chains around his ankles before he'd finished the sentence.

"Can you stand?" Stella had her arm around him as she helped him stand.

His entire body was covered in his blood, poison still pumping through him, but… "Yeah, I think so."

Harlow wrapped an arm around his other side and they helped him to the opening where the door had been.

"What's going on?" he rasped out, as he hobbled down the stone floor toward the exit—the one door into this blasted place.

"We're busting you out of here," Stella murmured, worry rolling off her in sharp waves. "While the others create a distraction."

"You shouldn't be here," he growled out even as he scooped up one of the fallen blades, gripped it tight. Ready to kill any fae that dared try to stop them.

"You don't get to tell me what to do, big guy."

He ignored that. "You should be back in your realm, safe."

"She's not leaving you to die, dumbass," Harlow growled, then stopped by an empty cell. She inhaled sharply, looked at him, her tiger in her eyes. "Was there another prisoner here?"

"No, just me."

She frowned, but nodded as they continued.

"I'm good," he said once they were almost to the door.

When they stepped back from him, both hovering as if they thought he might fall over, he knew he looked bad.

Felt like shit too. He rolled his shoulders once, called on his dragon.

His beast was under the surface, but he wasn't sure if he could shift yet. He'd built up a tolerance to fae poisons, but they'd shoved so much of it into him he was surprised he wasn't actually dead.

To his surprise, Stella veered off and...

"What the hell?" He stared as part of the wall moved back to reveal a smaller entryway and a narrow hallway. He could scent the damp stone, hear water in the distance.

"Secret entrance, come on." Stella practically shoved him forward.

He wanted to tell her that he'd bring up the rear but there were footsteps coming outside the prison door, so he ducked into the hallway. The two females quickly followed and Harlow eased the stone doorway back into place with a click.

"They might figure out what we've done," Stella whispered, nodding in the other direction.

He wanted to demand she go first so he could protect their flank, but there was barely any room to move.

He hurried as fast as he could, the stone cold against the soles of his bare feet. As he moved, he gained strength with each step, even if his lungs burned. It was as if needles had been embedded in them, but if his female had taken it upon herself to rescue him, he wasn't going to keel over and die.

He was going to make sure she got out of here—then he was taking her back to her realm. She was never putting herself in danger again.

"We're almost there," Stella whispered as the sound of running water grew louder, louder, a cacophony of noise.

When they stepped into a small cavern he saw the source of the thundering water—they were inside a waterfall.

Harlow motioned for the two of them to stay put on the slick stones as she pulled out a small blade, then eased through the waterfall.

A moment later, she came back through—somehow still dry—and nodded that it was safe. But then her eyes widened as she focused on something behind them.

Rhodes whirled, ready to blast fire at an attacker but Stella was lightning fast.

Her magical chains whipped out and sliced off the head of the fae who'd been torturing him. The male's head hit the stone with a thud.

He wrapped his arm around Stella. "Come on!" They needed to get out of here. It wouldn't be long before more fae arrived and he couldn't shift, couldn't reach his dragon. He could take on some fae, but not an army of them. He couldn't keep her safe.

They passed under the water, which he realized must be an illusion because they didn't get wet either.

On the other side, he saw they were in a forest of thick trees, the two moons of the Domincary realm peeking through the canopy of leaves.

In the distance he heard multiple screeches. Dragons.

"Can you shift?" Stella asked, her bicolored eyes filled with worry as she looked him up and down.

"Not yet," he gritted out.

"Okay. I'm going to shift and I'll scoop you up. Harlow, you want to ride me or run?"

"I'll ride you. Let's make this a fast getaway."

As panic hummed through him, he eyed the faux waterfall as Stella shifted in a magical shower of sparkling light. As she shook out her marble-colored wings, a fae male with a crossbow flew through the waterfall, bow and arrow primed to shoot her.

He moved without thought, drew back the blade he'd grabbed and threw it right at the male's face.

It embedded in the fae's eye without a sound.

Before the fae's body had even hit the forest floor, Stella scooped him up in her claws as Harlow raced up her body.

He bit back a cry of pain as she took to the skies, bursting through the treetops in a rush.

She blasted out fire and that was when he saw three other dragons wreaking havoc on the castle in the distance. When they saw her, they all stopped, turned and headed in the same direction as Stella.

Even as pain coursed through his entire body, the thought that she'd come for him after everything he'd done, everything he'd hidden, slammed through him.

He'd lied to her, had been hired to kidnap her, and she'd still come for him.

He might not deserve her, but he would always love this female.

Until the day he died.

CHAPTER THIRTY-THREE

Rhodes opened his eyes, realized he wasn't alone in the room in the healing center. Two large dragons—Ares and Soleil, the king and queen of the Nova realm—stood at the end of his bed.

Watching him as if he were vermin.

He sat up, preparing to be attacked.

But the queen stepped forward, her eyes glowing silver as she watched him carefully. She wore a simple tunic and loose pants, both with intricate stitching reminiscent of the Nova realm. She was tall, almost as tall as her mate, with the same silvery hair of the Nova females. "You saved my daughter and then she saved you. Now you are even and that is the only reason you still breathe. I know you were hired to kidnap her, to deliver her to that trash Dominic."

He swallowed hard, but held her gaze. "I *never* would have delivered her."

"Even so, you kill people for a living. You are not the right male for my daughter. She is all that is good and wonderful with our realm, you will not sully her."

"Where is she?" he demanded.

"She doesn't want to see you. She saved you out of a sense of duty." Soleil sniffed once, then leaned forward, her dragon in her gaze. "I could have killed you where you lay. But she doesn't want you dead because her heart is kind, so you will live. But if you ever come near her again, that will change. You've been given a second chance because of her so don't squander it. Leave this place and never return."

"What about the Domincary fae king?" King Dominic. If the king wasn't dead, Rhodes would be making sure that happened soon.

She lifted an eyebrow.

"Is she safe? They will not stop—"

"They will not exist soon," the female murmured, her low voice reverberating with rage.

Ares, her mate, simply watched him as if he was contemplating removing his head from his body, but otherwise the male didn't speak.

All Rhodes could focus on were the queen's earlier words. *She doesn't want to see you. She saved you out of a sense of duty.*

He wished she'd have just left him if she didn't want him. He could have just rotted in that prison cell.

He didn't respond, just waited until they finally left before he slid out of bed. He'd been more injured than he'd realized, had been running on adrenaline.

Once they'd been transported back to New Orleans, Stella had taken him immediately to the healer's place. And apparently she'd just left him to his fate. Her duty done.

He wasn't even surprised. He shouldn't have hoped for more, shouldn't have dared to dream that he had a chance with her. Goddess, he was a fool.

Throat tight, he gathered all his things and went to the window. For the first time in his life, he wasn't sure where to go, what to do. He felt lost in a way he'd never experienced.

Not since he was a child wondering why he was all alone on that snow-covered mountain.

As he opened the window, he breathed in the early morning air, could see the sun rising on the horizon.

And he decided he wasn't staying here one moment longer. Grabbing his stuff, he jumped down from the second floor to the grass, then shifted and flew away as he weighed his options.

~

GREER'S EYES widened as she watched Rhodes land in the backyard. She shut off the sink, ready to go ask him what the heck he thought he was doing when he suddenly shifted and took off. "Blasted dragon," she growled.

"Who is?" Reaper strode into the kitchen, headed straight for her. Her mate had been keeping the shifters who'd brought Rhodes in earlier company in the waiting room.

And sweet Stella was so worried about him, had only come downstairs when she'd heard her parents were arriving. "I just saw Rhodes fly away," she said as she dried her hands on a towel.

Reaper blinked. "Wait...what? When did he even wake up?"

"I don't know." She gave him a quick kiss, then hurried up the stairs to his room, wondering what the heck had happened to make him wake up and then just run.

Greer knew he loved the female down in the waiting room, it was clear as day. Oh goddess, hopefully he wasn't returning to the Domincary realm to kill the fae king. He was far too weak yet. As she stepped inside, Rhodes' scent was clear, as was Stella's. But there were some underlying scents, ones she didn't recognize.

"Do you scent that?" she murmured to Reaper, who'd walked up behind her.

"Yes. Someone was in here."

"We need to tell the others he's left," she said as she turned, worry eating at her.

She'd taken out the poison in Rhodes' body and even though he'd had more in him than Stella, his body had seemed to process it differently. His blood had been destroying the poison even as she'd pulled it out. She'd taken a couple samples of his blood to study because it was fascinating. There were similarities to phoenix blood and she wanted to examine it more. Considering how quickly he was healing, he should be fine on his own. But she didn't like that he'd left without telling anyone.

Reaper simply nodded, followed her downstairs. In the waiting room, Stella was talking to two unknown dragons—must be her parents. Both were tall, even taller than her and Reaper.

The female had the same silvery hair as Stella and the same bicolored eyes. The male had dark hair and the same warrior countenance as her own mate. They both nodded respectfully at her—healers were revered by shifters in all realms.

Everyone else had left by now except for Juniper and Zephyr, Stella telling everyone else to go home and rest.

As Greer stepped closer, ready to be introduced, she scented them.

And frowned. "Were you just upstairs in Rhodes' room?" she demanded, not worrying about being polite. If they had been, they'd had no right.

The queen blinked at her, her expression neutral. "Excuse me?"

Deflecting? "Oh, you heard me just fine." This was Greer's domain and it was pretty clear these two had done something to run Rhodes off. One of her patients had just jumped out a second-story window and flown off. "Did you run off my patient?"

"Wait, Rhodes is gone?" Stella's eyes widened, the scent of pain rolling off her sharp. "When?"

"Just now," she said as she kept her gaze on the queen.

The female sniffed once. "I'm not surprised he ran off. He's a useless male who targeted my daughter."

"Well, he also saved your daughter," Juniper said, her tone dry. "And he's definitely obsessed with her."

"And now Stella has saved him. They are even. It is good he has left. She can move on from him now."

"I'm right here," Stella snapped, drawing the attention of both her parents. "So please stop talking about me like I'm not. And I let you smother me, shelter me, but that is stopping *now*. What the hell did you say to him?"

Soleil cleared her throat. "It is not important. What matters is that you will return home and put this mess behind you. He is simply a mistake."

Juniper groaned, covered her face. "Oh man, that's the wrong thing to say," she muttered even as Stella's chains snapped out in clear anger.

They crashed into a chair, splintered it, making Greer wince. But she ignored the destruction—wasn't the first time a shifter had broken something at the clinic and wouldn't be the last.

"I'm not going anywhere without Rhodes. And I don't even know if I'm returning home. You don't own me! You don't get to make decisions about my life for me, especially not who I mate. Now what did you say?"

"We told him that you didn't want to see him anymore, that you saved him out of a sense of duty," Ares said.

"Oh, don't give me that 'we told him' crap. This has mother written all over it," Stella growled as she faced off with her mother. "You told him that?"

The queen sighed. "Fine, it was me. And I'm not sorry. That male was hired to kidnap you, to deliver you to those monsters! You are my child, I am allowed to be angry, to want to rip out his beating heart. By letting him live, I believe I've showed great restraint." And she looked quite pleased with herself that she'd done that.

"I...can't even talk to you." Stella turned, gave Greer an apologetic look. "Do you have any idea where he's gone?"

"No, I'm so sorry. If I hear from him, I will let you know."

"As will I," Reaper, her wonderful mate, added. "For the record," he said, addressing her parents. "That male loves her."

Stella ignored all of them, her expression stricken, as she stalked out of the sitting room and out the front door.

Letting out a huff, Soleil sat in the chair next to the broken one.

"You really screwed that up," Juniper murmured.

Soleil actually looked surprised as she focused on her other daughter. "You can't believe that."

"Goddess, Soleil! You guys have smothered Stella her entire life. I mean, yeah, Rhodes *royally* messed up, but so what? We're all messy and imperfect."

"He was hired to kidnap her! He stole her virginity!"

"I'm here to tell you, it wasn't stolen. And I'm pretty sure he was a virgin too."

Ares covered his face and looked away, clearly uncomfortable. "She is a grown dragon, a Nova female, we need to let her make her own decisions."

Soleil's expression turned murderous as she stood. "Seriously? It was your idea to confront that male."

Ares rubbed the back of his neck as he faced his mate. "I know. And I admit that the thought of ripping out the male's heart and tearing off his limbs is appealing, but...if this is who she has chosen, then we should respect that."

"We know nothing about him, or his clan or...anything!"

"Your parents said the same thing about me. Your mother threatened to throw me in a volcano if I remember correctly."

Greer started to ease back, Reaper with her. This was not a conversation she needed to continue listening to—no matter how interesting. She was going to call around instead, see if she could locate Rhodes.

Because no matter what, he was still a patient of hers and fine, she could admit that she genuinely liked the male. And she adored Stella. She wanted the two of them to make it.

Juniper and Zephyr followed after them, Juniper's expression a mix between apologetic and exasperation. "They don't know how to handle the fact that she's all grown up now," she murmured once they reached the kitchen.

"I gathered that. I'll start making calls, see if I can find him."

"I'll see if I can track him," Zephyr murmured, kissing his mate.

Juniper nodded. "I'm going to ask Harlow to come over here, see if she can track him too. She's excellent apparently."

"I'll join you," Reaper said to Zephyr, heading out.

Greer pulled out her phone, started texting everyone she could think of in the hopes someone knew where Rhodes was.

She just hoped he hadn't left the territory.

CHAPTER THIRTY-FOUR

"Thank you for allowing me to stay here." Rhodes finished loading up the last of the debris into a pile in Christian's backyard. Apparently a witch had come in and 'fixed' the issue of the busted-out doors, burned plaster and destroyed brick, since she'd owed Christian a favor. But that still didn't get rid of all the leftover destruction the fae had caused. Rhodes could easily dispose of it with his dragon fire.

"Of course. But I wish you would stop cleaning. I'm sure you need to rest. I will handle all of this. You are a guest."

"I'm fine." His heart was broken, but whatever. That wasn't going to change anytime soon—or ever. If he could stay busy, however, it might help.

The vampire made a scoffing sound, but said, "So, Axel just texted me. Wanted to know if I'd seen you. What should I tell him?"

Rhodes paused before he stepped away from the pile, wishing he had more to do. He'd gone flying for most of the day, had thought about leaving New Orleans for good. But his dragon half wouldn't let him. Finally he'd come to Christian's since the male had been part of his rescue crew and...Rhodes liked the male. And wondered if maybe they could be friends. "So what's up with you two?" he asked.

"What?"

"You and the lion. Is he your ex?"

Christian was quiet, contemplative.

"Apologies, you don't have to answer."

"No, it's fine. I don't know what we are. We certainly argue a lot."

Rhodes gave a half smile—but then scented danger. "Get inside!"

A huge dragon with scales that shimmered like a million diamonds suddenly appeared in the yard. Moments later, Ares shifted to human form, strode forward completely uncaring about his nudity.

"My daughter has been looking for you all day, and I cannot bear to watch her do this any longer. My mate and I made a mistake in telling you she didn't want to see you."

He narrowed his gaze as he stalked toward the other male, digesting Ares' words. "Your mate lied?" He hadn't scented a lie when Soleil had been talking to him.

"My mate is gifted in covering her scents."

Fire tickled the back of his throat, the urge to blast this male apart strong. But he was Stella's father and the only thing he truly cared about was getting to her. Because the truth was, he wasn't certain he'd have been able to stay away from her much longer anyway. "Where is Stella?"

The male's expression was dry. "I'm fairly certain she is two minutes behind me."

As if on cue, a dragon with shimmering, pale marble-colored scales descended straight for them, blasting out fire at her father—clearly missing intentionally—before she landed, shifted to her human form.

Unlike most dragons, she was able to shift with her clothing and now she had on simple black pants and a royal blue sweater as she raced at him. "I never said I didn't want to see you again!"

Rhodes was running at Stella the moment he'd processed she was flying toward them. "I would have understood if you hadn't." He wrapped his arms around her, buried his face against her neck, inhaled that sweet strawberries scent.

"I have eight guest rooms," Christian called out. "Use any one of them. We're both leaving so you'll have my place the rest of the night. I will see you before dawn."

Rhodes didn't look up, but he held out a hand, thanking the male as he continued holding her. "You came for me," he managed to rasp out against her neck. "In that dungeon."

"Of course I came for you. I love you." Her voice sounded watery as she gripped him tight. "I never would have just left you after saving you."

He squeezed tight, nipped once at her neck. "I've missed you, Stella." It had only been hours. But it might as well have been an eternity that they'd been separated.

Her chains snapped out suddenly, wrapped around both his ankles.

He looked down in surprise, then back up at her.

"It's my mating manifestation," she murmured, tears glittering in her gaze. "I guess it was suppressed because of the poison. I'm claiming you, so you better be okay with that."

Her words wrapped around him, made it hard to breathe. No one had ever claimed him, wanted him, not like her. "You're mine, Stella. Have been since the moment I saw you." His mating manifestation had already appeared—and had started up again, the dark fog starting to surround them as they stood in the backyard.

"Let's find one of those bedrooms." Her eyes went heavy lidded as they landed on his mouth. "But I do want to talk. Later."

He would do whatever his female wanted. "We're mating now," he growled against her mouth as he scooped her up.

She curled into him, wrapped her arms around him as he hurried up the short set of stairs to the back door. "That doesn't sound like a question," she murmured against his mouth.

"Because it's not." His instinct was to just kick the door in, but he wouldn't do that to Christian's place.

"You're bossy about mating now," she murmured again, "but were you just going to leave the territory? Not even fight for me?" Fury sparked in her eyes.

He shoved open the nearest bedroom door on the first floor, saw that it had a bed—which at this point, a flat surface was all that mattered.

He knew his dragon was in his gaze when he said, "I was contemplating just kidnapping you again. But I was trying to respect what you wanted, to be a better male."

"I'm so angry at my parents," she growled out, her dragon in her gaze.

"They love you," he said as he set her on the edge of the bed. "Want what's best for you—and I really don't want to talk about them now," he said as he stripped his shirt off. He simply wanted her naked.

Wanted to be inside her, wanted to claim her forever.

"Okay," she breathed out, her gaze tracking over him hungrily. "Are you sure you're okay after—"

"I'm good." He'd been tortured before, almost died multiple times and he was still standing. "I'll be better once I'm inside you," he growled, pinning her to the bed even as he told himself to take it slow.

She deserved more for their mating.

Even as he had the thought, her chains tightened around his ankles, making him smile against her mouth. Goddess, he'd wondered why she hadn't exhibited any sort of mating instinct, hadn't even thought the poison could affect it.

The knowledge that she wanted him as much as he wanted her, that her dragon accepted him as well, was everything to him. She was his female, his mate. His forever.

After a lifetime alone, he'd finally found his other half, the female he'd give up everything for. But he wanted to create a life with her, to have a family. Even the thought of that months ago would have terrified him.

He hadn't known Stella then.

"Too many clothes," she growled against his mouth as she shoved at his pants.

Laughing lightly, his heart full in a way it had never been, he leaned back and stripped her instead of him, quickly removing every scrap of her clothing before he shoved his own pants off.

Then he pinned her beneath him again but instead of kissing her, he looked down at her, drank in every bit of her face, her scents. "When I saw you in that dungeon... I know I said it, but I love you, Stella. And I never would have turned you over to the fae. Never."

She gently cupped his cheeks, her bicolored eyes bright. "I know that. And I might not love all of your past, but it brought you to me. So I guess I really do love all of you, even the darker parts."

Oh yes, this female completely owned him. "Well I love all of you, especially..." He reached between her legs, cupped her mound possessively.

She sucked in a breath as he teased a finger along her slick folds, and he forgot to breathe. She was already wet, and it was all for him.

It didn't matter what his past was, she'd still come for him, saved him. She loved him.

"I'm not letting you out of bed for a while." He nipped her bottom lip as he slid two fingers inside her, savored the way she tightened around him.

She dug her fingers into his back even as she dug her heels into his ass, completely wrapping herself around him.

The dark fog of his mating manifestation completely surrounded them so that all he could see was her.

Her silvery hair was splayed out around her, moving as if it had a mind of its own—maybe it did, maybe it was part of her magic. There was so much he had to learn about her and he couldn't wait for all those years together.

He gently wrapped his fingers around her neck, feeling her pulse as he devoured her mouth.

She flicked her tongue against his, the scent of her hunger wrapping around him as her tongue teased his, met his stroke for stroke.

He couldn't wait any longer, needed to be inside her. "Later, we'll take it slow."

"Not now," she rasped out, as if horrified by the thought. "I need you in me."

Hell yeah, she was right there with him.

Before he could move, she reached between their bodies, wrapped her fingers around his cock.

Just that touch, the feel of her hand on him, had his cock growing even harder. He was impossibly hard, ready to combust, and as she guided him to her entrance, he sucked in a breath as he thrust inside her.

As he buried himself fully inside her, he grasped her wrists, held them above her head as he kept her pinned to the bed. He wanted to savor this moment, to remember everything about it. And as he stared into her eyes, he knew without a doubt this was the female for him. Not that he'd actually had any doubts.

She brought out a possessive, protective side to him he hadn't known existed.

She rolled her hips against his, a not-so-subtle hint that he needed to move.

He pulled back, could barely think at the feel of her tight walls gripping him, then thrust inside her again.

She met him stroke for stroke, the sounds of her moans filling the air, making him crazy. When her inner walls started that familiar tightening, he knew she was close so he reached between their bodies and began teasing her clit.

He loved the feel of her coming around him, against his mouth, any way he could get her to climax. But this was probably his favorite, the feel of her tight walls clenching around his cock.

"Rhodes." His name sounded like a prayer on her lips.

And it was almost enough to completely set him off. He buried his face against her neck in the soft area where her shoulder and neck met —and bit down, releasing his canines into her soft skin.

Crying out, she started climaxing, her orgasm hard as she writhed against him.

As she let go, he allowed himself the same release, his orgasm hitting him hard. And as he came, she bit into his neck hard, her canines sharp and stinging.

It was the sweetest pleasure-pain as he came inside her long and hard, nothing else existing as he lost himself inside her.

Finally, they both came down from their high and he was aware of her fingers tracing up and down his back gently, softly, the way she touched him perfection.

"I might have lied about some things," he said into the quiet of the bedroom he hadn't fully paid attention to before. It was all masculine with large, dark furniture. "But I never lied about you being my first."

"I know." Her voice was slightly drowsy as she nipped his bottom lip, held him tight to her. "I know the important things. I had a lot of time to think, to replay some of our conversations."

"I thought about telling you the truth but I was worried you'd kick me out and I wouldn't be able to protect you."

She nipped his bottom lip again, didn't let go of him, simply held him tighter to her. His strong, wonderful female. "I kinda figured. And you're just obsessed with me," she murmured against his mouth.

"True." So very true.

"I'm obsessed with you too. When I thought you'd left today, left for good…" Her voice cracked on the last word.

"Never. I was never going to be far from you." He knew that much about himself. He wouldn't have been able to simply walk away from her.

"How do you feel about staying in New Orleans for a while?" she asked sometime later.

He wasn't sure how much time had actually passed as they lay on the bed, tangled up with each other. Normally he was aware of everything, but right now she consumed all his thoughts, especially now that they'd officially mated. Something he was still trying to process.

"I'll go wherever you want, including your realm." As long as he was with her.

"Honestly, I'd like to stay here for a while, spread my wings a bit more. And…I want time with just you away from my family. I'm angry at them, but I know my parents. The fact that my father came here to tell you where I was means he's accepted you. My mom is just stubborn and ridiculous."

"Maybe so, but she loves you and I was hired to kidnap you." If he was a parent…he didn't know if he would have showed as much restraint as her parents.

"Whatever," she grumbled against his mouth, arching her back into him, rubbing her breasts against his chest.

And just like that he was hard again—or harder, because his erection hadn't fully gone away. How could it when his gorgeous mate was naked and underneath him?

"I'd like to try you taking me from behind," she said into the quiet. "And a whole bunch of other things I've been thinking about."

"Things?" he growled. He was going to need them all spelled out.

She bit his bottom lip in response.

He would try every single thing she wanted, and then some. He wanted to have her in every way possible, any way she'd let him.

CHAPTER THIRTY-FIVE

"I'm not sure how I feel about leaving them," Ares grumbled as they stepped out onto the sidewalk.

Christian just snorted. "Doesn't really matter how you feel. She's mating him."

Ares shot him a surprised look.

"What?" He motioned toward the direction they should go.

"It's just interesting the way people speak to me here. As if I'm...not a king."

Oh. Right. Christian lifted a shoulder. He'd known enough royalty in his past lifetimes that they were normally assholes but... "Would you like that I bow to you?"

Ares snorted out a laugh and clapped him on the shoulder once—hard. Though Christian was almost certain he didn't mean it to be so jarring. Dragons were simply strong. "I think I like you, vampire. So where will we go?"

Ah... "Where are you staying?"

"The bloodthirsty tiger Harlow has invited us to stay at their place but my mate is there and not too happy with me. So, we need to kill some time."

"Why isn't she happy with you?"

"She wanted to battle with Rhodes before he mated with Stella, make sure he was worthy."

"Dragons," Christian murmured. "So violent."

Ares shrugged. "He was just tortured and poisoned so I simply pointed out that by the time he was healed enough, they would already be mated. And that if Soleil accidentally killed him, she would kill Stella in the process—so fighting was not the best idea."

Christian bit back a laugh as they turned a corner. "There's a little art walk up here, we can look at the vendors. Perhaps you can find something for your mate as an apology."

"I am not sorry."

Now Christian laughed for real.

"But I see your point. I don't think she actually wanted to fight him anyway, she just wants to kill someone and her mother has already gone to the Domincary realm to finish off the fae king."

Now he glanced at Ares in true surprise. "You and your mate didn't want to join her?" Dragons were a vengeful group by nature, with very long memories.

"We did, but her mother insisted she take care of it, make a big show of it. She's there now, has likely already burned everything to the ground." He gave an unconcerned shrug.

Christian simply nodded as they reached the beginning of the art walk. He'd wondered what would happen to the male who'd ordered Stella's kidnapping. It seemed that loose end was going to be tied up once and for all in short order.

As they reached the art walk, he glanced around, not surprised it was full of more humans than supernaturals. Though there were a few wolves manning booths.

He was glad that things like this still existed after The Fall. A line of booths were set up on either side of the street, with various art for sale —wood carvings, handmade jewelry, weapons, handmade plushies and blankets, quilts or other knitted or sewn things. Christian had no need for any of them, but still enjoyed looking at the wares.

"I would think they would have something like this during the daylight hours," Ares murmured as they passed a stand with intricately carved wooden bowls and other décor.

"It started around two and they keep it open later for vampires," he said with a smile. Just one of the things that had changed in this new world. "They'll shut down around eight or nine, depending on sales." There were solar-powered lights strung back and forth between each side of the street, giving everything a warm, cozy feel.

"Something smells good," Ares murmured, looking around.

"That'll be the food vendors. They're at the end along with various drink vendors. There's something for everyone." Even vampires.

"I will see you in a moment then," the king said, patting his stomach and looking like a mischievous kid as he hurried off.

Today had really turned out a whole lot different than he'd expected.

He stopped at a vendor selling all sorts of crocheted things—including a bunch of penises, which made him laugh. When he saw a small crocheted lion, he plucked it up on impulse. After agreeing on a payment with the vendor—he'd promised the vendor access to a table saw, of all things—he headed to the next booth, holding quite possibly the most ridiculous thing he'd ever purchased.

"Christian!" At the sound of a familiar voice, he turned and found Enzo and Legend, two seven-year-olds, soon to be eight, racing toward him. Both had copper-colored hair, golden skin and green eyes, but he could easily tell them apart because Enzo was the one with the wide open expression, while Legend hung back, always the more cautious one.

Christian shoved the little lion in his pocket when he saw Axel and Phoebe, the boys' teen sister, behind the kids. No need to let Axel's ego grow any larger. It wasn't as if Christian had bought the thing because of Axel. No, indeed.

"Children, how delightful to see you." He grinned as they reached him, Enzo going full steam as he jumped at him, secure in the knowledge that he'd be caught.

"Oof." He pretended to stumble back under the boy's hug, which just made Enzo giggle.

Legend gave him a shy smile and a simple, "Hey."

"Are you all out for the evening?" he asked as Axel and Phoebe reached him.

"Yep," Enzo answered. "Phoebe's meeting up with her *boooyfriend*."

Legend snickered but covered it up as his sister shot them both dirty looks.

"Really guys? After I bought you cotton candy?" She lifted an eyebrow. There was no denying she was related to the boys. She had the same copper hair, golden skin and green eyes. When he'd first met her and the boys, they'd all been too thin. They were all slender but thankfully they'd filled in thanks to being adopted by Axel and his crew.

"You are far too young to have a boyfriend."

Phoebe shot him a surprised look, her eyes flashing. "Wow, Christian, I expected more from you."

"You are fourteen."

"Almost fifteen." Her eyes lit up as she spotted someone behind him and when Christian saw who she was looking at, the tension in his shoulders eased. A gangly looking teen with thin arms and a big smile approached.

"Hey, Phoebe." He stared at her as if she hung the moon.

When the twins started making kissing sounds, she rolled her eyes and linked her arm with his. "We'll be back later, Axel. We won't go far."

Axel simply looked amused—and far too sexy for his own good. Annoying lion. His dark hair was pulled up into a bun—he cut it often, but since he was a lion, it just grew at an alarming rate. And it was thick and gorgeous. He had a perpetual tan no matter the time of year, his skin tone a stunning bronze. And...he was kind and giving. It would be easier to not fantasize about him if he were a true asshole. "Are you out by yourself tonight?" he asked, his tone even annoyingly polite.

"Ah, no, I'm with Ares. He wandered off to grab food a little bit ago."

Axel let out a low whistle. "Probably good he's here—Soleil is in a mood. It's part of the reason I'm out tonight."

"You're out because you promised us," Legend said, his tone oh so serious.

"I did indeed."

"I'm hungry," Enzo whined.

"All right, come on. You want to join us?" Axel motioned toward the direction of all the food vendors.

Christian knew he should say no, but... "Sure." He really was a fool when it came to this male.

At that thought, he shoved his hands into his pockets and grasped the little plushie, ignoring the pang in his chest.

CHAPTER THIRTY-SIX

S tarlena waited in the shadows of the huge Domincary castle, her dragon barely under control. She was an ancient, hadn't struggled to control her beast in millennia.

But someone had messed with her family. Had decided to come after her granddaughter.

A foolish little fae king who was barely grasping onto his power had decided to send someone to kidnap her granddaughter for reasons Starlena could only guess.

King Dominic of the Domincary realm—a pale replica of his father before him. Starlena had killed the male's father, but he'd been a worthy fighter at least.

From all accounts this Dominic, a child barely three hundred years old, had thought to come after Stella. And he'd hired someone—clearly not warrior enough to do it himself and get his hands dirty.

She'd entered his castle grounds with ease and after the rescue from Stella, the attack, this place should have been locked down much tighter.

Another example of how pathetic this king was.

Now she was in the private bedchambers of the king while he bathed. She was magnanimous enough to give him one last shower before she tore him apart.

The sound of running water stopped, then there was some rustling before a tall, lithe male with dark hair who most would consider handsome strode out completely naked. His wings were ethereal now, not fully formed as he moved around. He grabbed a dark blue towel from a chaise by a stained-glass window, wrapped it around his waist as he shoved the window open, stared out into the frosty night air. With a curse, he shut the windows and stepped back, muttering to himself.

"You never should have come after my granddaughter," Starlena murmured, her voice cutting through the quiet, insulated room.

Stella was her youngest granddaughter and Starlena held a special place in her heart for the fierce but kind girl. Stella had seen her cousins and siblings murdered before her when she'd been but a dragonling, covered in blood when Starlena had found her so long ago in the children's wing.

And this male thought to take her from all of them?

Dominic sucked in a sharp breath as he spun to face her, his dark eyes going wide, his wings snapping out fully. He opened his mouth...to call for help? She would never know—she released her magic faster than he could blink or speak.

Her white glowing chains shot from her wrists, slammed right into his chest. Her magic lifted him up as she slowly walked toward him, keeping him immobile. His wings disappeared, his magic withdrawing.

He opened his mouth again, but he was under her control now. His eyes glowed a brilliant pearl color as she injected her magic into him— injected sharp, stabbing pain to all his nerve endings.

Tears tracked down his face as he stared at her in horror, unable to speak or even scream.

"This will be quicker than you deserve," she whispered as she strode closer to him, lifting him higher in the air as she did. "You weren't even on my radar. You were nothing to me. Now you will die because of your hubris."

He tried to kick out, but the action was weak, a flop of his foot in the air.

Bathe him in fire, her dragon half whispered. *Burn, burn, burn.*

She rolled her shoulders, shoved back the impulse as she used her chains to shove him straight through the glass window.

It shattered and, moments later, horrified cries filled the air from below.

Then...the screams started.

She stepped through the broken window, onto the small balustrade and held the fae king high in the air, his entire body glowing with the light from her magic.

Then she let out a battle cry, a scream of rage—and the signal for her people.

Suddenly the night was filled with shimmering dragons of all colors in the air, surrounding the castle. Two hundred of her specially trained warriors.

They all blasted fire, but none of them made a move to attack, just filled the air with their fire as a very visible warning.

Still holding the king out over the balustrade for all his warriors along the battlements and the civilian fae below in the bailey to see, she shouted, "You have two choices! Leave the castle now while I raze it to the ground, or attempt to fight us and die. I'm showing mercy when you deserve none! Your king thought to kidnap, rape and kill my grand-daughter because of his ego," she snarled. "I will allow you all to leave if you don't resist. Choose now," she yelled as she ripped out the king's kidneys, tossed them below. Next she ripped out his spine. Then his heart. After, she sliced his head off with a sharp slash of her chains.

Then she tossed the body after his head.

More cries from below, but she ignored them, eyed the soldiers on the battlements.

One stood up on the crenellated stone's edge, held his palms up. "We will need time to get everyone out."

"You have one hour! Take yourselves and nothing else."

The male was perhaps fifty yards away from her, but she could see the fear in his eyes as he nodded, his wings pulled in tight against his back.

"Leave, now!" She whipped out her chains again, wrapped one

around a nearby tower and ripped it off its base. As the stone tumbled below, more screams greeted her—but it got the fae moving.

The fae in the castle moved like ants, rushing, and running in their escape, their wings making flittering noises as they moved about.

As they ran about, scrambling, she strode out into the hall, gave a feral smile as the soldiers avoided her gaze and raced past her.

There was no fight in these fae at all, not like the ones she'd fought in the past. They might not deserve her mercy, but her fight had been with the king, not everyone else. And according to what she'd heard, Stella's new mate had already killed the king's sons.

But the supernatural world had to know that if they came after the Nova realm, the Nova realm would come for them.

To her surprise the fae cleared out of the castle in less than an hour, no one taking anything with them as they ran. As soon as it was clear, she strode out into the deserted bailey and shifted to her dragon.

As her beast took over, she breathed deeply of the crisp night air and let out a blast of fire, destroying the nearest tower and part of an inner wall. She punched through another wall with the power of her wing.

Her dragons remained in the sky, simply watching as she breathed a raging, hot fire, destroying everything in her wake. Taking to the skies, she swooped around the castle, burning so hot the moat evaporated, the stone disappearing into nothingness as she burned, burned, *destroyed*.

The fae were on the run, would live, but they'd never build anything here again, would see her destruction and remember.

Don't fuck with the Nova clan.

When she was finally done, her dragon side settled, she shifted back to her human form. She kicked up the ash, her feet covered in soot as she strode around the former castle grounds, looking for anything she might have missed.

As she reached a deep chasm, she saw the dungeon below, ash raining down into it.

Perched on the edge of the abyss, she breathed fire, felt a push of magic.

But not fae magic.

Dragon magic, one as ancient as her.

She frowned, breathed fire again, wanting to feel the magic, to taste it.

Suddenly the ground rumbled below her, an earthquake starting as the chasm closed in on itself.

She called on her dragon, allowed only her wings to extend, she lifted herself into the sky as the ground fell away beneath her.

A roar louder than she'd ever heard ripped through the air as a dark-winged dragon burst from underneath the dungeon area, shooting into the sky like a rocket.

It moved swiftly, on wings of fire before it suddenly blinked out of existence. Not camouflage, but it actually...disappeared. Transported itself.

She blinked in surprise, but made the signal to her people, it was time to leave.

Time to go home.

She'd done what she'd come to do. Her clan was safe for now and these fae would spread the story of her destruction far and wide. Whoever had been trapped beneath that dungeon was now free—and not her problem.

CHAPTER THIRTY-SEVEN

Three days later

R hodes nodded at Stella, who snapped off the back door handle
with her magical chains. Then she eased the door open and to
her annoyance, he stepped in front of her, listening intently.

After everything that had gone down, he wasn't going to lose her by
not being careful.

As he stepped deeper into the New Orleans townhome, he could
hear...moans. He looked back at her, grinned at her smirk.

He felt a little bad about what they were about to interrupt, but only
a little.

They moved quickly up the stairs, and when they reached the top,
the sounds had abruptly stopped.

Though he knew Stella was annoyed at him for taking point on this,
he wasn't going to smother his protective urges. Not with her. He would
always protect her.

He kicked open the bedroom door, wasn't surprised to find the
vampire bartender they'd questioned with the female who'd very likely
stolen Stella's family crown.

The male had tossed on pants and his fangs were out as he prepared to attack.

"I wouldn't recommend doing anything right now," Stella said as she strode in behind him, her chains out.

The female with the bartender stepped out from behind him and Stella's chains shot out, looping around the female's neck and the male's neck. She held them in place as they clawed at their restraints.

Seeing her at full capacity, fully embracing all of her power, was hot as fuck. And he knew she was barely breaking a sweat now.

"I'm going to let you down now, Cassia. If you attempt to attack us, you'll regret it." Stella's voice was even as she loosened the chains completely, let the female drop.

The female was a dragon so neither of them would underestimate her.

"Why did you steal from us?"

Cassia's cheeks flushed crimson as she looked at her vampire lover, who was still thrashing around. Rhodes knew the male's name was Seamus from their intel.

"Let him go," Cassia begged.

"He's fine, he can breathe." There was no give in Stella's voice.

"I'd come to this territory a few times when Nova opened up their borders and I fell in love with New Orleans. I...thought if I sold the crown, it would help me start over. I was worried my family would come after me because my ex..." She trailed off, tears tracking down her cheeks. Her scent was off though, as if she was telling half-truths.

Rhodes eyed them both cautiously, trying to sift through the scents but it was difficult without knowing these two on a personal level.

Stella let the vampire go and he immediately pulled Cassia into his arms before he shoved her behind him in a protective stance. Didn't matter that she was likely more powerful than him.

"She didn't want to come to our relationship empty-handed," he rasped out. "Which is ridiculous. I only want her, but she was afraid her ex would come after her. She thought she might need funds to escape if her family tried to retrieve her." Again with the half truths. Some of what he was saying was true, just as when she'd spoken.

"Who is your ex?"

"Philo of the Carver clan."

Stella frowned slightly so Rhodes guessed she must know the male. She looked at Rhodes, said, "He occasionally works at the castle. He runs a few farms in one of our more distant territories." Then she looked back at the female. "Did he ever threaten you?"

"Yes. But he never laid hands on me. He just made threats, said that my family would suffer if I left him, that he'd make sure my father lost out on certain jobs."

"And you thought stealing from us would be smart? To what end?"

Her cheeks flamed bright red and she looked at her vampire. Then back at Stella. "Originally I was going to plant the crown on him, make it look like he stole from you," she whispered.

And Rhodes could scent the raw truth in her words. Okay, they were getting somewhere now.

"But then I felt guilty, even if he is a bastard. I'd already taken it, I couldn't give it back without getting caught. I thought that if I really did need to escape him, the funds from selling the crown would help us start over in another territory. But then you showed up asking questions and I saw you at the auction so we decided not to sell it."

The words were pouring out of her now and Rhodes could scent the truth, knew Stella would as well.

"We've been trying to figure out a way to give it back, especially since I heard your parents are in the territory." She whispered the last part, her eyes wide. "Are they that angry with me?"

That was when Rhodes realized how young she was, maybe twenty-five. Goddess, she'd lived in another realm, had probably been sheltered her whole life too.

"My parents aren't here for you," Stella said. "Do you still have the crown?"

Her expression miserable, she nodded. "It's in there." She pointed at an armoire.

Rhodes opened it as Stella watched the two. He opened a round hat box, found a glittering crown inside and showed it to her.

His princess eyed it, nodded, then sighed, withdrew her chains completely. "Is there a reason you didn't come to someone for help with your situation?"

"She was scared," Seamus snapped as he pulled the female into his arms again.

Stella looked at Rhodes once before focusing on the two lovers. "Do you truly wish to stay here or are you using this male as an escape?"

Cassia wiped away her tears. "I love him more than anything."

More truth.

"Okay, then stay here and I will wish you well."

Cassia blinked at them, surprise rolling off her. "You're not going to...bring me back for punishment?"

"No. I believe you stole because you were afraid. I do wish you'd gone to someone for help—and I will make sure my family investigates Philo. If you've lied to me, I will be back. But, I don't think you are."

"I'm not," she whispered, eyes still wide.

"Until you formally decide to leave the Nova realm, you are still a member of our realm, which means you're afforded certain rights. If you need any sort of financial help, it is yours."

Cassia continued to stare at Stella in surprise.

"The fact that this surprises you, bothers me," Stella murmured. "Someone from our realm will likely be by to speak to you further. If there's an issue in any of the outer territories, we need to know about it. Because this is something you should have been aware of. If anyone feels they're being treated unfairly or are being harassed or threatened for whatever reason, they *always* have a standing to come to the castle, to speak to my parents. You really didn't know that?"

"No."

"Well we're going to see ourselves out. Someone will be in touch, however."

"Thank you," Cassia's voice was still low, her expression cautious.

"Why did you let us take those cell phones?" Rhodes asked, looking at Seamus because hell, he was a dragon—always curious.

The vampire shrugged. "There was nothing on them and I figured if I was helpful, it'd throw you off the trail." He looked a little sheepish as he said it.

And Rhodes realized how young he was too, probably the same age as Cassia. Freaking kids, he thought.

Once he and Stella were outside, she wrapped her arms tight around him and buried her face against his chest. "That went differently than I thought."

He kissed the top of her head, inhaled deeply. He couldn't get enough of her scent, especially now that she smelled like him too. His scent covered her now that he'd claimed her so everyone knew they were mated, off limits. "I know. They're just kids," he murmured.

"Yeah. I don't like that she didn't realize how many rights she and her family have either."

"You'll get it straightened out." Of that he had no doubt.

"Or Juniper and Zephyr will. She's been kicking ass and shaking things up."

"Do you want to return to your realm? There's no reason we can't."

She looked up at him, her eyes bright with love. "Not yet, if that's fine with you? The past few days with you have been wonderful. I want more of that...I don't want to be a princess for a while."

"I don't think your location changes that," he murmured, his gaze zeroing in on her bottom lip. He wanted to nibble on it, then wanted to strip her down—

"Whatever you're thinking, you've got to stop because we're still in public," she whispered.

He looked at the backyard of the little townhome they'd just broken into. "No one's watching us."

She snickered lightly, then stepped back and picked up the hat box. "True, but we've got to get to that thing anyway. Unless you just want to bail?" She sounded oh so hopeful.

"No way. We're going." They were meeting with her parents tonight at Christian's, for a get-together in a neutral enough place.

She was nervous about how her parents would act around him, but he didn't care. Well, he cared about her feelings, but he wasn't worried how they would act. He hoped that they would one day accept him, but her acceptance and love was all that mattered. No one else's.

And her sister and Zephyr had already accepted him, which seemed to go a long way in smoothing things over for tonight's dinner. "Besides, Reaper will be there and he's bringing some new weapons."

Stella let out a startled laugh. "I love that you two are friends."

"I do too." Having friends was a foreign concept for him. Long ago he'd considered the humans he'd looked after as sort of friends, but the power imbalance had been so vast. He'd never put down roots after that, had always been adrift, never letting anyone into his life.

Until now.

All because of the wonderful female in his arms, his mate.

CHAPTER THIRTY-EIGHT

"I didn't get to properly thank you for helping out with the distraction the other night," Rhodes said to Prima, an ancient dragon female Reaper had just introduced him to. Officially.

"Of course, it was good to stretch my wings and kill some assholes." She looked over at Stella, who was talking to the snow leopard shifters. "I heard your female's grandmother killed that asshole Dominic," she said, nodding her approval.

"I wish I had been invited," Reaper said, practically grumbling. "I've never been to the Domincary realm before."

"I'll be glad to never go again." The only thing that mattered was that the king of the Domincary realm was officially dead, as were all his offspring. The male who'd hired him to kidnap Stella had been killed by Stella's grandmother. Who had then decimated the entire castle and surrounding area. Good riddance to them all.

Reaper snorted, then pulled out a leather sheath that looked like dragon scales. "This is what I wanted to show you. Look at the craftsmanship."

Rhodes ran his fingers over the leather, was surprised by how soft it was to the touch. "A human made this?"

"Indeed."

"I want one too." Prima frowned, plucked it from him and withdrew the blade. "This is beautiful," she said, turning it so that it glinted under the lights illuminating Christian's backyard.

"Excuse me," Rhodes murmured when Stella made eye contact with him, subtly called him over.

Both her parents stood there with her, in fairly formal Nova style garb—tunics and loose pants—with visible weapons strapped to their thighs. Not that they would need them, but it was a clear message that they were warriors.

Stella's mother eyed him, tried to smile and failed. But her father held out a hand in the way of warriors, shook it hard. "Thank you for meeting with us tonight."

"It's my pleasure."

"Of course it is." Soleil sniffed haughtily.

"Mother," Stella murmured through gritted teeth.

"Fine. I apologize for lying to you before. I thought I was protecting my daughter."

"No apology necessary. It is I who should be apologizing to you. I was hired to take Stella," he said, linking his fingers through hers. "Not that I would have, but you're her parents. Of course this will be difficult for you to forgive. I just hope that with time you will realize how much Stella means to me. Because she is my world and I will do anything to keep her safe and protected—not that my female needs it as she is fierce."

Soleil softened slightly, then her gaze turned calculating. "I don't think it will take much time to forgive you, especially if the two of you give us grandchildren. I would like dragonlings in the castle again and the sooner the better."

"Mother!" Stella looked horrified.

Ares ran a hand over his face.

Rhodes wrapped his arm around Stella's shoulders. "As soon as you're ready, I am," he said, looking at Stella.

Who just blinked up at him.

"Ah, see, you are forgiven." Soleil patted his cheek once before she was dragged off by Juniper, who was growling at her in undertones about boundaries and inappropriateness. Ares quickly followed.

Stella continued to stare up at him. "Are you serious?"

"I don't want children immediately, but…yes, whenever you are ready, I am too." The thought of Stella carrying his child…it terrified him a little, but he'd never had a family and he wanted to create one with the female he loved.

"Goddess, I love you too much," she growled, throwing her arms around him.

"Not too much, just enough." He pulled her close to him, covered her mouth with his, but forced himself to pull back before they got carried away.

Because he had control. Mostly.

A shout went up and they both turned to see that Bella, Lola, Marley, and Axel had all jumped in the pool—in their various feline forms. He thought cats hated water?

Stella snickered as she watched them splashing around like lunatics. "I think we're going to love living in New Orleans for a while."

"I do too." Because wherever she was, he would be. Forever.

EPILOGUE

One Month Later

S tella and Rhodes let themselves in the front door of Christian's
mansion—where she and Rhodes were now living for as long as
the vampire let them. It seemed to be open-ended as he truly enjoyed
having company. And for a vampire, the male could cook—made them
dinner regularly and he loved to experiment.

As they stepped into the kitchen, Stella blinked to find Juniper and
Zephyr there, since it was midnight. "Hey you two."

"Hey yourself." Juniper was up and off her chair in moments,
rounding the big island to pull her into a hug. "We're in town for a
couple days and I thought I'd surprise you. I told Christian not to say
anything."

Christian appeared in the entryway then, two bottles of wine in
hand. "I figured it was a secret worth keeping."

"It is." She grabbed Zephyr in a big hug, ignoring Rhodes' grumble
behind her.

He didn't like her touching any male but him, though he still liked
Zephyr, did that warrior handshake thing before he quickly tugged her
close to him.

219

"Are you staying here?" she asked, sitting at the island with Rhodes, automatically leaning her head on his shoulder. They'd had a very long day and she was glad to be home.

"Yep." Juniper grinned as Christian poured her a glass of wine.

"Oh, is that why you've been cleaning like a maniac?" Stella glanced at Christian.

Who just grinned. "Perhaps."

"So how was your meeting today?" Juniper asked. "Christian told me what you two were up to."

"Ah…" She glanced at Rhodes, who looked exhausted. "Long. Good, but long. The fae from the Latore realm have been incredibly kind but setting up a cross-realm visit for our peoples…it's simply exhausting. There are so many logistics to worry about." Now that she was temporarily living in New Orleans, her family had tasked her with something she was much more capable of—diplomatic relations.

She'd been in meetings with King's half-sister, Princess Cressida of the Latore Kingdom, for most of the day, and Rhodes had been on a rescue op with a handful of King's wolves and dragons. They'd found a bunch of humans barely scraping by a few hours away and had transported them all via air but it had taken multiple trips. She and Rhodes had only just met up half an hour ago—she'd waited at one of the pack's mansions for him to return.

Juniper snickered. "I'm so glad it's you doing all the heavy lifting."

Stella plucked a grape from the tray Christian sat down and chucked it at her head. "Mean."

"I'm kidding. That's actually why I'm here. Soleil thought it might go faster if the two of us worked together, though I think she truly wanted you to teach me diplomacy."

"That's rich," Stella said, picking up her glass.

Rhodes snickered next to her. "Soleil and diplomacy don't seem to go together."

"I'm glad it's not just me," Juniper murmured, laughing. "Oh, I've also brought a bundle of letters for you from people. Like, so many. Including one from the human painter, Mia."

"How's she settling in?"

"Wonderfully. Though Tiber is trying his best to court her. Apparently it's like a big deal or something?"

Stella's eyes widened. "Wait...*Tiber*, as in one of Starlena's deadliest warriors? That Tiber?" Their grandmother's personal army of assassins were terrifying, even to other dragons.

"Yep. The whole castle is abuzz with it, so that's the biggest gossip you've missed out on. I didn't read Mia's letter but I'm curious if she'll mention him. I left the bag of letters on your bed."

For the next hour, they all talked until Rhodes had to practically carry her to their bed.

"Too much talking tonight, my mate," he murmured, as he pulled her tunic off her. "You need sleep."

She flopped back onto the bed, sighing with relief as he started tugging her pants off. She didn't want to do anything at the moment. "No arguments from me, but I'm so happy my sister is here." Since moving here, she'd missed her family, but she'd been so busy—and she felt useful, really able to help her realm make solid inroads with possible allies. Something that was necessary now that they'd opened up their realm again. Especially since her grandmother had torched the Domincary realm. The more allies, the better.

Her mate sat on the end of the bed and started massaging her feet gently. And oh, when he hit that spot—a punch of heat rolled through her.

Rhodes paused, his eyes turning that beautiful obsidian. "I assumed you were too tired for anything tonight."

"Not possible. And you have far too many clothes on."

His dragon peeked back at her for a long moment as he stood, stripped his own shirt off. "How do you feel about a shower together? I don't want to touch you until I'm clean."

She didn't care about that, but understood. "A hot shower sounds amazing." But only if he was with her.

He scooped her up, something she was still getting used to. He simply loved to carry her around sometimes and okay, she loved it. Loved everything he did.

This male had stolen her heart, and every single morning when she woke up and saw his face, he stole her breath too. It didn't matter that they were officially mated, that mating instinct was still riding her hard. She couldn't get enough of him, wondered if that wild, raw feeling would ever abate.

Something told her it wouldn't. All she had to do was look at her parents—who were still wild for each other.

"My dragon really knew what she was doing when she picked you," she murmured.

"Your dragon, huh?" He turned on the shower, holding her close as he waited for it to heat up.

"Well, me too." He completely owned her, had practically from the moment he'd cut that dress off her. She buried her face against his chest, inhaled deeply. "I'm so glad we get to sleep in tomorrow." Well, today, technically since it was close to two in the morning.

"I don't plan on sleeping much," he growled as he held her close, lifted her into the hot shower. His erection was thick between them and yeah, she didn't think sleep was going to be in the cards either.

Which was just fine with her. Because she had Rhodes with her.

—THE END—

Dear Readers,

Thank you for reading Ancient Vengeance and going on this adventure with me! If you'd like to stay in touch and be the first to learn about new releases you can:

- Check out my website for book news: https://www.katiereus.com
- Follow me on Bookbub: https://www.bookbub.com/profile/katie-reus
- Follow me on TikTok: https://www.tiktok.com/@katiereusauthor

Also, please consider leaving a review at one of your favorite online retailers. It's a great way to help other readers discover new books and I appreciate all reviews.

Happy reading,
Katie

ACKNOWLEDGMENTS

I owe a big thanks to all my readers! Thank you for reading this series and asking for more dragons. I hope to keep writing this series for a long time. I'm also incredibly grateful to my editor Kelli Collins and proofreader Tammy Payne. Thank you! For Sarah, thank you for all you do (always). Of course I owe a huge thanks to Jaycee for her gorgeous covers, including the special edition hardcover edition (I'm obsessed with both versions). And my biggest thanks is to Kaylea Cross! Thank you for helping me whip this book into shape. You are a true friend and a fantastic critique partner. I'm also so thankful to my mom (who will never read this book) who makes it possible for me to get more writing in during the day.

ABOUT THE AUTHOR

Katie Reus is the *New York Times* and *USA Today* bestselling author of the Red Stone Security series, the Ancients Rising series and the MacArthur Family series. She fell in love with romance at a young age thanks to books she pilfered from her mom's stash. Years later she loves reading romance almost as much as she loves writing it.

However, she didn't always know she wanted to be a writer. After changing majors many times, she finally graduated summa cum laude with a degree in psychology. Not long after that she discovered a new love. Writing. She now spends her days writing paranormal romance and sexy romantic suspense. If you would like to be notified of future releases, please visit her website: https://katiereus.com and join her newsletter.

Complete Booklist

Ancients Rising
Ancient Protector
Ancient Enemy
Ancient Enforcer
Ancient Vendetta
Ancient Retribution
Ancient Vengeance
Ancient Sentinel
Ancient Warrior
Ancient Guardian

Darkness Series
Darkness Awakened
Taste of Darkness
Beyond the Darkness
Hunted by Darkness
Into the Darkness
Saved by Darkness
Guardian of Darkness
Sentinel of Darkness
A Very Dragon Christmas
Darkness Rising

Deadly Ops Series
Targeted
Bound to Danger
Chasing Danger
Shattered Duty
Edge of Danger
A Covert Affair

Protecting His Witness
Sinful Seduction
Under His Protection
Deadly Fallout
Sworn to Protect
Secret Obsession
Love Thy Enemy
Dangerous Protector
Lethal Game
Secret Enemy
Saving Danger
Guarding Her
Deadly Protector
Danger Rising

Redemption Harbor Series®
Resurrection
Savage Rising
Dangerous Witness
Innocent Target
Hunting Danger
Covert Games
Chasing Vengeance

Sin City Series (the Serafina)
First Surrender
Sensual Surrender
Sweetest Surrender
Dangerous Surrender
Deadly Surrender

Verona Bay Series
Dark Memento
Deadly Past
Silent Protector

Linked books
Retribution
Tempting Danger

Non-series Romantic Suspense
Running From the Past
Dangerous Secrets
Killer Secrets
Deadly Obsession
Danger in Paradise
His Secret Past

Paranormal Romance
Destined Mate
Protector's Mate
A Jaguar's Kiss
Tempting the Jaguar
Enemy Mine
Heart of the Jaguar

Made in the USA
Monee, IL
25 June 2023

37411277R00142